THE
INTERN

USA TODAY BESTSELLING AUTHOR

MARNI MANN

Visit my website at: www.MarniSMann.com
Cover Designer: Hang Le, By Hang Le, www.byhangle.com
Editor: Jovana Shirley, Unforeseen Editing, www.unforeseenediting.com
Proofreaders: Judy Zweifel of Judy's Proofreading, Kaitie Reister, and
Chanpreet Singh

ISBN-13: 979-8-9871060-3-7

To all the sexy, growly, dominant alphas like Declan Shaw.
Thank you for making us scream.
For making us wet.
And for telling us to always keep our heels on ...

ONE
DECLAN

Out of the thirty students in this classroom, there was one I couldn't take my goddamn eyes off of.

In fact, the moment I had stepped through the door of the Trial Advocacy class, I had caught eyes with her.

She was twenty-three. Twenty-four tops.

With long, wavy, dark hair and bright blue eyes. Lips that were full, plump, and covered in a shiny pink gloss. She wore a black skirted suit with the highest heels.

Heels I wanted stabbing into my back as I wrapped her legs around me.

Heels that were a solid four inches, still only bringing her up to the top of my chest.

She was small, petite.

But this girl had a fire.

A mighty personality, wrapped in a fucking delicious body.

And, *fuck me*, didn't I take in that body while she stood in the center of the classroom, facing the stand, cross-examining her witness.

I'd come in to mentor this mock trial, and several students had gone before her, cross-examining the witness. The difference was, their voices lacked confidence. They hadn't grown into their personalities, their fight didn't demand attention, their passion didn't match their lyrical drive.

When they'd stepped into the courtroom today—even if it was simulated—they didn't have what it took to gain them a win.

They weren't her.

With a posture full of assurance, she smiled at the witness before she verbally tore him apart.

It wasn't just impressive; it was sexy as hell.

Never in the last eight years since I'd passed the bar had I ever looked at a law student the way I was staring at her.

Aside from a few football games, this was the first time I'd returned to University of Southern California, the first time I'd ever agreed to sit in on a mock trial. But when Professor Ward, who had been my favorite law professor, had said she had a classroom full of students who emulated me, it was hard to say no.

Even if I was a ruthless bastard inside and outside the courtroom, I couldn't deny them this opportunity to learn from the best.

Ward's group certainly needed the training and practice and feedback.

Not this one though.

This gorgeous girl had something the rest couldn't compete with.

Of course, I wouldn't tell her that.

I wasn't here to stroke anyone's ego.

I was here to do the opposite.

"Stop," I said, cutting off her questions. I moved closer, the short distance allowing me to get a whiff of her perfume. A scent that was sweet, like vanilla and brown sugar. "Tell me your name."

Her stare glided from the witness to the professor and finally to me, an expression on her face that told me I'd caught her off guard.

No litigator wanted that, whether it came from the opposition or the judge; it interrupted the flow, the concentration.

It allowed for a moment of weakness.

Will she weaken?

I needed to see for myself.

"Hannah," she replied.

"Well then, Hannah, I want you to remember that in the jury's eyes, this particular witness is going to make or break your case. You don't want to come on too strong—you'd overwhelm the jury. You want to ease in. Gradually build up speed. Think of it like ..." I knew exactly what she was thinking of. I could tell by the way she was breathing, how her lips were parted. Her eyes narrowed as she gawked at me. "Writing the next best thriller," I continued. "Weaving tension and excitement into the chapters of the most suspenseful, harrowing tale, getting closer to the end that will tie everything together. As the author, what can you do to make the reader continue to the last chapter, to ensure they won't set down the book before then and never return to it?"

I didn't know if she was a reader, like myself. I knew nothing about this woman. But part of being a litigator was being intuitive, and I could see right through her.

The way she was dissecting me.

The way she was turned on by my charm.

My appeal.

If she were as experienced as me, she would know I felt the same way about her.

That, in my mind, I was already making her wet.

With my fucking tongue.

"You should end each chapter on a cliff-hanger," she replied. "Making them desperate to continue flipping the pages."

"Yes." I nodded toward the witness, but not before I glanced down her chest. The way it lifted as she breathed. I wondered how it would look if it was covered in sweat. How it would taste. What she would sound like if she was panting my name. "Now, build up that jury. Feed them crumb after crumb after crumb. And when you walk back to your seat, leave them clinging to your final word."

"I can do that."

"Show me."

I didn't return to the side of the classroom where I'd previously stood.

I wanted her to feel the intimidation of my presence like she was in a real courtroom and I was on the opposite counsel.

I wanted the pressure to pulse through her.

She set the folder she'd been holding onto the desk behind her, her arms falling to her sides, her posture now having a visual edge. "Is it true that on—"

"Hannah ..." I crossed my arms over my chest, the back of my suit jacket pulling as my shoulders flexed. I waited until her eyes met mine. "The witness is important, but the jury is who matters. They're the ones you need on your side. Don't forget to look at them. Engage them. Direct each point at them."

"The jury. Right."

"Start again."

She walked over to where the stand-in jury was sitting, her body pressed against the wooden half-wall of the jury box, and that was where she began to question her witness.

And in that moment was when Hannah really started to

shine. Where she courted the jury, dangling each carrot so methodically that they were fucking chomping for more.

Who is this girl?

And how the hell is she this good?

Already?

The moment she finished with her witness, she locked eyes with me the entire way back to her seat.

She didn't smile.

She didn't need to.

I saw it in her gaze, the satisfaction in each of her steps.

I couldn't look away.

I couldn't take my fucking eyes off her.

But once her ass was in that chair, I forced myself to glance away, and I went to the center of the room, the scent of her hitting me in the damn face. I didn't let it deter me. I didn't lose myself in thoughts, wondering if her pussy smelled just as sweet. Instead, I took inventory of the students while I raised my hands in the air and clapped.

"Congratulate her," I told them. "That's how it's done."

Professor Ward joined me, waiting for the room to quiet before she said, "I would like to thank Mr. Shaw for taking the time to join us today." There was a round of applause. "As I've said to you all before, he's become one of the most successful lawyers to ever graduate from USC, and as one of his professors, I would like to think I had something to do with that." She squeezed my arm. "For a select group of you—more specifically the top six performers in today's class—Mr. Shaw has graciously agreed to chat with you one-on-one, giving you an opportunity to ask him questions and discuss his experience."

There was a loud rumble among the group.

"Mr. Shaw, who would you like to pick for this evening's meetup?" Professor Ward asked.

Three women. Three men. That was the only fair way to do it.

The top performers were clear in my mind.

I mulled over the jury, where many of the students were sitting, and pointed to three familiar faces. Then, I shifted toward the back of the classroom, where the rest were standing, and I chose two more.

I finally landed in front of Hannah's desk.

Her scent was the strongest over here.

It was more than just vanilla.

It was like a fucking cake.

Something I wanted to eat.

Savor.

Ravage.

"And you, Hannah," I said. "The rest of you who weren't chosen can leave. The ones who were, please hang back, and I'll give you instructions on where we're going to meet." I waited until everyone was gone, except for Professor Ward and the six winners, and said, "I'd like to go to a place that's a little less formal than the classroom. Where we can relax and speak freely." If I was going to spend more time with Hannah, I wanted to do that with a scotch in my hand. "When I was a student here, Nikki's was my favorite bar. Let's meet there in twenty minutes."

While the six students shuffled out of the room, I grabbed my briefcase from one of the desks and turned toward Professor Ward. "Will you be joining us?"

"I'm afraid not." She coughed, her voice scratchy from age. "I think it'll be good for the students to have some time alone with you. A chance to speak without being surrounded by academia."

"I understand."

Her hand returned to my arm—a place she had never touched when she was my professor. "I appreciate you doing this, Declan. I know today didn't incur any billable hours, but it'll go a long way in their eyes."

I gripped the leather handle, feeling the slickness on my palm.

Anticipation.

That was what grew there.

The thought of seeing Hannah outside of a school setting, if she would be as enthralling when she wasn't standing before a jury.

"I'm happy to do it," I replied. "I just hope they learned something today."

"I assure you, every second you spent with them was invaluable." She lowered her hand toward mine, a grip that was so motherly. "How are things at Smith & Klein? You've been there since you graduated. I assume all is well?"

"They recruited me during my first year of law school with an offer I couldn't refuse. But I'll be honest, Professor; Smith & Klein had promised to make me partner, which should have happened almost a year ago, but they have made no move to do so. I've been dodging offers for years, but it might be time to entertain some."

She raised her finger and grinned. "Nothing wrong with dipping your toes in the shark tank."

"I think you're forgetting I'm a great white."

Her grin widened. "From the very beginning, I knew you were going to be something special, Declan." Her long gray hair fell into her eyes. She moved it away from her face before she looped her arm through mine. "Wherever you end up, they're going to be very lucky to have you."

I winked at her. "You're right about that."

7

She walked me to the door. "Be good to those kids tonight. Except for one, they weren't born with your sharpness or charisma. They could most definitely stand to learn a lot from you."

I couldn't help myself.

I had to know.

"Who's the exception?"

Her smile was warm and deliberate. "I think we both know that answer." She patted me on the shoulder as we reached the doorway, her arm leaving mine. "I'll see you next semester, Declan."

She wasn't asking.

I gave her a gentle nod and went down the hallway, exiting the double doors at the end, leaving the building that I had countless memories of, where I'd spent all three years of law school.

Rather than getting into my seventeen-year-old Toyota, like I once had all those years ago, I slid into the driver's seat of my McLaren 720S.

As I shifted into first gear, quickly leaving my parking spot, a call came through my Bluetooth. The center screen on the dashboard showed a name that made me chuckle.

Dominick Dalton.

Dominick along with his two younger brothers and parents were the owners of the largest law firm in California.

He also happened to be a good friend of mine.

There were only two reasons that motherfucker would be calling me at this hour.

Something in my gut told me it wasn't to meet up for drinks since requests like that usually came through a text.

That left option B, which meant things were about to get very interesting.

"Dominick," I said as I connected the call. "How can I help you, my man?"

"You can come work for me."

Damn, I was good—and always right.

I turned at the light, not needing to hide my smile since he couldn't see it. "Do you treat your girlfriend the same way? Not giving her even a second of foreplay, just sticking it right in, hoping she's wet?"

"You sick bastard." He laughed. "Don't act like this is the first time I've asked. Hell, I've done everything but fucking beg you to come join my team. What else could you possibly want, Declan?"

I wanted him to sweat.

There was no question Dominick's firm was the best. With the wealth of clients they represented and the different areas of law, it would be a litigator's dream to work there. They had several on their team, but what they lacked was a fucking pit bull. Dominick knew that. That was why he'd been recruiting me for years.

"I don't hear the need in your voice," I teased. "And I don't have a contract in my hand with a number that's going to make me hard."

"It's in your email."

I stopped at the red light and pulled up my inbox, quickly downloading the contract, scanning each line until I found the salary.

It was impressive.

I assumed it was also more than any litigator in his office made.

But they weren't me, nor did they have my reputation.

"I need you to double that salary." I continued reading until I reached the section where my hourly wage was listed and what I would be invoicing his clients if any of the cases went to trial. "You can double my hourly fee as well."

"We both know this isn't about money. If that was what you wanted, you would have asked for it a long time ago."

It wasn't often that I interacted with someone as perceptive and keen as myself.

"What is it about, then, Dominick?"

"You want me on my knees."

That was exactly what I wanted.

Dominick Dalton was the boss, but that didn't mean he dominated this friendship, and if I was going to work for his company, one thing needed to be clear.

I wasn't going to bow down to anyone even if that person's name was on my paycheck.

"If this is your attempt at that, you're doing a shitty job," I told him.

"Declan, Declan, Declan. In all these years I've known you, you've never changed."

I turned into the parking lot of the bar and found a spot, shutting the car off and raising the phone to my ear, the Bluetooth disconnecting. "That's why you want me. You know what you're going to get, and that's a ruthless motherfucker who's going to fight for your clients."

"Is that a yes, then?"

I opened the door and climbed out. "I've got to go, Dominick. We'll catch up soon."

"So, that's a yes?"

I laughed. "Not a fucking chance."

I hung up and made my way inside, finding the group of students congregating by the bar, several rows of empty shot glasses lined up in front of them. It looked like they had started without me.

"Does everyone have something to drink?" I asked,

checking their hands to make sure they were holding something.

I received nods and yeses from everyone besides Hannah.

She shook her head, and I asked, "Why not?"

"I'm just waiting for the bartender to finish making mine."

I moved in next to her, needing to place my order, the closeness causing my arm to graze her shoulder.

Goddamn it.

Even in here, a bar older than me, with an overwhelming stench of spilled beer and mildew and college-aged sweat, I could still smell her.

She tucked a chunk of her dark hair behind her ear, forcing me to notice her black polish and thin fingers, several decorated with gold rings—an edgy style that I really liked.

"Today was one of the best days I've had in law school." She paused to take the martini from the bartender and turned partially toward me. "We'd done mock trials in the past, but they were nothing like this one. This one made me realize I had been doing it all wrong. Addressing the wrong audience, focusing on the wrong elements." She moved the glass to her lips, where they slowly parted to take a drink. Her tongue swiped away the wetness the moment she was done. "Thank you for bringing this to my attention. I'm going to be a stronger lawyer because of you."

Fuck, this girl was sexy.

I looked at the bartender and said, "Scotch. Neat. Give me a double." When my gaze returned to Hannah, my dick started to harden.

I just wanted to keep her talking, so I could see her lips moving. I wanted to envision them spread wide, wrapped around my cock.

Sucking the cum out of my tip.

"How are you going to do things differently now?"

She pushed her back against the edge of the bar, holding the drink near her chest. "Well, for starters, I'm going to give the jury a lot more attention, and I'm going to gauge my questioning based on their facial reactions, and trickle those questions in lightly." She chewed the corner of her lip. It was brief, and if I hadn't been staring, I would have missed it. "I'll slowly build their interest, laying the foundation, before I leave them desperate for more."

I took the glass from the bartender's hand and positioned it in front of Hannah's, clinking them together. "Excellent. I'll cheers to that."

"It's funny; I'm used to performing in front of an audience but—" She stopped abruptly, her cheeks instantly reddening. "I just mean, law school has prepped me for situations like today," she clarified. "But to present in front of you, the top litigator in the state"—she swallowed, shaking her head—"was far more intense than I'd anticipated."

If she was going to stroke anything, I wished it were my cock, not my ego.

"That's what you need to be prepared for every time you walk into the courtroom, Hannah." I pulled at my tie, loosening the knot. "That someone cutthroat and merciless is going to be on the opposition, someone who's going to sink their claws into you. If you're prepared for that, then no one, not even myself, will bring you down."

"I don't know if I'll ever be experienced enough to face you … in the courtroom."

My stare must have been too much because she glanced away, giving me a view of her profile.

One that was as beautiful as her full face.

Freckles peppered the skin near her hairline, and her long, thick lashes fluttered. Lips that pursed without pouting.

This girl was a fucking vision.

She wrapped an arm over her stomach, the movement causing the top of her shirt to fold between her tits, giving me a line of cleavage to enjoy.

"I want you to know that I read the transcripts of the Garland case." She was referencing one of my high-profile cases, where I'd won my client so much in damages that he purchased a fucking castle in Ireland. "No one else would have won that trial. No one but you." Her tongue folded over her upper lip. "The transcripts were certainly impressive, but now that I've met you and experienced your personality, it all makes sense."

"Experienced?"

"Yes."

I let her response settle.

The one word ticked between us.

My lack of a reaction caused her to get slightly nervous, and she lifted her glass to take a sip but kept it between her lips long after she swallowed.

"How exactly have you experienced me, Hannah? Because this"—I glanced around the bar, seeing the students now sitting at a table nearby, waiting for their turn with me, and as I returned to her, my eyes took in her towering heels before gradually working their way up her body—"is hardly what I would define as experiencing me."

It took her several seconds to reply.

"There's something ..." Her voice trailed off. "Something unique about the way you look at a person, the way you speak to them. I can see how that would translate in the courtroom, the advantage it gives you over your opponent."

Interesting.

"You've read up on me ..."

She laughed.

She didn't find that funny.

13

She just didn't know how to react when my stare was so fiercely connected to hers.

"Of course I have. I've followed your career since I started law school—even before that, if I'm being honest. You've built quite a name for yourself, Mr. Shaw."

"Declan."

"Declan," she repeated.

A voice that wasn't light.

That wasn't raspy.

More like ... breathless.

"What else did you learn from your research?"

She glanced up at me through her dark lashes. "You have this ability to mesmerize people on the stand. You're like a magician. I'm positive you can't escape the water tank you're submerged in, where you're wrapped in a straitjacket and tied to a chair, running out of air and drowning." She glanced down at her drink but didn't raise it. "Yet you do escape." Her eyelids narrowed as she looked at me again. "That's more than talent. That's something you're born with."

If I were a magician, I would already have her panties off, my dick deep inside her pussy.

I was going to do everything in my power to make that happen at some point tonight.

But right now, I was just a confident, charismatic man who knew how to make a woman wet without even touching her.

"The skill that makes me a successful litigator, I believe, is my ability to see the truth in people's eyes. I don't need my witnesses to respond most of the time. I can see their thoughts, I can sense their fabrications, and I know when they're being honest or misleading. The same way I can see what you're thinking right now."

She sucked in a long, deep breath, tilting her body fully toward me. "And what's that ... Declan?"

Her chest opened as her shoulders pushed back.

Her legs spread as she widened her stance.

Check-fucking-mate.

I ducked my head, getting close to her ear. Her perfume took ahold of me, and as I exhaled, my air hitting her neck, goose bumps spread across her skin. "I think we both know the answer to that."

TWO

HANNAH

D*eclan Shaw*, I thought to myself as I watched him walk to the table of students. Followed by, *Oh God, that man.*

He had quite a reputation.

If you attended USC law school, you'd heard of him. Every professor spoke about him at some point during their lecture. They raved about his success. They gushed over his achievements.

There wasn't a single litigator in the state who wanted to go to trial against him.

Because when Declan stepped into a courtroom, he won.

Therefore, I wasn't surprised that women dropped their panties the moment he approached.

When I'd only seen him on paper and in photos, I had been positive that had to do with his accomplishments. He had more millions than he knew what to do with and a face that could model eyewear.

Of course, women couldn't resist him.

Now that I'd been in his presence, that his eyes had gazed

16

down my body, that I'd been lost in his words, I knew it went far deeper than just his finances and power.

He was the hottest man I'd ever laid eyes on.

When you mixed his charm and charisma with his ability to look right through you, the way he heated you with his stare and melted you with his voice, the combination was lethal.

And I felt it.

All the way down to my toes.

I'd struggled to find a response to his questions, to hide the way he was affecting me.

To mask how attractive I found him.

But he had seen the truth in my eyes—that I found his dusting of scruff so deliciously sexy. That his square jaw and perfect set of lips, strong nose and green eyes were some sort of magnetic sorcery. Not to mention, the man was at least six-three, appeared to be solid muscle, and with him in that black suit and red tie, my brain was conjuring up the naughtiest thoughts.

Thoughts that shouldn't have entered my mind.

Thoughts that were so uncharacteristic of me.

Thoughts that kept me frozen at the bar, watching him speak to the other students.

He even made conversation look easy.

Smooth.

He laughed when it was warranted, his focus never leaving the speaker, listening, processing, responding appropriately.

His attention was like a stage, where he placed you in the center with a spotlight over your head and a microphone in your hand.

You could feel his eyes inside your bones.

And that was what happened the second his stare shifted over to me, his tongue swiping his bottom lip as he took me in.

"Why don't you tell us what your plan is, Hannah?"

My plan?

Only feet away, but I hadn't been listening.

I'd been too lost in a fog of Declan.

But I needed to rein myself in before I made a fool of myself.

"I'm not sure what you mean," I said as I walked toward the table, my feet airy, my body tingly as I sat in the only open seat.

One that was directly across from him.

"Your plan for after you graduate," he said. "I've heard their aspirations." He pointed around the table. "Why don't you tell me yours?"

I swallowed, finding my breath. "I'll be prepping for the bar. I'm taking it twelve weeks after I graduate."

"And then?"

I held my drink with both hands, taking a quick sip. "I'm going straight to work." The vodka burned the back of my throat, the olive juice causing my tongue to pucker. "Assuming I land myself a job."

The chances of that were likely.

Mostly due to my last name being famous in the legal world and that my cousins, aunt, and uncle owned the largest, most successful law firm in the state.

But I wasn't going to mention that or that I knew he was friends with my cousins.

There was absolutely no need to.

Besides, I didn't want him to think, due to my family ties, I was a shoo-in.

Because that wasn't true.

My family had made it clear to me and Camden—my twin brother who attended law school in New York—that we needed to earn our positions at their company.

I'd never worked so hard at anything in my life.

"You'll be taking the California bar?"

I nodded. "This is home. It's where I'd like to stay."

I took another drink of my martini, surprised that the vodka and the two shots of tequila that I'd taken earlier were already hitting me.

Or am I?

It had been almost a day since I'd eaten anything, too nervous before class to really chow down, knowing I was going to be mentored and judged by Declan Shaw.

"Can I ask you a question?" The sound of my voice came as a shock. I hadn't planned to take over the conversation or take more of his time since it seemed I'd already gotten more than everyone else, but every minute I got with him was vital.

"Yes."

"Let's say you have a client you know is guilty, but you're skilled enough to get them off." I cleared my throat, cursing myself for phrasing every conversation I had with him in such a sexual nature. "Are you able to close your eyes at night? You know, sleep eight hours and wake up the next morning like nothing happened?"

He crossed his hands over the table. "Are accountants able to sleep at night, knowing their clients are embezzling money that's not reported to the IRS? Or how about a cardiothoracic surgeon who performs open heart surgery on a patient who will return home post-surgery and eat a stick of butter with dinner, washing it all down with a pint of ice cream?"

His fingers formed a triangular peak, drawing my attention to them. Their length, thinness. How masculine they looked with a slight dusting of hair on the backs of his hands.

Hands that I could picture running across every inch of my body.

Oh man.

"We can't control what our clients do or what they admit to or withhold from us," he said. "Our job is to get them a fair trial and win their case." His thumb grazed the length of several of his fingers. Back and forth. *Baaack* and *fooorth*. "We can't let their crimes—or lack of—affect us personally, nor should it change who we are as humans." He glanced around the table, addressing all of us. "This isn't a job for the weak. For the person who's going to rush into the restroom and throw up when the court breaks for lunch. You're either made for this job or it's going to break you." His eyes returned to me, causing my breath to hitch in my throat. "Remember, your reputation is everything. You'll be hired because of your ability to win. If you can't win, you're going to be paid what you're worth. And that's absolutely nothing."

The pressure.

I had been feeling it long before this meetup.

Now, it was intensifying.

Could I shut off my personal feelings when it came to these cases?

Did I have the skills to give my clients a fair shot?

Because I wasn't far from being in that position. I was graduating at the end of the semester, followed by a couple of months of studying, and then I would be practicing law, assuming I passed the bar.

It was so much to process.

I downed the rest of my drink, chewing the olives at the bottom.

I needed more food.

And more vodka.

With Declan speaking to one of the other students, I returned to the bar and waited until I could order, "An extra dirty martini, please," from the bartender. "With double blue cheese olives."

"Exactly the way I would order it."

Declan's voice made my back straighten until I was no longer slouched over the bar top.

I hadn't realized he'd left the table.

Or that he was behind me.

But I should have. The second he was in close vicinity, the air seemed to change.

It thickened.

It turned hotter.

I glanced over my shoulder. "Would you like one?"

"Yes."

"Make that two, please," I said to the bartender.

Before I could reach into my pocket to grab my credit card, he was already handing his to the bartender.

I put my hand up. "No, no. Please let me pay. It's the least I can do for everything you've done for us today."

"You're not paying for my drink, Hannah." His stare deepened. "You're not paying for yours either."

He leaned his stomach against the edge of the bar, the closeness sending me his cologne. I hadn't noticed it before. Maybe I had just been too absorbed by his handsomeness, obsessed with this perfect man the previous two times he was near me, that I missed that detail. But a richness was now filling my nose, one that was heavy, but not overpowering, with a hint of spice.

A scent that had a bite ... just like him.

With my breathing untamed, almost panting, I replied, "Declan, I don't mind paying."

His arms rested on top of the bar, his back hunched so we were eye-level. "Listen, I was in your shoes once. When you're in mine, you can buy me a drink." His stare dipped to my mouth. "So, remember this moment."

"It'll be impossible to forget."

That was the truth even though I wished I hadn't said it.

"I like that." He finally glanced up again, our eyes locking. "Tell me something, Hannah. Why do you want to be a litigator?"

I checked on the bartender, hoping she was almost finished with our drinks.

She wasn't.

"I—"

"Because no reasonable, calm, collected person wants to fight for a living," he said, interrupting me. "There are many other types of law that don't require you to be so argumentative, but to be a litigator"—he exhaled, a rush of excitement filling his eyes—"now, that takes a set of balls. I want to know where your balls came from."

I laughed.

This was an easy answer.

"I grew up in a family of boys. A twin brother. Cousins who were all older than me. I hung out with them every day of my childhood. Since I was the only girl, they never wanted to listen to me. They treated me like the runt of the litter. To make them hear me, I had to be better than them. I had to fight and claw and outsmart them." I pulled my hair to one side as a layer of sweat moved across my skin. "I couldn't run faster, I couldn't throw farther, but I could take any of them down with my words."

"You learned how to win."

"Exactly." My laughter faded to a smile as I recalled some of the specific times I'd left those boys in a cloud of verbal dust. "My youth prepared me for this job in every possible way, so there's never been a question about what kind of law I want to practice."

"Sounds like you not only enjoy winning, but you also *crave* it." His voice turned gritty when he emphasized the second-to-last word.

Was that true?

Did I have that competitiveness inside me?

When I had been younger, I'd felt such satisfaction because that was one less thing they could tease me about.

But now?

I tried to envision representing one of my cousins' clients in court—something none of them could do, as they weren't litigators—and this vicious pulse began to pump through me.

"Yes," I responded. "I suppose I do crave it."

"I can see it." He reached for our second round of drinks, handing me one and taking the other. "You're in the right field, Hannah."

As my fingers surrounded the glass, they briefly grazed his.

That was all it took to set my skin on fire. Just that small, subtle embrace, and every nerve ending was lit, throbbing, crying out in shock waves.

"Thank you," I whispered.

He signed the credit card receipt and tucked his card away. "Tell me something else, Hannah ..."

As he paused, I tried to remind myself that this was the time to ask him questions, to pick his brain, to find out the secrets of our trade—an opportunity that probably wouldn't present itself again.

But I couldn't.

I was completely locked up.

Speechless.

Drowning in a pool of Declan.

"When you walk into a courtroom, what's going to be your secret weapon?" He watched as I licked my lips, and it felt as erotic as stripping off my clothes. "I've told you mine. I want to know yours."

"My secret weapon," I repeated.

"You know, not only can I read people, but I also use my

reputation to my advantage. I don't give any motherfucker a chance. I find what it'll take to make them bleed out, and that's where I cut them."

I knew that.

I'd read the transcripts from his cases.

Declan gave zero fucks. He pushed limits. He tested everyone.

"A lot of girls in my class want to use their looks."

"Is that you?"

His stare slowly dipped down my body, and I felt every inch, his eyes like fingers stroking my skin. Taking me in. Teasing me. I'd never felt anything like it, and he wasn't even touching me.

"No." I shook my head, trying to breathe. "It's definitely not."

His gaze lifted unhurriedly. Each spot he observed—my thighs, my navel, my breasts—caused a stronger sensation to build inside me.

He was more than a magician.

He had powers, and if this was just his stare, I couldn't imagine what it would feel like to have his hands on me.

His lips.

His ...

Oh God.

"I didn't think it was." He brushed his fingers over his cheek, the friction against his short whiskers made the most appealing sound. "Even though it could be."

I took a large drink of my martini. "My plan is ..." *Do I have a plan? Do I even remember how to speak?* "I guess I'm going to find a piece of evidence that my opponent is unable to locate and use that to make my case."

He turned toward me. "How will you find it?"

"I'll dig. Hunt. Whatever it takes." But I knew I wouldn't

be alone. No litigator worked solo. They had a team of assistants, a paralegal, clerks who helped them prepare for court. "I know I'll only be as strong as my team, so I also plan to have the best."

A smile grew across his lips.

It couldn't have been sexier.

"An important part, yes," he agreed.

"Can I ask you something? Even if it's slightly inappropriate?"

"Go on."

I couldn't believe I had blurted that out. That my thoughts were so unhinged that I no longer had control over my mouth.

"Do you make all your opposing counsel feel this way? If they're women?"

His thumb traced around his lips. "What way is that, Hannah?"

My body hummed like he was breathing against it.

My hands squeezed the glass so hard that I was surprised it hadn't shattered.

"Connected." That wasn't right. I needed to better describe this. "Like you're on the verge of ..."

"Devouring them."

I nodded.

Because that was all I could do.

"As I've said, if they're facing me in the courtroom, I want their blood. I don't want their lips. I don't want their body. I don't want"—he gazed down again, stopping at my waist—"anything from them."

"Then, what's this?"

"This is the way I treat a woman when I find her so sexy that I can't take my eyes off her."

He knew I felt the same way.

Because he knew what I was thinking.

How I was feeling.

He'd told me so.

"In fact, if we had met under different circumstances, you would be coming home with me tonight."

I couldn't wrap my head around this news.

A night with Declan Shaw.

A man I'd studied since he'd begun making a name for himself in the industry.

A man I followed on social media.

A man I was so utterly, consumingly attracted to that I'd been wet since he had walked into our classroom.

But going home with any man wasn't something I usually ever did.

I'd dated in the past, but my current schedule was far too packed and daunting to even consider it. I went from school to babysitting my cousin's daughter to prepping for the bar. Even though my best friend and roommate, Oaklyn, was constantly pushing me to find a man, I wasn't looking.

But I was definitely looking at Declan.

"And you think I'm the kind of girl who would climb right into your passenger seat and let that happen?"

He leaned into my ear, something he'd done before.

I remembered how incredible his breath had felt against my skin.

And it did again.

"Do I think you're the girl who has one-night stands? No. But I think, eventually, you would find it impossible to resist me."

As I turned around, he stretched his arm across the bar, moving it behind me. A slow, torturous scrape across my shoulder blades with just enough pressure that I trembled. My nipples were so hard that I swore they were on the verge of breaking through my bra.

"I take that back. I don't think ... I'm positive you would."

"What makes you so sure of yourself?"

"I told you, Hannah, I can read you."

"And what are you seeing?"

His face, still near my ear, moved to the front of mine. For the briefest of moments, he glanced away, and when he returned, I realized two things.

One, I missed him, even during that brief break.

And, two, he really could see right through me, his expression telling me so.

"I see a woman who's trying to argue against her body. You don't want me to have this effect on you, but I do. You're shivering. I can feel it." His hand moved around to my arm, his finger running up and down the back of my bicep. "Your pulse is hammering away; your heart's pounding. You have to really focus on everything I'm saying because you find yourself getting lost in my words."

When he leaned into my ear this time, I was sure I felt his lips against my lobe.

"You're dying to know what my mouth tastes like. If my cock fits my body type—large, thick ... manly." I tried to fill my lungs as he added, "It does."

"Declan—"

He shifted, so our eyes met. "What would tomorrow feel like, Hannah, after I spent the whole night with you? How satiated ... how sore would you be?"

I wasn't thinking.

Because he'd sucked every thought out of me.

"Isn't that what's on your mind?"

I couldn't answer.

I couldn't even force the spit filling my mouth down my throat. But I knew I needed to give myself a second of something that wasn't Declan, so I glanced at the table of students, all deep in conversation, not a single one looking in our direction.

They hadn't been captivated by this vulture of law, by the god of turning women on.

"Hannah ..."

I looked at him again, knowing instantly it was a mistake. "Yes?"

"If I were to slip a finger up the bottom of your skirt and touch you, would your pussy be wet?"

I couldn't lie.

He would know.

He would see right through me.

"Yes."

He smiled, a grin so devilish that it made me wetter. "Then, the defense rests," he said, and he returned to the table, leaving me alone at the bar.

THREE

DECLAN

I was seconds away from lifting Hannah onto the bar top, tearing her skirt at the waist, and eating her in front of every patron in here.

I gave no fucks who saw.

Who watched.

Even though I hadn't kissed her, I could taste her on my tongue. Maybe it was the vanilla that I'd inhaled as my lips grazed her earlobe. Maybe it was just the anticipation of what she was going to taste like.

But the flavor in my mouth was positively hers.

A flavor I wanted more of.

A flavor I needed more of.

I'd told her that if we had met under different circumstances, she would be coming home with me. Words that were only bait. And not only had she swallowed the hook, but she'd also deep-throated the entire line.

I was ready to make her body mine, to hear the range of octaves in which I could make her moan, to have her nails scratching and stabbing my flesh because I was making her cunt scream.

I was quickly learning one thing.

Hannah was irresistible.

That was why I'd left her at the bar and returned to the table of students.

The moment my ass was back in my chair, I began fielding questions, the students waiting their turn to drill me. There was one who was going to use her looks, like Hannah had suggested, and a few who would rely on their charm. The rest didn't have a fucking clue what their secret weapon was.

Not a single one of them was Hannah.

The more I looked at her, the more I listened to her speak, the more I dug into her thoughts, the more I realized she was a dangerous woman.

When she joined us, sitting in the chair across from mine, I had to force myself not to reach under the table and dip my fingers beneath her skirt.

She was staring at me, nursing her martini, her lips spread across the edge of the glass.

That girl had no idea what I was going to do to her tonight.

Considering her age, I assumed she'd only been with college dudes, never a man, like me. I could make her shudder just by blowing on her clit. I would listen to what she needed. I would hear what she desired, unlike the selfish sons of bitches at this table who were trying to engage me in small talk. Whose clumsy fingers couldn't even tie a proper Windsor knot, so I knew they couldn't ever find a woman's G-spot.

"I have a question ..."

Hannah's voice was a welcome interruption from the conversation I had been in.

My gaze shifted to her. "Ask it."

"Do you take the courtroom home with you?" She glanced

around the group, her voice lowering as she added, "I think we're all in similar stages of our lives here, but I wonder what it's like for you. When you return to your house and Mrs. Shaw is waiting in the kitchen, a plate of cookies on the counter, can you eat the cookies and chat about where you're going to vacation the following weekend? Or do you spend the entire dinner recapping every moment of the day's trial before doing it again over coffee the next morning?"

Oh, Hannah ...

I see right through you.

I had a reputation.

Bachelor. Serial dater. Playboy.

Whatever the fuck they called me.

I liked to think of it as not being tied down.

I was surprised Hannah didn't know that about me.

Or maybe she did, and she was just confirming.

"When my driver takes me home every day, whether that be from the office or the courtroom, I leave work behind. Of course, there are evenings and weekends where I spend time doing paperwork or I take calls from clients. But when I'm out with friends, even if they're lawyers, we don't talk shop. When I'm eating cookies my private chef baked, I don't think about the questions I should have asked in court or the points I should have made." I gave Hannah a hard stare. "There's work time and playtime. I don't mix the two."

I was immediately bombarded with another set of questions, taking my eyes away from Hannah. It didn't matter. I could still feel her. Sense her. Smell her in the air.

Until I couldn't.

Since I'd placed my back toward her during the last round of examination, I glanced across my shoulder to find her.

She wasn't there.

I didn't know if she was getting another drink. If she'd gone to the restroom. Or if she'd left the bar.

What I did know was that this meetup was over.

I gave my final bit of feedback to the student next to me and turned toward the group. "I appreciate you all joining me. Unfortunately, our time is up." I decided to do one more thing to ease the blow. "Don't bother paying your tabs; your drinks are on me tonight."

Everyone stood to shake my hand, thanking me for my time and generosity. After I watched each of them trickle out through the main exit, I went over to the bar to pay their bill, ordering a scotch while I waited for the bartender to tally up the receipts.

That was when I scanned the room for Hannah.

But there was no sign of her.

Was our conversation too much for her to handle?

Did I misread what was building between us?

Nah, I didn't believe that for a second.

Then, where the fuck is she?

I signed the credit card receipt and walked around the perimeter of the bar, looking to see if I could find her. When I neared the restroom, I spotted her. Her body was hidden because the man she was speaking to was much taller, blocking her from most angles.

They weren't touching.

But Hannah was smiling, transfixed on his face.

Basking in his attention.

Only minutes ago, she had been doing the same to me.

And now, she was flirting with another guy.

Fuck that.

I downed the rest of my scotch and left the empty glass on a table before I headed into the restroom. I finished at the urinal and washed my hands, and as I was coming out the door,

Hannah was walking into the short hallway, just about to turn into the ladies' room.

Our eyes caught, and she stopped, leaning against the wall between the doors. "Where did everyone go? I just went to the table, and they're all gone."

"I sent them home." I shoved my damp hands into my pockets. "You would have known that if you hadn't been so tied up."

Her stare deepened, and then she smiled. "You mean ... with Gregory?"

"I don't know who the fuck he is."

She turned her face, giving me more of her profile. "Is that jealousy that I hear?"

I knew what she was trying to do. I wasn't going to fall for it.

"I saw you two on my way to the restroom, Hannah. I wasn't looking for you. Don't make this something that it isn't."

Her teeth ran across her lip in a way that I couldn't look away from. "Are you sure about that, Declan?"

Damn it.

She was pushing, attempting to control this conversation.

She would soon learn that the only thing she could control was the speed in which she sucked my dick.

"No, I'm not just sure," I growled. "I'm positive."

"Then, why do you appear so bothered by it?"

"I'm not."

She switched positions and now faced me by leaning her shoulder against the wall, her hand clasping her hip. "Do you want to know who Gregory is?"

I didn't like that she kept saying his fucking name, implying that his title mattered to me.

Before I could reply, she said, "He's one of my study partners and a good friend, and he also happens to be gay, so there's no reason to worry."

33

Fuck, she had a mouth on her.

"I wasn't worried," I told her.

But deep down, I felt relief.

I didn't know why.

But there it was.

"You know, it's funny ..." Her lips pulled into a seductive grin. "You told me earlier that if we had met under different circumstances, I'd be going home with you tonight. But from the way you're looking at me right now, it seems those circumstances have changed."

"And you can tell that from my eyes?"

She nodded. "Looks like you're about to ravish me against this wall."

She was right.

If my hands weren't shoved into my pockets, they'd be all over her.

I didn't know what was stopping me.

"Is that what you want, Hannah?" I paused. "Do you want my lips all over your body?"

"Yes."

Then, there was no reason to wait.

I took a step closer, halting directly in front of her, our bodies only breaths apart. I placed my palm against the wall above her head, her body caged beneath me. "Do you want me to make you scream so loud that everyone in the bar can hear you?" I leaned my face into her ear. "Is that what you want from me?"

She was quivering.

Panting.

When her teeth skimmed her lip this time, it was a slow, painful scrape. "I don't want an audience"—she took several breaths—"but yes. Yes to all of it."

I gripped her face, aiming it up to mine.

I didn't kiss women.

Lips were something I could easily get attached to.

They were the most personal part of a woman's body.

They expressed emotions. They spoke the truth. They even tried to mask and hide the real feelings inside.

I didn't fuck with them.

But as I gazed down at Hannah's mouth, it was so goddamn beautiful. Those full, pouty lips, silently begging for mine.

She was giving herself to me.

And I'd accept every bit, except a kiss.

I held her face tighter. "Is your pussy ready for my dick, or do you need my fingers to get you wet?"

"I want your fingers." Her teeth returned to her bottom lip but then left again, her tongue now licking back and forth across it. "I want every part of you, Declan."

It was like her tongue was soothing that lip.

Dragging me toward it.

What if I just went in for a taste?

A quick feel.

To know if her lips were as soft as I suspected.

If her breath was as sweet as her scent.

Fuck me.

I ducked my head, our mouths getting closer. The wetness that her tongue had left behind was enticing me, the throbbing in my cock pushing me forward.

I didn't know what the fuck was happening to me ... but I couldn't stop.

I was inching, closing in, until not even air separated us.

The moment we touched mouths, something inside me exploded.

A feeling I hadn't expected.

One so fucking powerful that it reached all the way to my toes.

Her body went limp, and I wrapped an arm around her back, hauling her up against me while I pushed her shoulders into the wall.

Her hands dived into my hair, yanking, gripping. "Declan …"

It was the sound of my name, the feel of her lips vibrating against mine, that made me pull back.

I touched my mouth, reminding myself of what I'd just done.

Of the rule I had just broken.

But, damn it, that taste.

I'd never had anything like it.

Nor had I ever felt this way before.

Who the fuck are you, Hannah?

And what the hell did you just do to me?

That had to be a one-time thing. Another kiss certainly wouldn't duplicate that feeling. It'd only happened because it was something I didn't normally do, my body's way of reacting to something so foreign.

I needed to be sure.

That was the only reason I held the back of her head and slammed our mouths together again.

While I took in her mouth, melding our lips together, I lowered my grip to get a feel of her curves. I started with her navel, rounding the whole width with my fingertips before I circled to her hips. Just as I took a breath, my tongue slid in between her lips, savoring the flavor bursting inside my mouth.

Jesus, fuck.

I parted us, holding her face so she couldn't move, staring into her eyes.

What had become more obvious than ever was that this girl had one hell of a fucking body and a kiss that set off every alarm inside me.

I needed her.

Now.

"I live about forty minutes from here. I can't wait that long to have you."

Her hand moved between our bodies, where it grazed my hard-on. "I can tell."

"Do you live around campus?"

She shook her head. "I'm about as far away as you."

The front seat of the McLaren wasn't large enough.

Another idea came to me.

One that I needed to run by her first.

"I know you don't like an audience, but are you adventurous, Hannah?"

Her thumb circled my tip. "If it involves this, yes."

I grabbed her hand and led her out of the hallway and through the bar, and once we were outside, I walked us to the side of the building. The only reason I knew about this alley was that my college roommate had been notorious for bringing women here. I now understood why. The area was closed off, the streetlights barely reached the space, and it was blocked from the sidewalk, giving total privacy.

The moment we entered, I turned Hannah toward me, guiding her back to the wall until she hit it, and then I lifted her arms over her head, holding her wrists.

That fucking mouth was taunting me.

I couldn't keep myself away.

I claimed her lips, my tongue instantly going in again, her heat causing my whole body to ignite.

They weren't just flickers.

They weren't even flames.

This was a fire.

And it was spreading.

I pulled away, my mouth hovering above hers. "You're never going to forget this."

"Why's that?"

"Because you've never been fucked by someone like me."

I pulled out my wallet, removing the condom I always kept inside, and stored it in my jacket pocket to make it more easily accessible.

"You come prepared," she voiced.

When it came to sex, yes.

I had plenty of friends who worked in family law.

Not using a condom was a gamble I wasn't willing to take.

"Aren't you thankful for that?" I hissed against her lips.

"In this moment, yes."

I kissed her neck, her skin tasting like the cake I smelled.

I felt her swallow.

And then she sucked in a deep breath.

"How badly do you want me, Hannah?"

I needed her begging.

I wanted her neediness echoing through me.

She tried to wiggle a hand loose, like she was going to steer one of mine toward her pussy. "If you felt me, you would know."

I didn't budge.

"I intend to, but I want to hear you tell me first."

"Declan ..." She rose onto her toes, nipping my bottom lip, catching me off guard. When she went in a second time, she didn't release it. She sucked on the end, running her tongue across the inside. The moment she let me go, she whispered, "My body is dying to be touched by you."

I could still feel her teeth even though they were long gone.

She was spicier than I'd thought.

I ran my hand across her stomach, going underneath the lacy red tank she had on beneath her jacket, her skin getting hotter and her breathing getting louder, the higher I climbed. I surrounded her tit, the hardness of her nipple poking into my palm.

I traced my thumb around her nipple, pinching it between my fingers.

"Oh God," she squealed. "Yes!"

"Now, I want you to show me how badly you want me."

I unshackled her wrists, and her arms fell. I took the opportunity to remove her jacket and lift her tank over her head before I sucked her nipple through her bra.

"Fuck," she cried, cupping my cock over my suit pants.

"Show me, Hannah. Show me how you want me to fuck your pussy."

She unbuckled my belt and popped the button through and lowered my zipper, reaching into my boxer briefs to fist my shaft. Her hand was slick, making it easy for her to pump me.

"My God, Declan." Despite the dark alley, I felt her eyes on mine. "You weren't kidding."

"Let's see if you can handle me." I pulled the bottom of her skirt up to her waist, not wanting to take the time to remove it, and I slipped her thong to the side. My fingers met her heat and wetness. "Goddamn it, you're perfect."

Each time I passed her clit, flicking it, she cried out louder.

Her hips rocked toward me.

She was ready, desperate to be touched, frantic to come.

"You're dripping." And that was only her clit. Once I lowered to her pussy, I found she was soaked there as well. I slid in a finger, going in as deep as my knuckle, the walls of her cunt already clenching around me. "Hannah, you're so fucking tight."

She wasn't a virgin—that much I could tell—but I wouldn't call her experienced either.

She'd certainly never been fucked the way she needed.

"I can't stop thinking about what you're going to do to me." She rubbed around my crown as though she were using her tongue. "How to even prepare myself for it."

My size, my power—I wasn't average.

And she wasn't the first woman to infer that.

So, I responded, "You mean, the pain?"

"That, yes."

I hummed against her skin, "I'll be gentle ... at first."

"But also how you're going to make me feel." She swallowed. "How loud I'm going to scream."

I pulled her bra down to expose her tit, taking the peak into my mouth, swirling my tongue around the hardness. I gnawed and then licked, a pattern of inflicting pain and then calming with pleasure.

That was what she did to me, what she caused—this urge to hurt and heal.

To own and mark.

She had a body that was everything I wanted.

She wasn't lanky and flat and straight.

Hannah had curves.

A body I would kill to see in the light, to watch the way her skin glowed as I kissed it, how she would dip and arch each time I plunged inside her.

But I wasn't going to get that right now.

Right now, all I could do was graze my way across her and memorize each spot, like her clit that I couldn't stop rubbing.

Aside from her mouth, a woman's pussy couldn't manipulate the truth. It couldn't lie. It couldn't deceive.

A cunt told you exactly the way a woman was feeling.

And Hannah's was fucking screeching.

Begging.

Yearning.

"Declan ..." She gasped. "*Ahhh.*"

So far, I hadn't gone in farther than my knuckle. But I pushed in deeper, curving upward, twisting, turning until I felt her G-spot. The second I touched it, I earned myself a howl louder than any she'd released so far.

"Oh God." Her hand stilled on my cock, squeezing. "What are you doing to me?"

I didn't know why my lips went to hers.

Why I wanted to feel the softness of them once again.

Why I wanted to taste her exhales.

But I locked us together, inhaling each of her breaths, rotating our tongues.

Hannah. Fuck.

She thought I was doing something to her ... but she was the one doing something to me.

Her fingers dropped from my dick, and her arms circled my neck, pulling me closer. The moment our lips parted, her head leaned against the wall, my mouth falling to her throat, feeling the purr that thrummed inside.

"I need to feel you come."

She wasn't far.

Every sign in her body told me that.

I left her throat and leaned down farther to take her nipple into my mouth, biting the end, sucking it as though she were feeding me. With my palm pressed against her clit, I worked my finger in and out, tapping that spot deep inside her, adding a second finger when she began to tighten more.

"Declan ..." Her nails stabbed the back of my neck, her body becoming slack. It only took a few more seconds before her moans turned higher, her wetness thickening as it coated my fingers.

"Fuck yes, Hannah." I picked up speed. "Give me that fucking orgasm."

As a wave of shudders moved through her, fluttering her

muscles and limbs, every exhale turned into a pant. She eventually became silent, her body frozen until a swish of air exited her lips, ending in, "What the fuck was that?"

"The very beginning," I growled. "That's all that was."

As I pulled my fingers out, her thong moved back to its original place.

A place that was in the way.

I held the lace strings at her sides and tore them off her, tucking the flimsy fabric into my pocket where I'd stored the condom. With the metal foil now in my hand, I bit off the corner of the packet and placed the rubber on her palm.

"Put this on me."

It had been minutes since she'd touched my cock, and the moment she returned to it, she spread the bead of pre-cum that glistened at the tip.

She didn't roll the condom over me.

Instead, she surrounded me with both hands and bobbed up and down my shaft, holding on tightly, mimicking what her pussy was going to do.

"Fuck"—I pressed my forehead against hers—"yes."

A hand wasn't normally enough for me, but Hannah's strokes felt incredible. So much so that I had to repay the favor, lunging back into her pussy—a spot still so fucking wet that she soaked my finger.

Typically, I never would have taken this long to bury myself inside a woman.

I certainly wouldn't be moaning over a hand job.

But I was lost.

Lost in the way her pussy sucked in my finger.

Lost in the way this gorgeous girl was making me feel.

Lost in the way I was craving to taste her wetness.

I didn't know where the latter had come from. My mouth

never dipped below the belly button of a woman I was having a one-night stand with.

If I was going to eat a pussy, that pussy was going to be mine.

Forever.

But I was quickly learning that Hannah was breaking every rule.

Especially as I found myself on my knees, the longing to taste her so overwhelming that I couldn't fight it.

My fingers left her, and I placed my nose at the top of her clit, taking a long, deep inhale. "Just what I thought ... fuck."

A scent so sweet that I would lust for it every day.

A scent I'd never be able to get enough of.

Her hand dug into my hair, shouting, "Oh fuck," as I gave her the first swipe.

That one was just for me—to know if I'd been a fool to kneel on this fucking pavement or if it was the best decision I'd made tonight.

And, *goddamn it*, it was.

The flavor of her cunt melted over my tongue.

It was so strong, so perfect that my eyes closed, my cock fucking throbbing.

This girl was a dream.

Now, I needed to stop being so selfish and make this about her.

My two fingers returned to their spot deep inside her, thrusting in and out, while I licked across her clit. Every few laps, I swallowed the heaviness of her arousal, the deliciousness enticing me to go faster.

"I can't," she cried. "I can't breathe. Oh my God."

That was what I wanted.

To take away her air, to make her feel so fucking good that she was as lost as I was.

She was twisting my locks, shoving her cunt against my mouth.

And I licked that treasure, flicking across it, wishing I could see her face when I made her come.

That wasn't going to take long.

Not with the way she was yelling, "Declan," through the alley.

I added more pressure, pointing the tip of my tongue against her clit, and within a few more strikes, she was gone.

Wriggling.

"Yes! Fuck!" She held the back of my head like she was about to fall, flexing her hips, grinding into my mouth.

The walls inside her quickly dampened, and I ate through her fucking orgasm, urging her cum down my throat with each lick.

When she became sensitive and motionless, I rose to my feet and took the condom from her hand. As I rolled it over my shaft, I licked her off my lips, getting one last taste of her, reveling in her flavor. Once the rubber was in place, I lifted her into my arms, wrapping her legs around my waist, and positioned her back against the building.

"What have you done to me?"

She sounded spent.

Satiated.

"*Mmm*," I exhaled over her face. "You've come on my finger and my mouth. Now, I want to feel you come on my dick."

"There's no way. Three times—that's ... impossible."

"Hannah, I've told you"—I probed her pussy, going in only to my crown, letting her widen and stretch, getting a solid feel for me—"you've never experienced anything like me before."

"So cocky," she teased. "But I'll admit, the second you kissed me, you proved that to be true."

I wasn't going to let that reminder get in my head.

So, I sank myself in deeper, giving her a few more inches to cling to. "Goddamn it, you're tighter than I thought."

It wasn't just a narrowness.

There was heat.

And a pool of her pleasure.

"You're going to break me."

"I am," I admitted. "And then I'm going to put you back together again. And again." I bit her lip. "And again."

I slid in some more, and she squeezed her arms around my neck, her breathing labored.

She needed something else to focus on.

I slowly moved the rest of the way in and aimed my cock upward. "You have all of me." As she pulsed around me, I pressed the short, coarse hairs above my shaft directly onto her clit. "Do you feel that?"

"I feel"—she swallowed—"everything."

I kept myself sealed to her, urging her to accept me, and it felt like she was tightening even more.

"Tell me when you're ready."

She stayed put, breathing into my face, her body as stiff as stone, holding me even though she wasn't going anywhere in my arms. And then, out of nowhere, she began to lift herself up, gently gliding me in and out.

Bouncing over my cock.

"Declan," she gasped after several plunges.

"You're fucking ready."

I didn't hold back.

I couldn't.

And when I felt like my hairs rubbing her clit weren't doing a good enough job, I reached down and grazed it with my thumb.

It was like I'd flipped a switch.

She began to go fucking wild.

"Declan! Yes!"

Each time I reared my hips back and dived in, she took every inch of me, hollering so loud that I could feel it in my goddamn chest.

The only thing that would have been sexier was if there were a light in the alley, allowing me to see her.

But what the darkness did was heighten my other senses—her vanilla still all I could smell, her beautiful curves and that amazing cunt all I could focus on.

"Hannah," I roared, twisting my way in, grinding, building that intensity, "you feel—"

Her mouth cut me off as it slammed against mine.

An unexpected kiss.

One that I didn't immediately end.

Because the more it deepened, the more I danced around her tongue, the better this all felt.

Fuck, I didn't know how.

Why.

But I knew I didn't want this to end right here.

I wanted more.

And I wanted more tonight.

I pulled away from her lips and growled, "You're coming home with me."

As I pounded into her, feeling like I was tearing through her, her pussy began to clench.

"Take me, then."

Not until the both of us came, and then I was putting her in the passenger seat of my car and driving her to my place, where we were going to continue this.

Where I could really take my time.

Where I could spread her across every surface of my house.

But first, I needed her to scream once more.

I could feel that she wasn't far from doing that.

She arched her pussy into me, squeezing me with a neediness that came from wanting one thing.

"You didn't think you could come a third time."

"God, was I wrong."

"If you think this is the last time you're going to come tonight, you're wrong again."

"Declan, I"—she sucked in air, closing in around my shaft—"I can't ... I can't stop it."

"Then, maybe I should." I slowed my strokes. "Maybe I should make you wait, punishing you for doubting me."

Her fingers stabbed my neck. "No. Please. I need it." She swallowed. "I need you."

I pressed my lips to her ear, and her hair tickled my face. A softness when everything felt so hard and rough. "Beg me."

Like a good submissive, she used her words, telling me how badly she wanted to get off, and then she kissed me, her actions backing up her pleading.

The sound of her was more than enough, but her kiss sent me straight over the fucking edge.

And as I hammered into her, my balls tightened, my movements turning hard, fast.

Relentless.

"*Fuuuck!*" I shouted against her mouth. "Hannah!"

"I'm coming!" she screamed, her voice breathless, as her wetness flooded my dick.

I wasn't gentle when I took her lips.

I ravaged them, fought them, disciplined them for wanting to kiss her.

And while her mouth melded against mine, her other set of lips milked me, pulling the cum straight out of my cock.

"God-fucking-damn it," I hissed.

We held on to each other until there was nothing left but

air, and I hugged her for several extra moments before I carefully pulled out my cock and set her on the ground.

"Get dressed. We're leaving now."

I heard her gather her tank top and jacket and put them back on while I adjusted my pants, clasping the button and belt. And just when I thought she was dressed, something fell onto the ground, her phone lighting up the moment it crashed.

She picked it up, holding the screen in front of her face. "Shit."

"Is there a problem?"

This was the first bit of light we'd had since we'd entered the alley, and her expression told me that whatever it was, it wasn't good.

"It's a BFF 911."

"A what?"

"I need to call my best friend. Something's wrong." She continued to hold the phone where it gave off enough glow that we could see each other. "Give me five minutes. That's all I need, and then I'll be right back. Don't move, okay?"

"Hannah ..." My cock was already getting hard again. "Hurry."

FOUR

HANNAH

When a BFF 911 text came through from Oaklyn, it meant drop everything and call her. So, that was what I did the second I got out of the alley, rushing inside the bar.

"Oaklyn, what's wrong?" I asked the moment she answered.

I really needed a drink, and as I waited for her to respond, I went over to the bartender and mouthed, *Water*.

Declan had fucked everything out of me, including the saliva in my mouth.

"Hannah, h-he broke u-up with me-e."

I gripped the edge of the wooden bar, my eyes closing, my head falling forward. "What? No. *Nooo!*"

"He d-didn't even h-have the decency to c-call me. H-he did it th-through text."

"That asshole. I'm going to kill him."

My heart ached for my best friend.

She loved Trevor.

Oh God, she loved him hard.

I lifted my head, opening my eyes, already wincing as I asked, "What did his message say?"

"You're n-not going t-to believe it-t."

But I would.

Six months ago, when they'd first started dating, every alarm went off in my gut, telling me that Trevor was bad news. I tried to warn my best friend. I'd done everything in my power to prepare her for a moment like this. But when moments like this came, my job wasn't to remind her of those conversations we'd had. My job was to pick up the pieces that Trevor had smashed and so carelessly left behind.

Thank you, I mouthed to the bartender when she set a cup of water in front of me. I quickly took a sip. "What did he say, Oaklyn?"

"That I-I wasn't worth w-waiting for."

I squeezed the cup, the plastic threatening to break as icy water sloshed over the side. "He didn't."

"He d-did."

My best friend—the drop-dead gorgeous twenty-four-year-old virgin—wasn't waiting for marriage per se; she was waiting for a prince to sweep her off her feet before rewarding him with the one thing she hadn't given to any other man.

Half a year later, the most romantic thing Trevor had done was book them a weekend away in Santa Barbara. Oaklyn had ended up paying for the hotel along with their food and drinks since Trevor's credit card had been declined.

She never picked the patient, sympathetic, nice guys.

She picked straight-up assholes who treated her like a conquest.

Oaklyn and I had been best friends since we were twelve, and this issue with boys had started in high school. It'd worsened in college. Now, at our age, it was an impossibly difficult challenge that she constantly had to hurdle.

Men, at least the ones she chose, didn't want to wear a crown.

They wanted to verbally fuck you at a bar and make you come in an alley.

My thighs, without prompting, pushed together, the delicious pain that sparked between them a reminder of how many times I'd screamed tonight.

Oh, Declan Shaw, you are nothing like I thought you were going to be and everything I didn't know I wanted.

Declan—*oh shit.*

I'd almost forgotten he was still outside in the alley.

Waiting for me.

"Hannah, I h-hate him," she cried. "I-I hate everyone."

"Me too. Especially a man named Trevor and that dimple of his that we thought was cute at first, and now, I just want to poke it with a nail."

"The d-dimple. I can't-t."

I downed the rest of my water.

There was only one way I could make her feel better, and that was by returning to our apartment, getting her drunk, and letting her vent for the rest of the night.

"As soon as I get home, we're purging every trace of Trevor from your room and finding a bar that has darts, so we can use his pic as a target and aim for that damn dimple."

"*Yesss-s.*" She sighed. "Screw that d-dimple."

"It's going to take me about forty minutes to get there, but don't worry; I'm coming."

"Wait."

I paused as I turned toward the exit. "Yeah?"

"Your car is h-here, and you're that far away?"

Before Declan had invited the top performers out for drinks, a bunch of us law students had planned to go barhopping. Since my intention was to crash at Gregory's apartment, where there was no parking, taking a ride-share to campus had just made my life easier.

"I'm just off campus," I told her. "I had that mentorship thing today for my Trial Advocacy class."

"Oh my God, that's right. I-I totally forgot. How did it g-go?"

I stopped at one of the open tables, leaning against the back of the chair.

This wasn't the right time to mention Declan.

Tonight needed to be about Oaklyn.

"It went *really* well," I told her.

"Is it over?"

It was over enough.

If things with Declan were meant to continue—and I hoped that was the case—then we would reconvene when my best friend wasn't bawling her eyes out. When she didn't need me to hand her darts and feed her wine and say all the things that would make her forget about that dick.

"Yes," I fibbed. "In fact, I was just getting ready to leave. I'll text you when I'm almost home, so you can open a bottle of wine for us." I had another thought. "Oh, and can you also turn on the oven? The brownies I made last night will be extra yummy if you heat them for about ten minutes. The caramel will ooze out and get all gooey and delicious."

"I love you."

"See you soon, babe." I slipped my phone into my pocket and rushed out of the bar and down the side of the building to the alley.

It was so dark. Quiet. Almost eerie and creepy.

"Declan?"

The only sound was my breathing and my feet swaying as this dreary space started to freak me out more and more.

"Declan, are you back here?"

When there was still no response, I took out my phone and turned on the flashlight, holding it up so I could see.

Our condom wrapper was on the ground, and I could pinpoint the exact place where Declan had held me against the brick building, pulling sensations out of me that I'd never felt before. But he wasn't here, nor was he on the other side of the alley or the small walkway that had led me here.

Didn't I tell him to wait for me?

Right here?

And not to move?

Or did I dream that?

Did I dream this whole thing?

I went to the front of the building and scanned the entrance and the sidewalk, searching for his handsome face, but there was only a bouncer and a few girls standing out here. The girls were holding each other up—a sign that they wouldn't be the most reliable source—so I walked over to the bouncer.

"Have you seen a guy in a suit with a red tie?" I asked him. "Dark hair, built, about"—I held my hand at least a foot above my head—"this tall."

"You're kidding, right?" He laughed.

I should have figured he was going to be no help.

As I went back into the bar, I ordered a car from the rideshare app and weaved around the small and large tables, looking at everyone sitting at them along with the people hovering at the center bar.

He wasn't in here.

He had to be in the restroom.

I went to the hallway where we had first kissed, my body all tingly as I recalled the way he had caged me in, how his mouth had devoured mine, how he had grabbed my hand and led me into the alley because he couldn't wait another second to have me.

Oh God.

I opened the men's restroom door just a crack. "Declan?" I waited, listened. "Declan, are you in there?"

When I got no response, I retraced my steps, glancing at faces in here, hoping I would see the familiar one I was looking for.

But I didn't.

Did he leave?

Would he really do that?

He was Declan Shaw after all, one of the biggest playboys in the industry, sharing the same reputation as my cousins before they got in serious relationships.

I had known that about Declan before my lips ever touched his.

Hell, anyone who was part of the LA scene knew that about him.

But I also knew the way he had made me feel before we kissed. And how badly he'd wanted to take me home, even while he was still inside me. And how he had wanted me to rush my phone call, so we could leave together.

Had I really read the situation that poorly?

Not realizing that he would just up and leave the second I left his sight?

A text came across my screen, telling me the ride-share had arrived and was out front.

I didn't know what to do, but I couldn't stay here, circling the bar, looking for someone who clearly wasn't here.

The disappointment caused my muscles to feel heavy and sluggish as I headed for the backseat of the car. I confirmed my address with the driver and slumped into the corner, resting my head against the window.

I couldn't stop racking my brain, trying to figure out what had gone wrong.

Things had seemed so perfect.

What would have caused him to leave?

Why wouldn't he have waited since being together for the rest of the night had been his idea?

Maybe I was looking at this all wrong. Maybe an emergency had come up and he had to run, the same way I'd had to immediately call Oaklyn.

There was only one way to find out.

One way that I knew of to get ahold of him.

At least it would show I was making an effort, but it would also reveal my last name. A detail I'd have to give him sooner rather than later if tonight ever led to something more. I just didn't love that this was the way he was going to find out I was a Dalton.

Since I saw no other option, I opened Instagram and found his profile, clicking on Message.

We weren't friends, so my note would appear in his Requests folder.

A folder I hoped he checked.

Hey, it's Hannah. I'm not sure what happened or where you went, but I'm on my way home. If you want to meet up later tonight or sometime soon, call me. I had a really great time tonight ...

I reread the message a few times, satisfied with what I'd written, and left my phone number at the bottom before I sent it.

I then exited the app and checked the texts that had come in since I'd gone to the bar. The most recent one was from Ford, my cousin, asking if I could watch his daughter tomorrow night.

Everly, his four-year-old, was my partner in crime. I would do absolutely anything for that little girl, which meant I was juggling classes and prepping for the bar and babysitting, all at the same time. It was far too much. Ford needed a nanny, and I could no longer fill that role as often as I was—a conversation I needed to have with him. Still, with how much studying I needed to get done this week, knowing I could do it after Eve went to sleep, I sent him a reply and agreed to tomorrow night.

I checked the rest of my messages, getting caught up on my email and social media, and texted Oaklyn a heads-up when I was about ten minutes away.

The moment I arrived outside our apartment building, I thanked the driver and went into the lobby, up the elevator, and down the hallway to our door. The second I unlocked it, I heard the music.

The kind you played when you hated men—or more specifically, the man who had stomped all over your heart.

Lana Del Rey.

My poor Oaklyn.

She was definitely going through it.

I took off my jacket, draping it over a stool at the bar, slid out of my heels, and joined my babe on the couch. There was an open bottle of wine on the coffee table, the smell of brownies coming from the kitchen, and every candle in the apartment was flickering.

"Hi," she cried as soon as we caught eyes.

"He sucks." I wrapped my arm around her, hugging her against me. "He doesn't deserve you."

Bunches of soggy tissues littered the table, and her face was soaked. She'd cried off most of her makeup. Only tiny specks of black mascara were left, and those were clinging to her eyelids.

"But I-I thought he was d-different."

"That's what we always think when something new and fresh and exciting starts. But the dickhead showed what he was really about, and we hate him for it." I twisted a chunk of her long brown hair around my fingers. "If there's a silver lining, it's that he showed his dickish side six months in rather than a year. Could you imagine how much we'd have hated him then?"

She looked at me, all doe-eyed. "I don't hate him any less."

"Of course you don't, but it's my job to find a positive in this situation, and that's the only one I can find." I cupped her cheek, wiping away the mascara. "Other than the fact that your future son won't have that dreaded dimple, like Trevor's."

She exhaled, her breath quivering from crying. "But I loved that dimple." The tears started to flow a lot heavier. "Am I not worth it? Am I asking too much?" She sucked in a breath. "Am I a nut to think that some perfect guy is going to sweep me off my feet, someone worthy of taking my virginity? Maybe I should just have sex with some random stranger—"

"No." I shook my head. "No, no. And hell *nooo*." I handed her the bottle of wine since she hadn't taken out any glasses and waited for her to take several gulps. "You've gone this long; you're not going to give it up to some selfish, undeserving stranger who won't take care of you in all the ways that you need."

And then there was Declan, who was mostly a stranger and had cared for me in every single way.

That man ... *my God.*

"I mean, I've done stuff with Trevor—"

"He's Dickhead now," I corrected her. "We don't use the T-word."

She attempted a smile. "Right. Dickhead. It's not like I left him miserable and unfulfilled. He got stuff; he just didn't get *that.*"

She'd set down the bottle, but I lifted it again, taking a swig, and then I held it toward her lips.

"Drink." Once she did, I continued, "Babe, in all honesty, it wouldn't have mattered how many times you'd sucked Dickhead's dick; he wouldn't have been happy until he got you. So, somehow, we're going to have to move on and forget Dickhead ever lived."

She wasn't convinced.

She wouldn't be.

She needed time to get over the hurt and betrayal, but I would do everything in my power to reinforce how special my best friend was and how unworthy Dickhead was.

"It wasn't even that good of a dick," she admitted. "You know, compared to the ones I've seen in porn."

I laughed. "Another reason Dickhead sucks. Fuck him."

Her cheeks blushed. "Yep. Fuck him."

"Brownies?"

She nodded. "Please."

I went into the kitchen and grabbed the pan out of the oven along with two forks from a drawer and returned to the living room, handing her a utensil. Both of us immediately dug in.

With a mouthful, I suggested, "Let's go out and get completely shit-faced and then stop by Anthony's Pizzeria and get slices of the best pizza in the world. How does that sound?"

She wiped off a smear of caramel from her lip. "I have work in the morning."

"When has that ever stopped us from getting hammered?"

"Solid point."

"And you've been working from home lately anyway, so there's no need for you to even go into the office tomorrow morning."

She finally gave me a real Oaklyn smile. One that was full of beautiful, straight white teeth. "You're such a lawyer."

"I'm not one of those yet, but I will be a damn good one when the time comes." I pointed toward our bedrooms. "Go put on something über-sexy and throw on a layer of lip gloss and mascara, and let's tear up this town."

She lifted a huge brownie from the pan and set it in her hand as she stood from the couch. "Give me fifteen minutes."

"Hold up." I paused, waiting for her to stop walking and turn toward me. "Before we go out, you're blocking Dick on every social media account and deleting him from your Contacts. There will be no drunk texting, IGing, DMing, tweeting, TikToking, Snapping, or calling him tonight. Do you hear me?"

She wasn't vindictive, she didn't hold grudges, and she was far too forgiving. If a mosquito bit her, she wouldn't even swat it.

Oaklyn was an angel, the calm in our relationship.

I was the storm.

"*Yesss*. I hear you."

I held out my palm. "Give me your phone. I'll do it while you're getting ready."

She reluctantly handed me her cell, and while she went to her room, I entered her password and went to work, starting with her social media apps. I was halfway through the folder on her phone when I felt a vibration. I'd set my cell on the couch beside me, and on the screen, I saw there was a text from Madison, one of the students who had gone to tonight's meetup with Declan. The text had been sent to all six of the top performers, and half of them had already responded to what she'd written.

Look who I'm with

Instead of a period at the end of her caption, there was a fire emoji.

And underneath her words was a photo that made everything inside me start to shake. It was of her and Declan, their faces close, almost cheek to cheek, smiling into the camera as she snapped a selfie. I couldn't tell which bar they were at—

59

they all looked the same in that area—but they were certainly out.

Together.

All cozied up.

As I zoomed in, there was a piece of her long red hair stuck to the whiskers of his beard. I certainly couldn't ignore that her lipstick was a bit smudged. Even his lips looked red and swollen, covered in a color that was similar, if not exact, to the one Madison was wearing, like they'd just finished kissing.

That fucker.

Instead of waiting for me in the alley, he'd found her.

Maybe he'd gotten her number while they were talking at the table, and he called her the second I left him.

Maybe he'd found her inside the bar.

It didn't even matter.

The point was, he was with her and not me.

And he'd definitely been with her all right—or things were quickly leading in that direction. Madison had a reputation for sleeping with anyone to get ahead, including two of our law professors; she'd even been with Dominick at one point last year before he started dating Kendall.

I wasn't the least bit surprised she'd made Declan her next target.

What surprised me was him.

That he'd stoop so low. That he'd go to her after he was with me.

But should I really be surprised with a reputation like his?

No.

What should surprise me was that I'd ever thought Declan was interested in me. That we had a connection. That whatever had happened between us had potential to lead to something more.

He was as disgusting as Trevor.

I opened Instagram and pulled up the message I had sent him earlier, noticing that it was *unseen*.

Of course it was. He was too busy to check his phone.

I unsent the message and deleted the entire conversation.

I didn't want that dick to have my number.

I didn't want him to know that I'd made an effort.

I never wanted to see him again unless it was in the courtroom, where I would show him what happened when you messed with a woman as fiery as me.

"What are you going to wear?" Oaklyn yelled out from her bedroom.

I glanced up from my phone, my hands still trembling. "Something black. Tight. Short. And extremely revealing."

FIVE

DECLAN

Dominick held out his hand, waiting for me to grasp it, a cocky-ass grin growing over the motherfucker's face. "Welcome to The Dalton Group."

He was the oldest.

The lead.

I knew how that worked—with age came seniority—and that was why I was shaking his hand first, why the communication, the contract negotiations, the demands I'd requested had solely been between him and me.

Not that Ford and Jenner, his younger brothers, were any less important. The two of them represented the top billionaires of the world and certainly weren't slouches when it came to success.

But Dominick would be the man I bitched to if a problem arose.

I released his hand and moved on to Jenner and Ford. "It's good to be here, gentlemen, especially now that you've agreed to my terms."

"Your fucking terms," Dominick barked, "were some of the most ridiculous I'd ever seen."

He'd wanted me, so he'd had to give me everything I'd asked for—and what I'd asked for was a fast track to making partner. According to my terms, they had two years to make that happen.

He had known I wasn't going to come easy.

But he'd agreed.

And now, I would be the firm's top litigator, and within the next two years, I would become a partner at The Dalton Group.

With Dominick as the top entertainment lawyer in the state, Jenner a real estate lawyer, and Ford an estate lawyer, I would be representing their portfolio of clients if any of them found themselves in court—trials they were now guaranteed to win.

That was why they had been willing to get on their knees and beg me to join.

Why, when I'd asked for the goddamn moon, they had given it to me.

"Listen, you get what you pay for," I countered. "You know there isn't a litigator on your team who has even a tenth of my skills." I took the contract out of my briefcase, holding it inside the folder I'd placed it in, and pushed the pile across the table toward Dominick. "You won't be disappointed. You know that."

"We do," Jenner said. "That's why you're here and why we tried to recruit you for years."

Dominick opened the lengthy contract, scanning each page, probably ensuring I had initialed and signed each appropriate spot. After flipping to the end, he nodded to his brothers.

"Now that we have the formalities out of the way, how the

hell are you?" Ford asked. "I haven't seen you in a couple of months. Still single, I'm assuming?"

"We've been out plenty," I said, pointing to Dominick and Jenner. "You're the one who's been locked at home with a little one."

A life I couldn't fathom right now.

I didn't even have a woman holding me down, never mind one who didn't reach up to my waist.

"Don't even get me started on him," Dominick said. "It's getting impossible to drag him out."

"That's going to change now that I'm here," I told them, resting my arms on the table. "Ford will be coming out all the time and staying longer than for just one round of drinks."

"And how do you plan to make that happen?" Jenner asked me.

"It's impossible to say no to me." I nodded toward Dominick. "Your brother is a prime example, and that contract is proof of what I could squeeze out of him." I grinned. "Ford's no different."

"Jesus Christ," Dominick groaned. "This room isn't big enough for your ego."

I rubbed my hand over my beard. The whiskers that I'd shortened for today's meeting were soft from the oil I'd drenched them in. "It's not ego, my friend. It's confidence. I've got far more game than all of you."

"At this point, I don't doubt that," Jenner said. "We're settled down and off the market. Well, except for Ford." His eyes narrowed at me. "And you."

"Which is why you need a woman," Dominick chimed in. He pointed at Ford and added, "Both of you do." He glanced back at me, continuing, "Someone to tame your wild ass."

I crossed my hands over the thick wooden slab, my cuff links breaking the silence. "Who says I need to be tamed?"

Dominick chuckled. "I didn't think that was what I wanted. Shit, look at me now."

"Practically married," I replied, accurately describing his relationship with Kendall.

She'd had a brief role as a reality star, and Dominick had not only scouted her, but turned her into his client and girlfriend as well.

"And happy as hell," he shot back.

"That's you." I twisted my hands together, remembering how slick they had felt that night, just a week ago, when I waited in anticipation to rub them over Hannah's body. Fuck, I couldn't get that girl out of my head. "Me, on the other hand? I'm good with the way things are in my life." I'd been reminding myself of that each passing day since meeting her. "Real good in fact."

"That's the face of a dirty, dirty dog," Jenner said.

"I've never claimed to be a saint."

"That's the truth," Jenner huffed. "A flavor of the week—I remember those days."

I nodded toward him. "Another one who's on the verge of signing a marriage license, handcuffed to your relationship."

"I'm not complaining one bit," Jenner replied.

He'd shacked up with his largest client's daughter, and I was the fucking dog at this table.

Dominick took a drink of his coffee. "Who's the catch of the week? Tell us about her."

My arms crossed behind my head as my brain returned to that night in the alley. "She was so fucking hot; we didn't even make it back to my place." I smiled as I thought of the warmth that I'd felt inside her pussy, how her cunt had pulsed around me. The way she had fucking screamed out her orgasm. "Man, she was a fierce one. Captivating. Charming. Stunning." I smiled. "A law student."

"A thirty-two-year-old, slumming it up with law school girls," one of them said.

My brain was re-creating her body, her tightness, her sounds—too lost in Hannah's memory to focus on who had spoken.

But I'd heard the words, and I responded, "I fuck anyone who's over the age of eighteen and meets my criteria, and, oh hell, she exceeded them."

First at the mock trial, where she'd really impressed me.

Then at the bar.

Again in the alley.

"Besides, Jenner's no better," I added. "Let's not forget Jo was in college when they first met. That bastard was flying back and forth to Miami to get a piece of ass."

He flipped me off after I reminded everyone of that important detail.

"So, back to this twenty-something-year-old," Dominick said. "What, you hit it and quit it?"

"Don't tell me it's been so long that you don't remember what single life looks like." I waited for him to respond. "Dude, you're not a fucking dinosaur."

My phone started to vibrate in my pocket, and I slipped my hand in the fold to send the call to voice mail. But as my fingers skimmed the hard plastic case, I felt something else. Something almost soft, silky, weightless.

What the fuck?

Wanting to see what it was, I pulled it out just a little bit, my heart instantly hammering in my chest once I glanced down.

Out of the hundred-plus suits I owned, I'd chosen the same one that I'd worn to USC a week ago.

The same one that apparently still housed the thong that I'd torn off Hannah's body.

The same one my housekeeper was supposed to take to the dry cleaner and neglected to do so.

I shoved my hand back in the pocket, fisting the flimsy fabric, dying to see if it still smelled like her.

Damn it, that girl had been different.

She'd gotten things out of me that no woman had in the past.

My lips on hers.

A desire to have her more than once.

An invite back to my house.

But that situation hadn't worked out, and Hannah was long gone from my life.

"No, I'm not a dinosaur, but I've been out of the scene for a while," Dominick said. "Tell me, why didn't this one make the cut for a second date? Too young? Too innocent?"

"Too good for you," Ford added, laughing.

"She probably is," I admitted. "Girls like her"—I paused, thinking of that gorgeous body, squeezing the thong like it was going to make her appear—"they deserve a guy who can commit." I glanced around the table. "Like you assholes, but that's not me."

"He'll never change," Jenner joked.

"You've got that right." I released the thong and ran my fingers under my nose, taking in the slightest hint of vanilla. *Fuck.* I needed to get that scent out of my head; all it did was tease me. "Let's go out tonight. I'll show you exactly how it's done and what it looks like since it appears that you fools have forgotten."

Dominick slapped his hand on the table. "I'm in."

"You know I'm in," Jenner voiced.

We all looked at Ford.

"I'll ask my cousin if she can watch Everly. If she's available, then, yes, I'm in."

"Make it happen," I told him.

Dominick looked at each of his brothers and then took in a long, deep breath. "Before we get too far into planning this evening's drunkfest, I have something to tell you, and it might change the way you feel about going out tonight."

I stared at the three of them.

I couldn't imagine what would change my mind. It certainly wouldn't have anything to do with work; everything had been spelled out in my employment contract, leaving zero room for surprises.

"All right, lay it on me."

Dominick lifted a pen from the table and tapped it over the file that held my contract. "We have a bit of an initiation process when new employees start at the firm. Experienced ones, like yourself, that is."

I cocked my head to the side. "Okay ..."

"We don't find it necessary to outline this duty in the contract. One, because it's only for a semester, and that's such a tiny smidgen of time, and two, because we look at it as an advantage."

"A hidden bonus," Ford added.

"A semester?" My brows rose from the verbiage he'd used.

Dominick's pen stilled. "You're going to mentor an intern."

I shook my head. "Fuck no."

"It's not a choice, Declan."

I glanced at their faces, their expressions backing up this new tidbit of bullshit.

"You're kidding ..." I sighed, waiting for one of them to crack a smile, laugh—anything that would tell me this was a goddamn joke. "You really aren't kidding."

"It's only for a semester, Declan. That's it." Jenner shifted in his chair. "Look at it like having another personal assistant. This one, you'll just have to give a little extra attention to."

We'd had interns at my last firm. I refused to work with one.

I didn't have the time or patience to mentor and develop someone so green.

I'd passed them off to the estate and trust department or family law—attorneys, like the bastards in front of me, who sat on their asses all day.

That wasn't me.

That wasn't even close to describing my job.

"Since you're so good with law students, this'll be right up your alley." Ford smirked.

"You didn't." I huffed air out of my mouth. "I know you didn't just go there."

"All the new hires get an intern," Dominick added, like he was trying to soften the blow. "We're not singling you out. In fact, if we didn't assign you one, it would look like we were playing favorites."

"But I am a favorite. The three of you are my friends. That must count for something."

"Oh, it does," Jenner replied, tapping his hand over the folder. "We gave you everything you asked for—things you wouldn't have gotten if you weren't our friend."

I bent my fingers together, gripping them with full strength. "You gave me what I deserve—you all know that. What I don't understand is how you're not going to give your top litigator a pass. Do you have any fucking idea how busy I'm going to be?"

"Precisely the reason why an intern would be so helpful. Aside from your regular team, that'll give you another set of hands to help out."

"You're a shitty salesperson, Jenner. Not a goddamn thing you just said has sold me on any of this."

"Declan," Dominick started, wrapping his hands around

his coffee cup, "this isn't negotiable. You're going to get an intern whether you want one or not."

I took a breath, trying to calm myself before I exploded. "Show me the candidates." I lifted my hand in the air, circling my finger. "Line them up right now, so I can hear their qualifications and pick the smartest, most submissive one you've got."

"Submissive." Jenner laughed. "Jesus."

"Can you picture me with someone type A?" I paused. "Do you really think that would be in the best interests of your firm and the intern's future here?"

"We'll pair you with someone appropriate, I assure you," Dominick voiced. "It's a random selection, but we'll make sure the two of you are a good fit."

I turned my chair toward my friend. I'd never wanted to choke his ass out more than I did right now. "You mean to tell me you're not even going to let me choose my own intern?"

He shook his head.

"Oh"—I laughed—"you've got fucking balls."

The boys had known this would piss me off.

That was why they'd had me sign the contract first.

I ground my teeth. "You know, I could get you for breach of contract. Nowhere on those papers"—I stopped to point at the thick folder—"does it state anything about an intern."

Dominick grinned, goading me. "You're going to take me to court?"

"I might."

"It's a semester—that's it," he reminded me even though Jenner had said the same thing just moments before. "You'll survive."

I didn't want a shadow.

I didn't want to have to explain myself to anyone, especially someone who was going to test my endurance and tolerance and require so much finessing.

I wanted to come in, do my job, and have the support of an efficient, well-oiled team.

If I had wanted to become a goddamn teacher, I would have joined Professor Ward's faculty.

I took my time glancing into each of their eyes. "Are you looking for me to say yes?"

"How about some excitement instead?" Ford joked.

"You like to test me, don't you?"

The youngest brother adjusted his tie, smiling. "We only pick the best, top students. Our program is extremely exclusive. Whoever gets to work with you, you're going to be changing their life, so keep that in mind."

"Yeah, yeah." I pushed back in my seat, rocking the leather, but it did nothing to soothe me. "You can save your pep talk. This is going to be hell, and you all know that." An idea came to me as I continued to rock in the seat, forcing it to bounce. "You're going to make this better by adding another clerk to my team. That way, I can get some extra help with the intern."

"That's not part of the deal," Dominick said.

"Neither is the intern."

He exhaled loudly. "You're fucking relentless, you know that?"

Now, I could smile. "You're going to love that about me when I'm in the courtroom, representing one of your clients, getting them exactly what I promised." I stood from my seat and shook Jenner's and Ford's hands. When I reached Dominick, I continued, "I'll see you tonight." As I got to the doorway, I said over my shoulder, "And you're picking up the whole fucking tab."

SIX

HANNAH

"Hannah, the time has finally come," my uncle said as he sat across from me in the boardroom. "On behalf of your aunt and your cousins, I'd like to offer you an internship at our firm."

This was a moment I'd thought about for as long as I could remember. Now that I was here, I hid my hands underneath the table, clenching them together, squeezing each finger, reminding myself that this was really happening.

That I wasn't dreaming.

That every bit of my hard work and determination had finally paid off.

My uncle, looking at me so warmly, slid a folder in my direction, stopping once the manila was within my reach.

"In there, you'll find a description of the program, your compensation, and our commitment to you as your employer."

Every word my uncle spoke echoed in my head.

I made it.

Of course, Oaklyn would say I should have expected this. Maybe a part of me had, but that didn't diminish the work it had taken me to get here or how I'd strived to overachieve to show my family how badly I wanted to be a part of their firm. Not just because it was theirs, but also because it was the best.

I released my fingers, lifting them onto the table, flattening my sweaty palms against the folder. "Thank you." I glanced at each of their smiling faces. "I'm so honored to be here, you guys."

My aunt beamed as she said, "Your uncle and I are so tickled that you're here. We've watched you achieve everything you've set out to accomplish—first with your undergraduate degree and now with law school. You've had some notable scholarly achievements, young lady, and we're so proud of you, Hannah."

"It's been impressive to watch," my uncle added. "Even though you will always have a place at the family table, you've earned your place here as much as your fellow interns."

They noticed. Oh God, they noticed.

I took a deep breath, trying to calm my heart. "I appreciate that, Aunt Sue and Uncle David."

"And now, we're throwing you straight to the wolves, so you can work your ass off again," Ford teased.

My aunt smiled, shaking her head. "I wouldn't have put it in those terms, but, yes, Ford is right. The next several months are going to be extremely challenging."

Before I could respond, Dominick said, "I'm not sure how much you know about the internship program, but you're going to be working under one of our litigators for an entire semester. We feel that's an adequate amount of time to get an understanding of our operations. Aside from learning the ins and outs of the department, you'll be assisting all members of the attorney's legal team. We want to emphasize that this is a support role; you'll be required to do everything that's asked of you—within reason, of course."

"In other words, if you're told to pick up coffee, drop off dry cleaning, make reservations, book travel, do it." Ford winked.

I could always count on him for keeping it real and spelling everything out in layman's terms even if I didn't need it.

Still, I couldn't help but laugh at his reply. "Trust me, I get it, and I know what will be required of me."

"And that sounds good to you?" Jenner asked.

It sounded like a dream.

All I wanted was a chance, and they were giving me one.

"It sounds perfect," I told them.

"Good. Then, you won't be offended when I tell you that we don't play favorites in this office, nor do we give any special treatment even if you are a Dalton," Dominick voiced, the gentleness in his tone now gone.

"I would never want you to." I didn't feel as though I'd said enough. My family needed to know how much I wanted to be here and what I was willing to do to stay and how I wouldn't take a second of this for granted. "I didn't walk into your building this morning, anticipating a red carpet or favors or for my last name to get me any kind of special privileges. I don't want this job to be easy. I want to work my butt off, and that's what I plan to do." I took a breath, my stomach in knots, my hands even sweatier than before. "I don't want anything handed to me. I want to be awarded a role because I've done everything in my power to earn it." I scanned each of their faces. "I know you all have expectations of me, and my plans aren't to meet them, but to exceed them." I paused. "Just you wait and see."

The hardness in Dominick's expression began to fade just a tad. "We're excited to see what you're going to bring to your team and watch you grow throughout this program."

I noticed an exchange between him and Ford before Ford added, "We've randomly placed you with a litigator we think will be an excellent fit. Someone you're going to learn a great deal from. The experience will be much more beneficial than anything you could learn in the classroom."

My family didn't do anything that was random. If I was going to have an opportunity to work here full-time, then they would make sure I was assigned to the best. That person was Christopher Allen, their top litigator, someone I'd researched extensively. Although I hadn't met him personally, I'd asked Ford enough questions to know the type of demeanor I would be facing and just how much of a hard-ass Christopher was. With Christopher at the helm of my internship, Ford was right when he'd said this would be better than anything I'd learned in school.

I lifted a pen off the table, holding it between my fingers. "I can't express how excited I am to start." I opened the lid of the folder, flipping to the last page of the thick packet. I knew there was no negotiating the terms; I wasn't in that kind of position yet, nor was there any reason to fear that my family was going to screw me, so I scratched my name across the last page. "I'm ready to start today."

"Excellent," my uncle said. "Your mentor is certainly ready for you, and I'm positive an extra set of hands will help him tremendously; he has quite the caseload."

Every word he said was just adding to this incredible dream.

I closed the folder and pushed it toward my uncle. "Where do I find this mentor?"

"Office number eighteen ten," Jenner said. "Take a right outside the door, and it's the last office on the left."

Eighteen ten, I repeated in my head.

His office was on this floor, the same floor where my cousins, aunt, and uncle worked. That meant they had definitely assigned me to Christopher since he was the head of litigation, and each department head was located on the executive-level floor.

I smiled, the anxiousness erupting in my chest. "I'll be on my way, then." I stood from the table and froze. "I can hug you all, right? Handshakes just feel so wrong right now."

My aunt opened her arms, holding them in the air. "Get over here, my girl."

She wrapped them around me, and my uncle and cousins did the same as I made my way around the table. Once I thanked everyone, I walked to the door and carefully closed it behind me.

I needed just a second, so I leaned my back against the wood and closed my eyes, taking a giant breath.

I didn't care that it was only an internship. I'd still signed a contract; I would receive a paycheck.

Therefore, in my eyes, I was an employee of The Dalton Group.

Oh God.

This is really happening.

Everything I've ever wanted is finally coming true.

I didn't have time to waste or celebrate or even shoot a quick text to Oaklyn to tell her the news. If my mentor was expecting me, then his office was where I needed to be.

I walked down the hallway, following Jenner's instructions, watching the numbers increase as I passed each doorway. Most were closed, and even though this walkway was a defined space, there was a bank of admins to my right, working in an open area, assisting the executive-level staff. I smiled and nodded as I made eye contact with them, stopping when I reached the closed door to office eighteen ten.

There were name plaques outside all the other offices.

But not this one.

I wondered why. Considering Christopher had worked at

the firm for the last eight years, it seemed odd that his was missing.

I took another deep breath and knocked on the door.

"Come in," I heard from the other side.

I didn't know why I was racked with nerves or why my body felt so weak, my limbs numb. This was just an internship; it wasn't like I was about to step into court for the very first time. Hopefully, I'd feel better once I got a sense of Christopher and his work style and what this process was actually going to look like.

Knowing I was already taking too long, I turned the knob and slowly opened the door. I was fully expecting there to be a tall, almost-lanky, blond-haired, light-blue-eyed man behind the desk—details I'd captured during my research of him.

But Christopher's eyes weren't the ones staring back at me.

These were green.

Magnetic.

And they pulled so many memories from my mind, ones that had started during the mock trial, ones that continued at the bar, ones that had locked with mine before he led me to the alley.

Declan Shaw?

Is here?

No.

He couldn't be.

He wasn't employed by The Dalton Group.

He worked at Smith & Klein.

Doesn't he?

I blinked.

Again.

And again.

Every time my eyes refocused, Declan was still there. His strong, broad shoulders taking up the whole width of the chair.

His square jaw, a literal work of art, was taunting me, as were his perfectly thick lips. The dusting of scruff on his face had now thickened into a fuller beard.

When I realized my eyes weren't playing tricks on me, my mouth parted, and instead of saying something to greet him, I gasped.

Oh shit.

That sound hadn't just happened in my head; it was audible.

But it turned out, I wasn't the only one surprised; the same look was registering on his face.

"Hannah ..."

The shock didn't last long, and what replaced that expression was hunger. His lips opened, and his tongue licked across them, his eyes becoming feral.

After the disappointment and hurt that I'd felt from that photo, I would have thought my body would have zero reaction to him.

But my body wasn't on the same wavelength as my mind.

Almost instantly, there was a wetness between my legs, my body aching for his fingers. I caught a glimpse of his hands, remembering the way they had tugged my nipples, twisted, and instant memories from that night in the alley were suddenly making me breathless.

"What are you doing here?" he asked.

My fingers fell from the doorknob, my feet frozen in place.

I couldn't take another step.

I couldn't sit.

I'd planned to never see this man again unless I faced him in the courtroom, where I would be forced to address him professionally and fully intended to whip his ass. That was what he deserved after ditching me for Madison. The aftershock of seeing that photo still rattled me.

But now, he was here.

In Christopher's office.

Which meant only one thing.

I was staring at my new mentor—a piece of information my family hadn't given me before I walked down the hallway. Based on his question, I figured they must have kept him in the dark as well.

Oh God.

How? Why?

And what am I going to do?

The dryness on my tongue made it almost impossible for me to swallow. "I work here." *No, that's not really true.* "I'm an intern."

"Since when?"

I couldn't tell if he was pleased by this news or pissed.

"Since today," I replied.

If he had been given my information prior to me walking through his door, then he would have connected the dots by now, and he would know I was a Dalton. Therefore, I had to assume he still didn't know.

Oh boy.

Today keeps getting more interesting by the second.

"Declan, when did you start working here?"

I hoped this was just a temporary situation, that Christopher was on vacation and would replace Declan in a couple of days or hours—the latter being my preference.

"A few days ago."

I tried to fill my lungs. "And you're going to be my ... mentor?"

His eyes narrowed. "Looks that way, doesn't it?"

"It ... does."

He pointed at one of the chairs in front of his desk. "Sit."

I encouraged my feet to move even though they didn't want to, and once I was safely seated, his stare intensified.

I couldn't continue to hold his gaze.

It was too much.

I just wanted to run and never return to this office again.

But I couldn't. I had to say something. There were just so many elephants in the room; I didn't know which one to start with.

My name seemed like a solid place, but I needed to find a way to ease into it.

Make light of it—somehow.

"You know, it's funny; my cousin always tells me about the firm's new hires," I said. "At least the lawyers who come on board who have quite a name for themselves, like you. I wish he'd mentioned something, especially since you're such a celebrity at our law school."

I wondered why Ford hadn't told me, considering I'd watched his daughter the past two nights, giving him a perfect opportunity to bring it up.

Declan was quiet for a few moments. "Your cousin works in HR?"

"No." Strands of my hair fell into my face as I shook my head. "Ford is one of the partners. As are Dominick and Jenner —all my first cousins."

"Wait." His arms landed on the desk, moving his body closer to me. "You're related to the Daltons?"

My hands were practically dripping with sweat. As I recrossed my legs, I shoved my fingers between them, hoping my skirt would soak up the wetness. "Their father and my father are brothers."

More silence passed.

"That makes you ..."

"A Dalton." I bit my bottom lip. "I'm Hannah Dalton."

"Hannah Dalton," he repeated. He dropped his gaze to the desk, appearing like he was processing the news, exhaling loud enough for me to hear. "A bit of information that would have been helpful to know that night."

That night.

A night I wished I could take back.

A night that had obviously meant much more to me than him if he'd so easily left me at the bar to go to Madison.

A night I didn't want to discuss with the man who was now my mentor, whom I would be working closely with for the next semester.

And a night I never wanted my family to find out about. I wouldn't be fired—I knew that much—but I didn't know what would happen if my aunt and uncle or even Dominick, Jenner, and Ford found out that Declan had fucked his future intern. That he'd left me alone at a bar. That he hadn't even had the decency to make sure I had a way home.

I couldn't have that evening hanging over us.

I couldn't let on that I was upset about what he'd done.

I certainly couldn't acknowledge that I'd fallen for him in a matter of minutes, and even though I'd tried pushing him out of my brain, I couldn't, and I'd thought of him every day since.

There had to be a way out of this. To avoid the conversation altogether. To start fresh as two people who had just crossed paths in a classroom, nothing else.

And then it hit me.

Why couldn't I have been too drunk to remember what had happened between us?

In order for Declan to prove I was lying, he'd need to bear the burden of showing that I was guilty beyond all reasonable doubt.

The only evidence that existed was the dirt I'd found on my suit jacket and tank top from him stripping them off me and throwing the clothes to the ground. He didn't know I'd found the stains the next morning and sent them to the dry cleaner.

He also didn't know there had been an ache between my legs when I woke up, the soreness a constant reminder throughout the day of the pleasure he'd given me and just how large he was.

The last thing he couldn't prove was how alcohol affected me, that after several shots and a few martinis on an empty stomach, I could have been a forgetful mess.

The way I saw it, he had no case at all.

But, *oh man*, lying wasn't the angle I wanted to take. It wasn't the way I wanted to start this internship. It made me sick to think that I was going to be this dishonest about the sexiest night I'd ever experienced in my life.

As I stared into Declan's eyes, melting from a gaze so strong, I knew there was no other option.

So, I clasped my hands in my lap, trying to look as innocent as possible, and said, "That night? I remember our time in the classroom when you were mentoring me, and from the little bit I can recall from the bar, I believe we had an enlightening conversation. But, admittedly—and this is so embarrassing—I don't remember anything we spoke about." When I shook my head this time, I tucked the loose strands behind my ear. "I definitely shouldn't have drunk that much on an empty stomach."

"Hold on a second ..."

His eyes scanned me, and I knew he was trying to read me. Something he'd done so easily before, but I wasn't going to allow that now. Layers of masks covered my face, blocking his penetration.

"You don't remember ... anything? Or just our conversation?"

"Anything, honestly." I winced like I felt bad about it. "Wait, that's not true. I think you said something about blue cheese olives." I paused. "That you liked them? Or maybe hated them?" I shrugged. "Oh gosh, I don't know." My eyes widened, and I put my hand over my mouth. "I hope I didn't make a fool of myself. Or do something silly. Or—*oh God*—inappropriate. That would make for a terrible first impression ... and I'd be mortified."

I didn't even sound like myself. I sounded like Madison, except she'd be twirling a piece of her hair around her finger, chewing a piece of gum.

I hated this.

I hated myself.

I hated the way I felt.

I hated the way he was looking at me.

But I certainly wasn't going to address how much I'd loved the way my wetness tasted on his lips or why he hadn't taken me home or how I knew it would be almost impossible to find a man who made me feel the way he had.

I needed my new boss to treat me with respect, not someone he'd thrown away.

I needed him to know I had skills other than the ones I'd shown him in the alley.

He meshed his fingers together, his fists clasped. "You didn't ... make a fool of yourself."

"Are you sure I didn't say anything inappropriate?" I needed to ensure this was all squashed, his response not satisfying me enough. "Sometimes, when I drink, I get a little flirty." My hand flew to my chest. "Please tell me that didn't happen. I would die."

Madison had nothing on me.

He huffed out a bit of air, breaking eye contact to look at his hands. He licked across his lips, his brows furrowed as he glanced at me. "There's no reason for you to worry."

"Great." I swallowed as the dryness faded, saliva finally

entering my mouth. "Well, I'm ready to get started. Whatever you need, just tell me. I'm here to help in every way. And, Declan"—I put my hand on his desk, not far from where his were, wanting to emphasize this point in any way I could— "even though I'm a Dalton, I expect you to treat me like I'm any other intern."

His arms left the desk, and he pushed back into his seat, his eyes roaming as though he were taking inventory of me. "You can take this folder to my paralegal. She'll know what to do with it." He lifted the folder off his desk and reached across the space between us.

I grabbed it from his hand, the position causing our fingers to collide.

The quick graze only lasted a second, just long enough for our heat to blend, for me to be reminded of the control he'd had over my body.

Once we parted, a surge erupted inside me—this sexy, over-whelming dominance that took me off guard.

Tingles licked across every inch of me.

They were strong enough to cause my breath to hitch.

To send me to my feet.

To not just dampen, but soak me.

This man ... fuck.

"I'll be back," I whispered.

I was relieved when I could turn away from him, but that feeling didn't last more than a moment because I felt his gaze move to my ass.

As I walked out and closed his door behind me, a thought marinated in my head.

He knew exactly what my ass felt like.

What I smelled like.

What I tasted like.

This was going to be the longest semester of my entire life.

SEVEN

DECLAN

uck me.

F That was the thought that had run through my head every time I looked at Hannah over the past three days.

It had been seventy-two hours since she'd walked into my office. Every morning was a different outfit of the same variety. But each one showed her beautiful, bouncing tits, her lean, toned legs that looked endless in a pair of sky-high heels. Her long, hanging hair that framed the hottest face I'd ever seen.

And her goddamn scent.

The vanilla that I could taste even though it was no longer in my mouth.

Is this some sick punishment?

The world's way of getting back at me for hooking up with a student I mentored?

For finally kissing a woman after all these years?

To find out she was a Dalton ... now, that was a fucking blow. If I had known that before, I wouldn't have laid a hand on her. I certainly wouldn't have kissed her. The truth was, I wouldn't have gone anywhere near her.

After she had given me her last name, she'd told me she didn't want me to treat her any differently.

That was laughable.

Her name was on the sign outside the building.

Her name would be on my paycheck—a firm that I would one day become an equity partner of.

Even though The Dalton Group didn't have a nonfraternization policy in their contract, it was a relief that we hadn't hooked up while either of us was an employee. Even if we had, Hannah would have had nothing to worry about. If things somehow went south, those brothers would throw out their best litigator long before they reprimanded their own blood.

Still, I found it interesting that during the conversations I'd had with her—the ones when she was sober, especially the ones when she was drunk—she hadn't mentioned her last name. Even during the talks that had been centered around her future, that would have been a perfect opportunity for her to slip in that she was a Dalton.

Yet she hadn't.

When, as a Dalton, her future was already written.

A position would automatically be made for her at this firm.

But those weren't things she had said at the bar. In fact, it'd sounded like she wasn't sure where she'd land; she'd just hoped it would be in California.

Of course, she didn't remember any of those chats.

She remembered nothing at all.

How had I missed all the signs that she was that drunk? I didn't recall her slurring her words or stumbling. If I had sensed any of that, I wouldn't have touched her. Consent was my middle name. I wanted my women coherent, so the next morning, they'd remember who had put that ache in their pussy.

But Hannah didn't.

Now, that was some shit.

Especially since every goddamn moment of that night replayed in my head each time I looked at her.

Like it was doing now as she walked into my office.

"Good morning," she sang.

Would she still be singing if she knew what had happened between us?

Fuck, I didn't know.

And I didn't plan on telling her; that wouldn't lead to anything good.

But I was still going to admire the hell out of her, especially in today's outfit, which was a black dress that hugged every curve, red heels that accentuated those sexy calves, and a pair of diamond earrings that made me want to suck on her earlobes.

Her presence was a fire that burned straight to my cock.

A dick that had been hard for three days, and this morning was no different.

I hadn't gotten any work done since she had started here.

I probably wouldn't today either—and that was some bullshit.

I was Declan Shaw, top litigator in the state. I needed to pull my head out of my ass. Women didn't throw off my game, and neither would Hannah.

But the fucked-up thing was that this was only the very beginning.

We were going to be together for an entire semester.

She took a seat, her legs crossing, a notebook on top of them, hiding the part of her thighs that her dress didn't cover. "Looks like my desk still isn't ready, so I'm going to have to spend another day in here." She smiled awkwardly. "Sorry."

The maintenance department had promised it would be delivered this morning.

I was getting punished.

Again.

"That's unacceptable." My hand went into my hair, pulling at the roots. "I need you to call maintenance and have them find you a desk today."

"I tried—"

"Try harder."

As she nodded, I took a long, deep breath. "See those boxes?" I pointed at the row of cardboard that took up a whole corner of my office. "They're filled with folders that you can file into those cabinets"—I shifted my finger to the cabinets that had been built into the wall behind me—"over there."

I needed her out of my hair.

I needed her attention focused on something other than me.

She got up from the chair, sauntering over to the first box, bending to open the lid. The position caused her dress to ride up well past her knees, the top loosening enough that it showed the swell of her tits.

Jesus Christ.

"Are these your previous cases from your old firm?"

I ground my teeth together, the anger building.

Why hadn't she told me her last name?

Why had she drunk so much?

Why the fuck couldn't I get her out of my head?

"Yes," I replied. "And don't stop until they all have a home."

"I'm on it."

"Can you do it silently?" The growl erupted in my throat. "I don't need you talking while you're in here. Understood?"

Images of her already owned my mind; the last thing I needed was her voice too.

Once she nodded, I turned toward my computer and tried to ignore that she was directly behind me, that I could almost feel the heat from her body. That every time she returned to the box, she bent over in my direction. That every time she came back to the cabinet, she was close enough that I could touch her.

"Wow, I remember studying some of these cases."

She was only inches away, practically on top of me, her words vibrating through me.

I fucking loved how that made me feel.

And I hated it.

I fucking loved that Hannah had this kind of effect on me, more than any woman ever had.

And, *goddamn it,* I hated it.

"Hannah, what did I say?"

"No talking ... *sorry.*"

I reached for my coffee, needing something to put out this fire, and when I went to take a sip, I realized the mug was empty. I gripped the ceramic in my hand and stood, heading for the door.

"Declan ..."

Her voice.

It never stopped.

It just echoed.

I paused in the doorway and faced her. "What?"

"I can get that for you." She nodded toward the mug. "A cup of coffee, I mean." She held out her hand even though she was still on the other side of the room. "Give it to me; I'll do it."

She'd done enough.

My fucking dick was hard.

Unless she planned to get on her knees and open her mouth, I needed her to stay put.

"I'm good," I told her, and I went into the kitchen.

I filled the mug and took a long drink of the strong, bitter black brew.

As I went back to my office, I stalled in the doorway, watching Hannah on her knees in front of the cabinet. The fabric of her dress was tight across her ass, showing the outline of her thong.

She glanced over her shoulder, catching me staring. "Everything all right?" She waited. "Do you need something?"

So giving.

Attentive.

All it did was make me angrier.

"I need you to finish that filing," I barked. "I have weeks' worth of work to catch up on, and I need access to those cases."

"I'll move faster."

As I neared my desk, she rose from the floor and must have gotten up too fast because she wavered on her heels, her arms shooting out at her sides as she attempted to gain her balance.

I didn't know if she was going to fall, but I surely wasn't going to let that happen.

With one hand still gripping my mug, I wrapped the other arm around her back and hauled her up against my body to steady her.

My cock instantly pounded inside my suit pants.

My heart fucking exploded as she molded against me.

As she glanced up, her lips wet and open, her eyes wide, it took everything in my power not to brush the hair out of her face.

Not to grab the back of her neck and smash our lips together.

Not to place her on my desk and thrust my face up her dress.

What the fuck is wrong with me?

"Thank you ... for catching me." She was breathless. Her expression spent, like I'd just finished giving her an orgasm.

I swallowed. "You need to watch where you're going."

Those words didn't even make sense.

I didn't care.

"Right. Sorry ... again."

My arm dropped, and I backed up until I reached my desk, placing the coffee on top of it.

When I glanced across the space, she was digging into the box to add more files to the cabinet, the dress now high in the back, showing her gorgeous legs.

Legs I wanted wrapped around my face.

I needed to focus.

Not on her.

I opened the top drawer of my desk to grab a legal pad, so I could jot down some notes on a client, and her thong was sitting inside it. The one I'd found in my suit pocket on the day I started at the firm, that I'd set in here because I didn't want to carry it around all day.

I shut the drawer, shoving my hands through my hair to stop them from shaking.

I couldn't do this.

I couldn't look at her every day, remembering what had happened and what I wanted to happen again.

I needed to get the fuck out of here.

"Do you want me to organize the Drake folders when I'm done?"

I stopped at the sound of her voice, turning toward her when I reached the doorway.

Drake was a client of Ford's—a case that I should be working on now.

"Why would you do that?" I asked.

"It's a lot of information, and your paralegal is sorting through mountains of—"

"Just focus on the filing." The frustration was making its

way into my skin. I could feel myself starting to sweat. "I'll give you your next assignment once you're done."

"Whatever you say, boss."

Boss ... fuck.

Followed by a smile that was far too satisfying on her gorgeous face.

This wasn't okay.

I couldn't have her.

And that wasn't okay either.

My clients needed my full attention.

They needed me at my best.

And for three days, I'd done nothing but fantasize about her.

"I've—" I cut myself off, staring at her, wondering what the hell to say. "I've got to go talk to Dominick."

I headed toward the opposite end of the floor. Dominick's door was open when I arrived at his office, and fortunately, Jenner and Ford were sitting in there with him.

I went in and closed his door behind me, taking the only open seat.

"Everything all right, Declan?" Dominick asked. "You look ... on edge."

"I need a new intern."

Dominick laughed. "For what reason?"

What the hell can I say to them?

"She's your cousin. She's probably going to become a partner here. I don't want that kind of pressure. You know me; I do things unconventionally. I'm reckless. I'm unethical at times, immoral even. Having her learn from me"—I shook my head, thinking of all the upcoming one-on-one time I'd have with her —"is a bad fucking idea. I'm no role model, Dominick."

"You're the top litigator in the state for a reason," Ford said. "Why the hell wouldn't we want you mentoring our cousin?"

They weren't buying my bullshit.

I needed to be more persuasive.

"Listen, I'm just not the right person. You've got a whole department of litigators. You've got Christopher Allen, who's excellent."

They knew I'd never call him that. Christopher was far from excellent. He lacked balls and charm, and I could destroy him without even saying a word.

"He follows the book; he'd be perfect to mold and coddle her. This isn't what I do. I produce evidence, I defend, I raise hell in court." I glanced around at all three of them. "I don't mentor ... I just fucking don't."

Jenner folded his hands on his lap. "You're not the typical mentor—I won't deny that fact. Patience certainly isn't your strong suit, but I want Hannah to learn from the best. I want her to see every angle of litigation—whether that's straddling the line or going directly by the book. She's one of the brightest women I know, and when it comes time for her to enter the courtroom, you'll make sure she's ready."

A good girl.

If they only fucking knew.

If she only knew what she'd done.

They weren't listening, or they weren't hearing me.

I needed to be more direct.

I cupped the edge of Dominick's desk and looked him straight in the face. "I don't want her as my intern. I'll take someone else. Anyone. But not Hannah. Reassign her." I took a breath. "Today."

EIGHT

HANNAH

"I don't want her as my intern. I'll take someone else. Anyone. But not Hannah. Reassign her. Today."

With my hand on Dominick's doorknob, I was frozen outside his office, my body instantly shaking as Declan's words hit me.

His voice was stern, assertive.

Insistent.

He doesn't want me?

But I didn't understand. Over the last three days, I'd done absolutely everything he'd asked for and more. I doted on him, ran errands, picked him up breakfast and lunch, made multiple coffee trips that weren't always to the kitchen, but to cafés in the area. I organized his office; I assisted with research.

I never said no.

In fact, I was constantly asking what he needed, what I could help with, what he wanted from me.

I'd just spent the last thirty minutes on my knees, emptying a few of his boxes, and I'd moved faster after he expressed how badly he needed those files.

And now, I wasn't good enough?

Why hadn't he voiced that to me instead of going to Dominick? He hadn't complained even once, so I'd had no idea he was so unhappy.

Sure, he'd barked.

He'd been dickish.

There had also been times when he was quiet, rarely engaging me in conversation.

But I understood that. That was the type of person Declan was—busy in his own head, demanding in his words, in control of all actions around him, with no patience for nonsense and bullshit.

But to just dump me? After three days?

Dominick was going to think I was inefficient and unprepared for this internship, that my family had made a mistake by bringing me on—or worse, that I wasn't good enough for a full-time position when the time came.

Declan ... how dare you!

Why would he do this to me?

Because of what had happened between us? Because I'd claimed to not remember?

But he was the one who had fucked me and then gone directly into Madison's arms.

Despite all of that, I was still giving him my best at the office, and I wasn't letting that night define my job.

Unlike him, who was clearly affected by something or he wouldn't be treating me like shit.

For such a seasoned lawyer—an adult for that matter—he was certainly acting like a baby.

"She won't be transferring to another litigator," Dominick replied. "She's staying put."

"You're telling me that for the next four months, you're going to keep me with an employee I don't feel like I can properly mentor? Or work with?" Declan asked, his voice rising.

My fingers tightened on the silver knob, my entire body shaking.

"Don't you think you're being a little harsh?" Ford asked.

Ford?

Oh God, Ford's in there too?

"Harsh?" Declan replied. "From the very beginning, I was upfront and honest that I didn't want an intern. Now, you give me someone who has no skills, zero experience. Whose hand I need to hold. I just don't have time for it."

No experience—I could accept that.

But no skills?

That's what he thinks of me?

I glanced down at my arm, where a folder rested on top of it, my finger lodged in between two heavy sections of paper, marking a specific area. I'd practically screamed when I came across this during my filing. Since my first day here, everyone on his team had been scrambling to find information for one of his upcoming trials, staying at the office until past midnight every night, constantly on edge, all because no one wanted to disappoint Declan and his desire to win. They all had been looking for the information I was holding.

And now, I had it.

A precedent that wasn't just going to help him with the trial; it was going to ensure he won.

But I have no skills, right?

We'll see about that.

Game on, dickhead.

I knocked on the door.

"Come in," I heard.

While twisting the doorknob, I pushed every bit of emotion

out of my body—the anger, the resentment—and I walked inside Dominick's office.

"I'm sorry to interrupt," I said when all four sets of eyes landed on me. I was surprised to see that Jenner was in here too. "But I found something and had to share it with you." I spoke directly to Declan, moving closer to where he was sitting.

I hated that his rich, spicy cologne immediately hit my face and that I loved the scent so much.

It didn't matter how awful he was; his gaze affected me in the most outrageous, powerful ways.

Like the way he was looking at me now.

Like he wanted to bend me over his lap and spank my bare ass.

"You've been so concerned about the Kennedy trial ..." I referenced the case, which happened to be Dominick's client, so my family would know the importance of whom I was speaking about. "Your whole team has been scouring every resource, looking for precedent, but they've been unsuccessful in locating one that will really sway the jury."

I opened the folder to the place where my finger was wedged inside and set it on his thighs. "While I was doing your filing, I came across this case. It's from seven years ago, but it's one I studied heavily while I followed your career." I let that bit of information sink in. "In this case"—I nodded toward his lap—"you used a precedent that I believe will be more than sufficient for the Kennedy case."

"Is she right?" Dominick asked.

Declan looked at my cousin and then back to me before his stare dropped to the folder. I watched his eyes skim several lines before he flipped through a few pages.

He slowly glanced up. "Yes."

One word.

That was all he would give me.

I smiled. "I'll get back to the filing now."

I didn't wait for anyone to respond.

I didn't look at any of their faces.

I didn't even pick up the folder from his lap.

I just walked out into the hallway, feeling all their eyes on me, and returned to Declan's office, going right back to the cabinet, where I resumed my duties.

As I placed the folders inside in alphabetical order, I couldn't escape my thoughts.

Declan Shaw wasn't the man I'd thought.

At this pace, I truly didn't know how I was going to survive this. It would be one thing if he didn't show appreciation, if he was constantly grumpy and demanding—I could deal with that. But knowing he didn't want me here, that he would rather have anyone but me, that hurt. And that was a feeling I couldn't overcome.

"Why the hell would you rush into Dominick's office, interrupting our meeting?"

Surprised by the sound of his voice, I shot my attention toward the doorway where Declan was standing, his shoulder leaning against the frame, his hand clutching the folder.

"Your team has spent days looking for a precedent. I thought you'd be pleased with what I'd found."

"You thought wrong. In fact, just stop thinking altogether." His stare penetrated my chest, wrapping around my heart, squeezing with a strength that made it hard for me to breathe. "Don't ever interrupt a meeting to give me a piece of information that I would have found myself." He walked in and tossed the folder onto his desk.

I wasn't going to apologize.

I didn't believe I'd done anything wrong.

If he had known the precedent existed, then his team wouldn't have wasted the last three days researching.

He just couldn't stand that I'd found it.

That I'd made him look like an asshole in front of my family.

I got up from my knees to grab another handful of folders. "Understood."

He took a seat at his desk, putting his back to me. "How long were you eavesdropping outside Dominick's office before you came in?"

Was the big, bad wolf worried that I'd overheard his bitch session?

Only a guilty person would ask that question.

That was Law 101.

Dickhead.

"I wasn't." I put my back to him as I reached into the box, bending so my ass was high and visible from where he sat. I stayed in that position for a second and then glanced at him. "Why?"

Of course he had been looking at me. Declan was a pig— the photo of him and Madison had proven that.

"Should I have been eavesdropping?"

"You should have been completing the task I assigned. I asked you to hurry the hell up. You clearly didn't listen to anything I said."

I'd listened to every word.

He had told me he needed me to finish the filing because he had weeks' worth of work to catch up on and he needed to access his cases.

I'd told him I'd move faster.

Which I'd done.

"What made you rush down the hallway and barge into Dominick's office like that?" He turned his chair toward me, spreading his fingers wide and pressing them together, like he was palming a basketball. "Why couldn't you have waited to show me the folder when I came back to my office?"

I straightened, holding a hand on my hip, the stack of folders resting in my other arm.

He was looking for an argument.

I wasn't going to give him one.

"I won't do it again."

"You're not the lawyer on this case, Hannah. You're not the one who has to stand in the courtroom and present a believable argument. I can't for the fucking life of me figure out why you did what you did today."

I felt the same way about how he was acting and what had warranted this kind of reaction.

"I was excited for you," I admitted. "I've watched how hard you've been working on this case, and I wanted to offer some relief."

"Relief?" His eyes narrowed, his hands dropping as his arms crossed his chest. "Don't get excited for me. Just do your goddamn job. If I tell you to file, do it. If I send you on an errand, don't text if you're running late; I don't need the constant updates of where you are and when you'll be back. If I give you the assignment of finding a precedent, that's when you're allowed to look for what I've requested. I'm not here to fucking babysit you, Hannah." He sighed, like even the sound of my name disgusted him. "If you want to be a litigator—and a successful one at that—you have a lot of work to do."

My heart was beating so hard that my throat was vibrating.

I couldn't believe he was treating me this way.

That my bringing a folder into Dominick's office had set him off this badly.

What Declan didn't know was that I was a storm and he'd just ramped up the wind inside me.

As I stared at him, all I felt was anger.

Frustration.

Repulsion.

I held his gaze for several seconds. "Then, I'd better get back to work." I didn't hesitate. I just returned to the cabinet, moving at the same speed as I had before.

Several minutes passed before he grumbled, "You asked me not to treat you like a Dalton, so I'm not."

Did he feel remorse?

Was his conscience actually kicking in?

"That's right," I said as I faced him again. "I want you to treat me like I'm any other intern."

He wiped his lips, although he hadn't eaten anything. "Then, you need to understand something. We have four months together. The last thing I need is you hovering in my fucking office like you're a goddamn child."

That's what he thinks I'm doing?

Hovering?

My eyes widened as I tried to fill my lungs. "Okay—"

"I need you to tell me you understand what I'm saying." His hand stayed by his chin as he took me in like I was his patient. "I need to hear you say yes, Hannah."

It took everything in me to nod and whisper, "Yes."

"Good." He pointed toward the area where I had set my purse and the few personal items I'd brought to the office. "Now, get your things and go find a different place to work. My office is no longer your girl cave."

NINE

DECLAN

I couldn't get over how much Hannah and her twin brother, Camden, looked alike. They had identical eyes and mouths, dark chocolate hair. They even fucking laughed the same.

I also couldn't get over that he was sitting across from me at the bar. No matter how hard I tried, something was always reminding me of her.

At work, it was her presence.

After hours, it was thoughts of our one night together.

Now, it was her fucking brother.

"I can't believe there's two of you," I groaned.

I'd already given him plenty of shit tonight about his sister. Another remark shouldn't surprise him.

It didn't seem to as he stared at me, laughing. "You're saying I look like her?"

I nodded. "Spitting image."

"I would hope so. We are twins."

This was the first time Camden had tagged along for one of our guys' nights. He lived in New York and was finishing up his last year of law school. He told me once he graduated, he'd be moving back to LA to work for the family's firm.

I hoped to hell that, once he returned permanently, his attendance for our nights out wouldn't become a regular thing.

The more Daltons didn't necessarily mean the better.

I clapped his shoulder. "I'm sorry you have to bear that burden."

"It's a good thing I have no interest in being a litigator." He ran his hand over his beard. "I have a feeling you and I would go twelve rounds on the daily."

I pulled my hand back, chuckling. "Listen, if you're self-sufficient and you don't require a pacifier or an afternoon nap and you don't need your bottle warmed, then we'll get along just fine." I rolled my eyes, making sure Dominick saw. "Your other half needs all those things."

"He's on fire tonight," Dominick said to Camden, referring to me.

"I'm only speaking the truth." I glanced around the table at all their faces but eventually landed on Dominick. "And since I'm in the middle of saving your client the millions he's being sued for after breaching his contract, I'd think you'd be a little more sensitive to my needs."

The brothers still hadn't listened.

They still hadn't reassigned her.

"You mean, the case in which Hannah found the perfect precedent?" Jenner asked. "The one you're going to win because of her?" He eyed me down. "I think you owe some of the credit to our cousin, my friend."

I shook my head, trying to force her name out of my mind. "I would have won without it."

"You haven't even gone to trial yet," Dominick countered.

"I'm telling you"—I ground my teeth—"we would have won without it."

I would have done everything in my fucking power, but I did question if that would have been enough to persuade the jury. Hannah's findings certainly made it easier, and now, I wouldn't have to work so hard.

That changed nothing.

I wasn't going to give her a goddamn medal for snooping through my files and bringing something to my attention that I would have figured out at some point anyway.

I brought the tumbler of scotch up to my lips. "Reassign her, I beg you."

"Dude, relax." Jenner rubbed my shoulder like he was a masseur. "You'll survive, I promise."

Dominick looked at Camden and added, "He's been chirping since the moment we even mentioned he was getting an intern. If it wasn't Hannah, he'd be bitching about someone else."

"Not true." I sighed. "She's going to be the death of me."

"I spent eighteen years under the same roof as her," Camden said, checking out a group of girls walking by our table. "I'm not saying my sister's the easiest. We both have quite a mouth on us. But you just haven't figured her out yet."

"Elaborate."

"She'll end up surprising you," he continued. "Just you wait and see."

She'd already done that.

When I'd observed her in the classroom and the night at the bar along with the time we spent in the alley. The morning she walked into my office for the first time. And the moment she had told me she was too drunk to remember anything.

All surprises.

"The only thing I'm waiting for is for this internship to be over." I drained the rest of my scotch and looked around the room for our waitress. "Fuck, I need another drink."

I pushed back my chair and went over to the bar.

"Scotch, double," I said as the bartender approached. "You know what? Make it a triple."

She poured the booze into a glass, and I brought it up to my mouth, taking a long drink. As I swallowed, I turned around, facing the main area, and that was when I noticed Dominick walking over to me.

"You all right, buddy?" He moved in next to me, leaning his back against the edge of the bar.

"Me?" I didn't bother to make eye contact with him. "Why? Does it look like I need to be tended to?"

He placed a drink order and then said to me, "I wouldn't call it that. You've just been a bit ... feistier the last week and a half."

It was no secret what that time frame marked.

Dominick knew that; he wasn't a fool.

"I'm always feisty, you motherfucker." I clinked my glass against his. "That's why you hired me."

"That's true." He paused. "But something still feels off."

"Besides the intern issue, I'm good."

When he looked at me, he stared deeper than I would have liked. "Your issues with Hannah aren't matching up to what your team has been saying about her." He gave me a small grin before it faded. "My assistant checked in with your clerks and paralegal after Hannah's first week of employment. We check on all the interns; it's standard protocol. Their feedback was glowing; in fact, they couldn't have spoken more highly of her."

I drew my brows together, my jaw clenching so hard that I thought one of my teeth would break. "Are you calling me a liar?"

"Far from it. I'm wondering if there's something else that's bothering you, so I can fix it."

If this were any other circumstance—a clerk, an assistant, a paralegal—I would tell him the truth.

But, fuck, I couldn't say a goddamn word.

So, I just stood there, drank my scotch, and lied, "Nah, man. Things are fine."

"All right, I'll take your word for it." He scanned the room. "Maybe what you need is her." He nodded toward the chick who was across from us, swirling her tongue around her straw. "Looks like she's got the skills to give you exactly what you need tonight. She can suck out some of that hotheadedness."

I laughed. "You think that's what I need, huh?"

"It certainly couldn't hurt."

I turned my back to the girl and rested my scotch on the bar top. "I assure you, I'm not hurting for women."

"You just won't settle down with one."

My head dropped, and I focused on the amber waves colliding across the top of my drink as I swirled it. "Correct."

"And your plan is to stay single for the rest of your life?"

"Maybe." I shrugged. "Or maybe the straw-sucker will become my bride."

"She'd probably settle for half a carat."

"Damn, that's a bargain." I exhaled all the air from my lungs. "I'm not saying the right woman for me doesn't exist. I'm not saying dating is out of the realm of possibility. I'm just saying it would take a fucking miracle."

He shook my shoulder. "Miracles can happen, my man."

In the meantime, there was plenty of ass to check out.

Aside from straw girl, there was a blonde in the corner, who had been eyeing me all night. A redhead across the bar, who couldn't stop looking at me as she licked her lips. A brunette a few tables away, who was pretty decent.

But if I was being honest with myself, none of them were Hannah.

Shit, not a single girl in here had anything on Hannah.

"You know what I'm really going to be doing tonight?" I asked him.

He nodded again toward the deep-throater. "You mean, instead of her?"

"After this drink, I'm heading back to the office. The Kennedy trial is going to be a goddamn media frenzy because of the people involved."

Dominick only worked with high-profile celebrities, and this case was no exception. According to my clerk, my social media had been blowing up all week over the anticipation of this trial.

"And the opposing counsel"—I quickly took a drink—"he's fucking ugly."

"You're better."

"I don't deny that fact. But the motherfucker is still ruthless." I loosened my tie. "My team is doing a hell of a job preparing, but I still have to comb through the notes and make sure I have everything I need. I'm worried ..."

His brows rose. "About what?"

"A piece of evidence is going to appear, something none of us have thought of." I smiled. "I happen to know one of the associates on the plaintiff's team."

"You're saying she's going to tip you off?"

I put my hand up in the air, not at all surprised he'd assumed it was a female. "I'm saying I might have benefited from sleeping with her a few years ago when she worked at my firm."

"Does anyone know about this? Hannah? Your team—"

"Fuck no. No one knows." I pounded his chest as I sensed his worry. I would never incriminate any of his employees—that was what he was asking and why there was concern in his voice. "Even you don't know, Dominick, because we never had this conversation." I pulled my hand back. "I don't always play fair, but Kennedy is going to win because he deserves to."

"Jesus, this could get you disbarred."

"It won't, I assure you."

He glanced around the bar, finally looking at me. "I give you a lot of shit for being an asshole, but deep down, you're a good man, Declan, and you're doing right by my client." He clinked his glass against mine. "I appreciate that."

"You know me; I don't fucking lose."

At least when it came to law.

When it came to Hannah ... that was a whole different story.

TEN

HANNAH

I brought the large, heavy glass of wine up to my mouth and took a long sip, groaning the moment I swallowed. "This has never tasted so good."

"Long day?" my brother asked.

The sound of his voice was usually so comforting.

We were in the exact same place in our lives. Although we had different perspectives, he understood how difficult this stage was and everything we had to balance.

But instead of comforting me, his voice was a reminder of how much I'd missed him. He'd flown in for only three nights, and he was leaving in the morning, and this was the first time I'd gotten to see him.

That was all thanks to Declan.

Due to the upcoming Kennedy trial, we were putting in eighteen hours a day.

"A long week and a half." I adjusted the pillow behind me to get a little cozier, held the glass against my lap, and kicked my feet onto our coffee table. "If I fall asleep, just nudge me. But take the wine out of my hand and save it—that's vital."

Oaklyn snorted from beside me. "God, do you need a pedicure."

"I need more than that." The polish had chipped from each toe. "Let's go to the spa this weekend and get rubbed and fluffed and scrubbed."

"Fluffed?"

I turned my head toward her. "Yes, extra fluffing."

She laughed. "I can't with you."

"You're not still babysitting Everly, are you?" Camden asked.

I moved the glass up to my chest, so it was closer to my mouth. "Ford's going to get a nanny. It's happening soon. We had the talk."

"Man"—he sighed, shaking his head—"Han, you need to start saying no. You're going to crash."

I yawned. "Isn't that what I'm doing now?"

I didn't think an earthquake would even pull me from this couch.

"She's the busiest person I know." Oaklyn spoke like I wasn't in the room. "From babysitting to school to prepping for the bar to working at the law firm—"

"Interning."

She rolled her eyes. "Same thing."

It was my time to snort. "If I were *working*, working there, I wouldn't be on Declan's team. And my paycheck would be much prettier than it is now."

"I hung out with him last night." My brother brought his beer up to his lips, staring at me as he sipped.

"Oh yeah?"

I'd watched Everly last night, so I knew Ford was going out with them. Plus, Camden had mentioned a guys' night was happening. But until now, I'd had no idea Declan had joined them.

"He's an all right dude," Camden said. "Super smart, the type of personality that shows me why he's a hell of a good litigator. He likes to talk a lot of shit—no different than our cousins. It's no wonder they're all so close." He pushed the hair out of his eyes, the top the longest I'd ever seen it. "Declan and Dominick are pretty much the same person."

I didn't disagree.

Both were dominant, so matter-of-fact, with the patience of a gnat.

I held my breath while I asked, "Did he say anything about me?"

Camden shook his head. "Nah."

I knew he was lying.

My brother couldn't hide anything from me. I knew him as well as I knew myself.

"Nice try." I tossed a pillow at him. "What did he say?"

He swatted the pillow, sending the furry white square to the ground. "Nothing. Really."

"I don't believe you." I leaned my head all the way back and closed my eyes. "I also don't have the energy to try to get it out of you."

When my eyes opened, I saw all the books that were on the table. The notebooks that were piled high next to them. The pens and highlighters.

All signs that I should be studying right now.

This wine wasn't nearly enough.

"I need a brownie." Somehow, I pushed myself up and went into the kitchen.

"When the hell did you find time to bake?" Camden asked.

"She gets wicked insomnia when she's stressed and bakes at, like, three in the morning," Oaklyn answered for me. "Or when she's watching Everly, they do it together."

"Jesus, Hannah," Camden groaned.

I ignored them.

I didn't require eight hours of sleep like most people. I could function with about five.

The good news was that I'd perfected my brownie recipe over the last week. The caramel ones I'd made were a tiny bit dry, but these were delicious.

I stuck the plate in the microwave for thirty seconds, and once they were done, I returned to the living room with enough napkins for all of us.

"Wait until you try these." I held the plate out to Camden and Oaklyn and then set it down after grabbing one for myself. "They're Nutella, and they might just be my best invention yet."

"Better than your cupcakes?" Camden asked.

I moaned as I took a bite. *"Mmhmm."*

"I don't know; your cupcakes are pretty serious, but—" Oaklyn licked the Nutella off her lip. "Hannah, what the heck are these?" She looked at the brownie in her hand as though it were an alien. "My God, girl. Damn."

"I know." I took another bite, eyeing my next victim—a middle piece in the center of the plate that was gooey on all four sides. "Everything about them is everything I need at this moment." I took a drink of my wine.

"If you weren't such a good attorney, I'd be telling you to open a bakery," my brother said, going in for his second brownie.

"Calm down with the attorney title. Neither of us can use that quite yet." I licked the chocolate off my fingers as I finished. "Besides, I might not even pass the bar—ever. So, there's a chance I might never get that title." I picked up the brownie I'd been eyeing and took a bite. "If all else fails, you can loan me the money to open the bakery. With you billing out at least four hundred an hour, you'll definitely be rich enough."

He laughed.

But the noise was interrupted by the sound of a fire alarm.

Not one that came from our building.

This was the ringtone I'd designated for Declan.

Because if I didn't answer, he'd have my ass, and that sound was impossible to miss.

"Ugh," I cried. "It's him ... the dickhead."

"Are you going to answer it?" Camden asked.

"I don't want to, but I have no other choice."

Camden wiped his mouth with the napkin. "Does he usually call you this late?"

I checked the time. It was past nine.

"If he needs something, there is no timetable. He calls at any hour." I reached for my cell and held it up to my face. "Hi, Decl—"

"I need you to come to the office right now."

I glanced down at what I was wearing and the almost-empty glass of wine in my hand. "Right *now*, now?"

"Did I not speak clearly enough? That means you get your ass in a vehicle within the next ten seconds, drive to the office, take the elevator up to the eighteenth floor, and march your ass into my office."

"Okay, but—"

"I'll see you in twenty minutes. Not a second later."

The phone went dead.

I'd just wanted to give him a heads-up that I'd been drinking.

He hadn't given me that chance.

"Shit," I said, glancing at my brother and then my best friend. "Have I mentioned how much I hate him? Because I do. With a passion that I can't even describe."

"He's making you come in?" Oaklyn asked.

As I pushed myself off the couch, I guzzled the rest of the wine, leaving the empty glass on the table, and ran into my bedroom. "Of course he is," I yelled from my closet. "He wants me there in twenty."

I heard the two of them mumble something as I threw a zipped sweatshirt on over my tank top and slipped my bare feet into socks and sneakers. The messy knot I had on top of my head was too wild, so I pulled out the elastic and braided my hair before sticking on a baseball hat. Once my bag was hanging over my shoulder, I went back into the living room, where Oaklyn met me.

"Take this." She placed a small soft-sided cooler in my hands. "You know, in case you get hungry since something tells me you might be there all night."

"What's in it?"

"Brownies. Fruit. The leftover pizza we had for dinner."

I dropped the cooler into my bag and threw my arms around her. "I love you."

"Go kick his ass. Or better yet, show him why you're an ass-kicker."

"I like your plan." I released her and hurried over to my brother. "If you want to stay and hang instead of going back to Mom and Dad's, just crash in my bed. If I'm lucky enough to come home before morning, I'll climb in with Oaklyn." I hugged him, and when I pulled away, I added, "I don't know if I'll see you before you leave, and I hate that. Hard."

He placed his hand on top of my hat, lifting the brim a little to look at me. "Hang in there. You're going to get through this."

"See you at spring break?"

"I might go to Mexico with some friends."

My brother had completed his internship at the end of his

fall semester, so now, he only had to focus on his last semester of school and prepping for the bar.

While he was drinking mojitos in Cancun, I'd be in Declan hell.

God, I envied him.

I sighed. "You mean, you might come home and hang with your sister because she's your fave."

He smiled.

I didn't have time to negotiate, but that didn't mean I was dropping this topic.

"See you guys later," I said.

As I headed out the door, I ordered a ride-share, and by the time I got outside, fortunately, the car was already parked along the curb. It was a short trip, and I walked into Declan's office close to the twenty-minute mark.

"What took you so long?"

He was too focused on his computer to even look at me.

"How can I help you, Declan?"

He finally glanced up from his screen, his gaze starting at my feet, slowly rising to my hat. "I see you got dressed up for the occasion." He laughed like he wasn't impressed. "You could have at least worn clothes instead of pajamas."

"It's almost ten o'clock at night. I had a massive glass of wine. I was in the middle of something." I paused. "I did the best I could."

His eyes narrowed. "In the middle of what?"

Did he have the right to even ask that?

And did he deserve an answer?

"I was hanging out with my best friend and my brother. He's only been here for a couple of days, and he's spent more time with you than he has with me."

I probably shouldn't have said that.

But the wine was making my lips a little looser than normal.

"Am I supposed to feel bad for you?" His brows rose. "Welcome to the life of a lawyer, Hannah. This is what happens when you're successful. Things come up at all hours, and you have to make yourself available."

I cleared my throat, holding the doorway, wishing I hadn't barked back at him. "What do you need me for?"

He pointed at one of the chairs. "Sit."

I set the bag on my lap as I settled in the seat.

He placed his arms on the desk, his teeth piercing his bottom lip as he looked at me. "We have a problem."

God, I wished he weren't so good-looking.

His hair was a tad messy on the top, his tie loosened.

His scruff was even thicker than it had been this morning.

Those were the only problems I could see.

There was a folder in front of him that he pushed toward me. "Read."

I lifted it into my hands and opened the top, scanning the first few lines. "What is this?"

"Evidence."

There were only three sheets of paper in the stack, each showing several different email exchanges between Kennedy and the plaintiff. I scanned the contents of the emails. They didn't exactly prove that Kennedy had known he was breaching his contract, but they certainly didn't help his case.

"How did you find these?"

"You're not asking the right question, Hannah."

I thought for a moment. "Is this evidence they're going to use against us?"

He took several breaths, and every exhale sent me his delicious, spicy scent. "Still the wrong question."

This was going to throw a massive wrench in our defense.

It was going to change everything.

We needed to kill this evidence before the judge and jury saw it.

"How do we make this go away?"

"Again," he snapped, "wrong question."

I glanced back at the papers, taking my time to read each word, seeing if there was something I had missed. "We find a way around it?"

He got up and went over to the bar he'd had built in his office. A glass company had installed the shelves this afternoon, and his assistant had fully stocked both levels with glasses and multiple bottles of liquor. He poured what looked to be scotch into a tumbler and returned to his desk. "How?"

I closed my eyes, my brain flipping through the evidence and research that we'd put together for the upcoming trial. "We prove that Kennedy didn't send those emails."

"And how do we do that?"

I shrugged. "I ... have no idea."

"Well, you'd better figure it out, and you're not leaving this building until you do." He brought the glass up to his mouth. "It's going to be a long night. Get to work."

ELEVEN

DECLAN

Hannah had set up shop in the conference room, needing the large space to spread out all the files and evidence, a whiteboard to track her notes, and—unlike my office—an area that wasn't filled with distractions.

Thank fucking God for that.

The last thing I needed was that perfect ass parading around my desk, bent over and taunting me.

Women thought they were doing themselves a favor by wearing yoga pants for comfort.

Really, they were doing men the favor, allowing us to see every curve and dip of their gorgeous bodies.

My dick had hardened the moment I saw Hannah this evening.

The gap between her thighs.

Her toned legs.

That heart-shaped ass, her sweatshirt not long enough to cover it. She wore the sweatshirt unzipped, and when she had first walked into my office, it had fallen to either side, her tank top underneath showing her small, rock-hard nipples.

I was doing everything in my power not to go into the restroom and jerk off, just so this aching, throbbing intensity would lighten.

I checked the time on my watch. She'd been in the conference room for an hour.

I wanted to go in there and bark every reason why she should have found the loophole already. But dragging her in here tonight was an invaluable lesson. She needed to feel the weight of the pressure; she needed to connect all the evidence as though this were her case.

True, successful litigators shone during times like this.

Some would allow this type of evidence to defeat them, their client never standing a chance in the courtroom.

Some would use it as fuel to create fucking magic before they walked in for the trial.

I knew what I wanted for Hannah.

Now, I wanted to see how badly she wanted this.

As I sat at my desk, draining several glasses of scotch, my stomach wouldn't stop growling. It had been hours since my last meal, the booze intensifying the hunger. I got up from my desk, and as I was about to head toward the kitchen, I smelled something interesting in the hallway.

Chocolate?

The only place that could be coming from at this hour was the conference room.

Now clutching my drink, I headed in that direction, stopping in the doorway. Hannah stood at the head of the long oval table, the space in front of her littered with books and papers, folders and highlighters.

"What is that smell?" I eventually asked.

She jumped from the sound of my voice, her hand going straight to her chest, and she gasped, "Oh my God, you just scared the life out of me."

I had known she didn't notice me.

That was why I'd taken a few extra seconds to admire her before I spoke.

As she turned around, grabbing something off the chair behind her, she gave me a view of that fucking ass again.

Goddamn it.

"When you heat up my homemade brownies, they turn extra gooey. That's what you smell." She nodded toward the other side of the room, where there was a kitchenette. "I used the microwave." She set the container she'd taken from the chair onto the table and pushed it toward me. "Here, have one." She licked a chunk of something off her thumb that must have accidentally dipped into the dessert. "Before you say it, I wasn't getting distracted by my stomach or paying more attention to my hunger instead of this case. Chocolate actually helps me focus."

That fucking mouth.

That was my distraction.

Not what was coming out of it, but what it looked like.

The thickness of her lips. The way she licked them.

How she chewed the inside of her cheek when she feared what my response was going to be.

"Tell me how chocolate helps you focus."

She pointed toward the container. "Try one. Trust me."

"You want me to trust you?" I chuckled.

Trust wasn't what had been built between us.

There was a brownie sitting in front of her, resting on a napkin, and she lifted it toward her mouth. "I didn't poison them, if that's what you're worried about."

I wasn't worried.

I just wanted one thing on my tongue right now.

It wasn't chocolate.

It was her cunt.

Since I couldn't elaborate, I took a brownie out of the container and chewed off the corner. The rich, fudgy consistency made my mouth water, the Nutella layer melting over my tongue.

"Fuck ..." I took another bite, shocked at how good it was. "This is incredible." I even winked to add emphasis.

"I know." She smiled. "Now, don't you just want to scour over every piece of evidence and help me solve this mystery?"

"Ah, brownie points, quite literally." I wiped my mouth. "Is that what you're after, Hannah? Earning yourself some answers by feeding me?" I swallowed the rest of the dessert, not allowing my face to allude to the satisfaction I was feeling. "Or is this your way of testing me?"

Her grin faded. "Not at all. It's just ... I'm stuck." She flattened her hands on the papers in front of her. "And I'm overwhelmed."

"Not the answer I want to hear."

"But an honest one."

"Are we shooting for honest?" I gripped the back of the nearest chair. "This is one of Dominick's high-profile clients. This is going to garner so much media attention; my face is going to be everywhere on the first day of the trial. I promised Kennedy a win. Do you think I can walk into the courtroom without an edge?"

The vein in my forehead was pulsing.

I could feel it as I snapped at her.

"No, I don't think—"

"Then, what the fuck are you going to do about it aside from feeling sorry for yourself?" I lifted the back of the chair, the legs floating in the air, and I slammed it on the ground. "Are you going to sit here and pout about being overwhelmed? Are you going to eat an entire container of brownies? Or are you going to buckle down and figure out the fucking loophole?"

Her hands folded in front of her, making it easy for me to see how badly they were shaking.

When she saw that I'd noticed, she hid them under the table, her chest rising like she was panting.

"I can tell you what I want to do, but that's not going to change anything," she whispered. Her eyes left mine, darting around the room before they settled on the table. "I'm not trying to bullshit you. I'm in over my head. I don't know how to find this answer. Where to look. How to search." Her hands lifted, and she picked up the edges of the nearest notebook. "I'm trying. I'm looking. I'm digging. I am ..."

I hadn't expected her to locate the answer immediately.

She was too raw, too much of a novice to know where to find it.

What I wanted was to see the desire on her face.

The drive.

The look of longing that was staring at me right now.

I walked over to her, stopping when we were inches apart, facing the evidence that she had spread out in front of her. "These are pieces. One"—I tapped the first bit of evidence my team had logged—"two, three," I said, counting as my finger grazed each one. "I don't want you to look at the individual pieces, Hannah." My eyes eventually met hers. "I want you to look at the entire picture."

The brownie had only intensified the vanilla scent coming off her body.

I took a long, deep inhale.

Fuck me.

I was close enough that I could touch her. That I could skim my fingers across her cheek, taking in the softness of her skin.

Would she slap me?

Or would we end up naked in the conference room?

She's your intern, I repeated in my head, *and a Dalton and your friends' cousin.*

I lifted one of the folders off the table and handed it to her. "You're trying to find a reason why Kennedy would send that email." I gestured toward her hands. "Did you ever consider why he wouldn't?" I could see her brain rolling through the different options, her expression changing as she began to bounce around ideas. "That's it. Now, you're on the right path."

She took off her sweatshirt, dropping it onto an empty chair, the movement in her arms showing the muscle in her biceps and the narrowness of her waist. She slid her braid to the other shoulder. She wasn't happy with that placement and shifted it again.

Silky, dark strands that would look incredibly sexy, wrapped around my wrist.

"You're close, Hannah. Almost there ..."

She glanced up, her eyes pleading with mine. "Declan—"

"Don't say it."

She suddenly looked defeated. She was tired. Hungry. She had wine flowing through her veins—I could see the tiny hints of burgundy on her lips. It didn't matter. What mattered was that she was going to push through.

"You've been studying this case since your first day here. Analyze each of the different viewpoints. Work backward if you have to." I had an idea, and I placed a brownie on her empty napkin. "What made me put that there, Hannah?"

"The brownie?"

I nodded.

She gazed at the dessert. "You want me to focus."

"What other reason?"

She took several deep breaths. "You had a motive."

"Yes." I waited until her stare met mine. "Now, take it further. Did I put that brownie there for my advantage? Or because there were too many in the container and I wanted to make room for something else?" I paused, waiting. "Not everything is what it seems."

Her mouth opened, teeth stabbing her bottom lip.

"Remember, there's going to be times when the opposition presents something you're unprepared for. You have to go into court, expecting this, or you'll risk the chance of being destroyed. So, when it happens, are you going to roll onto your back and take it?"

Goose bumps rose over her bare arms.

"Or are you going to spin what's presented and dominate the trial?" I lowered my voice and said, "What kind of lawyer are you going to be?"

She turned her body toward me, releasing the lip she'd been gnawing. "The kind that wins."

"Show me." I placed my hand on the folder she was still holding. "I'll be in my office."

I walked out of the conference room and stopped the second I reached the hallway. My hands balled into fists, and I held them tightly, forcing my feet not to move so I didn't turn around and go back inside and pull her into my arms.

I pushed air through my lungs.

I tried to tame my fucking cock.

There was just something about Hannah that I found impossible to resist.

Maybe it was her scent. Maybe it was her innocence. Maybe it was the determination I saw in her eyes.

Maybe it was the fact that she made me want to growl and fucking scream at the same time.

Maybe—

"Hi," she said, instantly interrupting my thoughts.

I turned toward the doorway of the conference room, and she wasn't there.

"Yeah, I'm still at the office," she said. "Ugh, I'm so tired."

She wasn't talking to me. That meant she was on the phone.

My anger suddenly flared.

Why the fuck was she speaking to someone right now when she should have been working? Was she not taking this seriously?

"Trust me, I'd rather be eating brownies with you." She laughed lightly. "And finishing that yummy bottle of wine."

Did she not realize how important this case was? To the firm? Dominick? Me?

"Are you okay? You sound ... tense."

I adjusted my position to hear her better.

"Oh no, babe."

Babe?

Who the fuck is she calling babe?

"I wish I were there too." She paused. "As soon as I get out of this hell, I'll be there." She exhaled. "I love you."

I heard the clunk of her phone as she set it on the table.

I love you?

Had she started hooking up with someone since the night at the bar?

Or had she already been dating him?

Whoever he was, he was important enough to be loved.

I didn't know what the fuck to think as I walked into my office, but I knew I needed a goddamn refill. I'd left my glass in the conference room, so I grabbed a new one and poured several fingers of scotch, bringing the tumbler over to my desk.

I didn't know why I was allowing this to bother me.

It shouldn't matter if she had a guy in her life.

But for some reason, I couldn't stand the thought of another man making her smile.

Of his hands touching her.

His lips.

For him to make her moan—

"Declan! Come here!"

At least when she interrupted my thoughts this time, it was because she was talking to me.

Or trying to.

I brought the glass up to my mouth, the scotch burning the remnants of chocolate off my tongue.

If she had something to tell me, she could come to me.

I wasn't a fucking dog.

I didn't move from my desk. I busied my hands, replying to an email, staring at my computer screen as she walked in breathlessly.

"Didn't you hear me calling you?"

"I heard you all right, but I'm not going to drop everything and come running to you." I took my hands off the keyboard and surrounded the drink. "You got my attention, Hannah. What do you want?"

She didn't move from the doorway. "Please come back to the conference room. I want to show you something."

"You can tell me in here."

She came closer, holding the edge of my desk. "Please?"

She'd asked nicely.

I even liked the neediness in her tone.

"This had better be good," I sighed and followed her down the hallway into the conference room.

She had taped the newly found evidence to the whiteboard and had several stacks of papers piled on the table—an organized layout, unlike the mess that had been in here before.

"I can't tell you how many times I read those email exchanges, looking for the answer in their conversations. I couldn't understand why I wasn't seeing it." She moved over to the whiteboard. "I thought maybe the emails had been edited.

Maybe they had been Photoshopped. Maybe there were more emails not included here; therefore, the proof was really taken out of context."

I took a seat. "And?"

She smiled. An expression so beautiful that I felt it all the way in my fucking gut. "I realized what I was really looking at."

"Don't waste my time, Hannah. Get to the point."

She flattened her hand sideways against the board, using her pinkie like a ruler. Even though I was too far away to read what was above her finger, I knew it was the area where the email addresses and subject line were listed. "That isn't Kennedy's email address." She pointed to each of the sheets, emphasizing her point, and then she lifted the stack of papers off the table and walked them over to me. Her finger went to the top of the pile, where she'd highlighted text. "This is his email address."

"You might be able to entertain your babe with your theatrics, but you're boring me to death."

Her brows rose. "Wait. My ... *babe*?"

"Your voice carried into my office," I lied. "First, you bitched about being here. And as if that wasn't enough, I had to hear your goddamn love confession."

"Oh." She swallowed.

"Do you think I want to be here, spending my evening with you? My fucking intern, who doesn't know her ass from her elbow? Watching you flail around like a fish I just plucked out of the water? Please, Hannah, there are a million other things I'd rather be doing right now."

"Fuck you, Declan." Her stare changed to a glare. "Not that it's any of your business, but it was my roommate. The fire alarm had gone off in our building. She's hanging out with my brother, and they had to evacuate. She was just letting me know." Her hands balled into fists. "She sounded stressed, and I told her I loved her—that's what you heard."

Fuck ... *me?*

She was playing naughty—and I liked it.

At the same time, the relief came in hard and fast.

I didn't know why. It shouldn't matter.

But it did.

"Stop deviating. You're wasting my time." I nodded toward the stack of papers. "What does this revelation—as you would call it—have to do with the evidence?" I ignored the way my hard-on was pressing against my zipper. "Our client has two email addresses. Most of us do. So what?"

As she took a deep inhale, I glanced down her body, seeing her nipples were even harder than they had been before.

She caught me staring, and I pushed the chair back, getting ready to stand.

"Maybe you called me in a little prematurely."

"No."

"Then, tell me, Hannah, what have you found?"

Her work-assigned laptop was open near the head of the table, and she brought it over to me. "I tracked the IP address from where this email had been sent. It's not from Kennedy's home or his office." The data on the screen showed a location in Northern California—an area that wasn't associated with Kennedy at all, but a region that had come up numerous times in our research. "The question isn't why he sent it. It isn't how he sent it. It's if he sent it." She shut the laptop, our eyes locked. "And the answer to that is no."

"What are you saying?"

"I'm saying the plaintiff knew he was going to lose this case, and he created false evidence, hoping that we'd be caught off guard so we wouldn't be able to authenticate it. It's not Kennedy's motive, Declan. It's the plaintiff's."

Now, she was playing the fucking song I wanted to hear. "Keep going."

She walked to the whiteboard, slowly taking the papers off that she'd taped there, placing them one by one on the table. "Kennedy has been painted as the villain of this story. The one who breached his contract and is being sued for millions. But he's not the villain here."

She had found the loophole.

She had shifted the power.

But it was a situation that was merely hypothetical, a scenario I'd created an hour before she arrived.

Had I wanted her heart to drop, her entire body to shake, experiencing the stress of what she would soon face in the courtroom once she passed the bar?

Or had I just wanted to spend more time with her, alone, in a setting that would test my strength?

Fuck, I didn't know.

I raised my hands and clapped them in the air. "You did it."

Her eyes instantly brightened. "I did?"

"Yes, Hannah. You found the answer I was looking for."

Her head tilted back, her mouth opened, her hands pressed against her chest. "Oh my God, I did it."

The second her eyes left me, I craved the closeness.

I needed it.

I stood and moved toward her, stalling a few feet away.

The moment her head straightened, she processed my new placement. The way my hands were holding the table. How I was leaning against it.

Her breathing sped up as she scanned my face. "Did I forget something? Did I do something wrong—"

"No."

I needed to back up.

I needed to return to my fucking office.

I needed to tame the thoughts consuming me.

But I couldn't.

My hands clutched the table and released it.

"Then, what's wrong, Declan?"

My jaw clenched and unclenched. My toes ground against the bottom of my shoes. My breath came out like huffs from a raging bull. "I'm fighting something—something I shouldn't even be thinking about."

"Me."

Her voice was so soft. At first, I wasn't sure she'd even said the word or if it had been in my head.

But then she added, "You're trying to stop yourself from touching me."

How the fuck does she know that?

Especially since she thought I'd never touched her before.

How would she have connected the way I'd been treating her to my desire of wanting to fuck her?

"Yes." I took a step closer. "But you're my intern and a Dalton." My feet moved again. "Someone I haven't wanted on my team—still don't." My hands hovered in the air above each side of her face. "Someone who has put me through hell since the moment you became employed."

Her eyes bounced between mine.

"Someone whose mouth has challenged me in so many fucking ways."

"But don't you love that about me?" She was almost timid when she spoke, yet she still closed the distance, her body barely pressing against me. "Isn't that why your eyes devour me at the same time you're screaming at me? Why you clench your hands whenever I'm within reach to stop yourself from grabbing me?"

She noticed.

"Yes, Declan, I've noticed."

And now, she was in my fucking thoughts, the same way I'd been in hers on the night we met.

Maybe she needed a refresher of what she couldn't remember from that evening.

The way I'd made her feel.

The octave in which I'd made her scream.

Since she could see it anyway, there was no reason to keep this in. "I'm not going to be able to leave this conference room unless I lick your pussy."

She rose to her tiptoes. "But you despise me."

My palms landed on her cheeks, and I aimed her mouth up to mine. "At times ... yes."

"And you want me on someone else's team."

I ran my thumb across her bottom lip. "I've all but begged your cousins to reassign you."

"But you can't stop thinking about what it would be like to fuck me."

I knew what it would feel like.

That was the goddamn problem.

"That thought often crosses my mind."

"What's stopping you, Declan?"

I lowered my face, placing my lips close to hers. Not touching, just within a hairbreadth. "You."

"Why?" She paused. "I haven't said no."

"But you haven't said yes either." I set my ear next to her mouth. "Tell me you want me, Hannah."

Each of her breaths echoed inside me as she teased the folds of my ear with her tongue. "I want you ... but you're such a dick to me."

"But don't you love that about me?" I asked, using her own words. "When I treat you so roughly, you can't stop thinking about what else I might do that's rough. Would my teeth bite as hard as my shouting?" I cinched her waist, feeling her breath hitch again. "Would my tongue whip you the same way as when I bark at you?"

"Love ... that's a strong word. Especially given that all you do is treat me like shit."

I raised my hands to her neck, wrapping my fingers around both sides. "You're not the only one who notices, Hannah. I see the way you look at me. The way you watch me. The way you get lost in your thoughts, your mind wandering."

"And you think those daydreams are all about you?" She was gnawing the same lip that I'd touched earlier. "Such a cocky dick."

"A dick that you're fantasizing about right now." I leaned into her neck, speaking right above the spot where her throat pulsed. "Wondering how many times that fucking dick is going to make you come tonight."

As I glanced up, her eyes closed. "Yes."

"So, you want me?"

She connected our gazes. "I shouldn't ... but I do."

"Say it, Hannah. I need to hear you fucking say it."

"I want you."

Fuck yes.

But since she didn't remember our first time together, she needed the warning again.

"I'm not going to be like the guys you're used to. There's nothing nice about me."

A coy smile came across her face. "You don't think I can tell that by now?"

That fucking mouth.

I saw no reason to wait at this point since she had given me no signs that she would stop me. So, while keeping our stares connected, I knelt to the floor and yanked down her yoga pants, pulling off her sneakers and the tight black binding from her legs. Once I had them off, I was surprised by the sight.

"A bare cunt ... like you knew I was going to eat you tonight."

She snickered. "I don't like wearing panties with yoga pants." Her laugh turned to a grin. "I'm glad you approve."

I needed her smell.

I needed my nose soaked in it.

"Goddamn it, Hannah." I moaned as I inhaled her, drenching myself in her heat. My eyes closed as I filled my lungs with her. I remembered this smell, the way it had captivated me. And it was doing that now, holding me fucking hostage. "These are the only lips I'm going to kiss tonight." I looked up at her after I spoke, running my tongue up and down her smoothness.

I'd kissed the other set.

All that had caused were these incessant thoughts of her, my brain obsessing about every way I wanted her.

I didn't need that again.

I just needed this.

Her fingers ran through my hair, gripping, pulling. "What are you saying?"

"After tonight, this can't happen again." My tongue swiped her. "I'm your boss. Mentor. The guy your cousins and brother would never approve of you dating."

"What's this, then?"

Her voice had changed.

There was a sultriness to it now.

"This"—I licked across her clit, swallowing, savoring—"is just a taste."

"And my mouth isn't good enough for that?"

"Oh, it is." And it had been—that was why I was staying far away from that powerful beast. "But these are the lips I prefer." I licked harder, inserting a finger into her pussy, instantly hit with her tightness. "Unless you have an objection to that—"

"Don't stop."

Her hunger made me laugh, but the only thing she heard was the swishing of my tongue and the wetness that sloshed against my finger as I reached, back and forth, to her G-spot.

"Fuck yes," she hissed.

I stayed toward the top of her clit, circling, flicking with the very tip of my tongue.

Since this was my second go-round, I'd thought it would be familiar.

But this time, we were in the light, not the darkness of an alley. I could actually see the creaminess of her skin, the color of her clit, the way she watched me with her raging eyes until it became too much and her eyelids closed.

She was even more perfect than I had imagined.

The taste, texture.

The scent.

I wanted more.

"Oh God, Declan."

Even her sounds were enticing.

Erotic.

Hannah Dalton wasn't just a presence.

She was a statement.

A mood.

And I wanted to worship her.

Every graze across her clit caused her hips to buck, and when I sucked that sensitive spot into my mouth, she pulled my locks. The moment I released her and increased the speed of my tongue, her breath hitched. When I slid over her G-spot, she moaned.

I wanted her to come.

But I didn't want this to end.

"Oh fuck," she cried, as though she were listening to my thoughts again.

This was my battle, not hers.

I was the one in control.

And if I wanted to draw this out, punishing her for that naughty little mouth, for not remembering our night together, for dropping that precedent in my lap while I'd been meeting with her cousins, then I had that authority.

"Don't you dare come," I threatened as she tightened around my finger.

My tongue stilled.

My hand halted.

"Declan! Please!"

I waited several seconds before I started up again, allowing the build to fade. But as soon as I resumed the licking, her hips picked right back up, rocking against my face, bringing her orgasm to the surface.

Once I sensed its arrival, I pulled back.

"Ah! No!"

It was a game.

But this wasn't about winning.

This was about ownership.

Hannah's orgasms were mine.

I decided when they happened.

But that didn't mean she wasn't fighting for one, wringing my hair like it was a fucking sponge, screaming like she wanted security to hear.

"Declan," she gasped as I dived back in. "Yes!"

She was too close, so I slowed.

A cycle I continued to repeat.

A pattern I didn't want to stop.

"Please," she urged, staring down at me, lips wet and parted. Feral. "Please let me come."

Maybe I just wanted to hear her beg.

Or maybe I wanted to reach the point where my dick couldn't wait another second to sink into her.

Both of her hands were in my hair now, and, "Oh God, yes," was filling my ears.

It would only take a few more swipes, and she'd be shuddering.

Was that what I wanted?

To have her cum pool on my tongue?

Or did I want her first orgasm to be on my cock?

Knowing her pussy was so tight that it'd felt like I was taking her virginity even though I knew I wasn't. But still, she had a cunt that felt as though it had been molded just for me.

I wanted that cunt squeezing my shaft.

I wanted her wetness soaking me.

I gave her one final lick, and as I stood, I wiped her off my cheeks but left my mouth alone. I wanted her to dry there, on that bit of skin, so I had something to smell when I got home.

Her eyes penetrated me as I took a step back. "You're vicious."

"I warned you."

She tried to inhale. "But that was ..."

"I know what that was, Hannah."

I took out my wallet, where I kept a spare condom. Once she noticed what I had in my hand, her eyes changed.

They darkened.

"I want you naked, sitting on the table with your knees bent, feet clinging to the edge."

She didn't move. She just let the words simmer into her smile.

"Now."

TWELVE

HANNAH

Declan Shaw was an asshole. He took his anger and frustration out on me. Maybe I could rationalize that behavior as my punishment for lying to him about being drunk. But what I couldn't rationalize was the evidence I had of him and Madison. A photo that still lived on my phone—his lips red, matching hers. Nor could I excuse that he had left me that night for her.

But there was wine running through my veins, and the desire to come was thundering inside my pussy, my needs charged like I was plugged into an outlet. And, *oh God*, this man could fuck like the thoroughbreds my parents invested in. I'd be an absolute idiot to pass up a dick like Declan's.

So, I was making an exception.

I was thinking only with my body.

Besides, he'd made it clear that this was never going to happen again.

I could accept that.

I could focus on the now.

Because, now, he was going to make me feel the best I ever had.

That was why, when he told me to get naked and sit on the conference room table, I obeyed his order.

I tossed my tank top and sports bra, the only things I had on, and climbed onto the cold, smooth wood.

This was the table where my family had offered me my internship.

Where my aunt and uncle had told me they were proud of me.

Where, as a little kid, I'd colored with Uncle David's highlighters on the days that Dad visited his brother and dragged me with him.

Would they be proud of this?

"Touch yourself."

That question was immediately answered the second his command hit my ears.

He stood only feet away, fully dressed. His lips wet, his fingers damp—from me. His eyes ravenous as he took me in.

Touch myself?

Something I'd only ever done in the privacy of my own bed, never in front of a man.

This was just another thing that I could add to the growing Declan List, underneath having sex outside, against a building, in the dark, with practically a stranger.

"Now," he growled.

As my knees bent, my feet rounding the edge of the table, I stared into his eyes.

A man who, more or less, had become my enemy.

But in this room, I'd felt something different from him.

A hint of softness when he was coaching me through finding the loophole, the relief on his face when he found out it was Oaklyn I'd been speaking to on the phone.

His expression had changed again.

It was untamed, his stare dripping with lust.

My hand dropped down my breasts to the bareness of my navel before I stopped at the top of my pussy. I sucked in a mouthful of air as the pads of my fingers gently touched the spot he had just licked.

And sucked.

"*Ahhh*," I gasped, surprised by how good it felt even though it was a touch I had been expecting and even though it was a touch I was extremely familiar with.

What made a difference was Declan.

"I want you to finger yourself while you're rubbing your clit." His eyes bored through me. "I want your wetness coating your fingers." He gradually glanced down to my breasts, hips, calves, even my toes. "And then I want you to feed those fingers to me."

Dirty.

Delicious.

And—at this moment—all mine.

Redness swept over my cheeks as I teased the area he wanted me to enter. I circled a few times, my hips sliding forward to meet the peak of my finger, to push myself in.

But I didn't.

I stopped.

I let the want grow.

The pressure mounting, especially as my palm rubbed my clit.

"All the way in, Hannah."

Was I taking my time or testing him?

Before I could decide, he stepped forward, his hands flattening on the table on either side of me, his face inches from mine. "Show me how good you can make yourself feel." His focus was on my lips—the ones on my face. He was ogling, flirting with my pout, even if he wasn't going to kiss me. "Show me how badly you want my fucking cock."

All I could smell was him.

And it was that scent, his passionate presence that caused me to glide in. I was so wet; it was like he'd drenched me in lube.

"Fuck yes," we both hissed at the same time.

It quickly became too much.

Not just the euphoria spreading through me, but also being under his watchful eye.

His gaze wasn't a normal stare.

It was power.

Pleasure.

"Fuck yourself, Hannah."

My neck fell back as his words collided into me, my hand beating between my legs. His mouth had already brought me so close; it wouldn't take me long to return.

"Look at me, Hannah." The sweetness of his breath breezed across my face. "Stare into my eyes while you fuck your pussy."

A bolt of energy blasted down my chest as my neck straightened.

I couldn't breathe.

All I could do was hold on to the sexiness of his face, those wildly beautiful green eyes, his carnal temperament that I could feel in the air between us.

"Harder."

I listened.

I followed.

And I observed him pulling off his tie, unbuttoning his shirt, a swishing sound hitting my ears as each item of clothing fell to the carpet.

Each bit of his body that he revealed was even more of a

turn-on. Ripples and cords of muscle, grooves etched across his abs.

He spent hours in the gym, and I appreciated each one.

A bead of pre-cum was at the head of his cock, glistening under the overhead light.

My God, that dick.

I remembered it.

There was no way I could ever forget it.

But here, we weren't surrounded by darkness.

Here, I could see the bulge of his crown and the thickness of his shaft and the short, coarse hairs that ran along the bottom of his stomach.

More man than I'd ever seen before.

He wrapped his hand around it and pumped.

Hard.

Even though he had torn off the corner of the metal foil and had the condom ready in his hand, he climbed onto the table, kneeling beside me. "Suck my cock while you finger yourself."

There was so much vigor in that creamy droplet that I wanted it on my tongue.

I wanted to mix his taste with the wine and brownies, adding to the desire that was keeping me so wet.

But there was something else, something that was also taking over.

"Declan"—I inhaled sharply—"I'm going to come."

"Do it with my dick in your mouth." He held my chin, his thumb tracing my lips. "Let me feel it on your tongue."

The saltiness immediately hit my taste buds, a flavor so masculine that it made my mouth water. I swallowed the small bead and lowered down his tip as far as I could go.

It was one thing to look at his cock in the light.

It was a whole other thing to have it in my mouth, my lips stretched wide, my throat too narrow to take most of it in. But as my orgasm started to take shape, the tingles working their way through my pussy, I filled my mouth with him.

Bob, swirl, suck.

A pattern.

He grabbed the back of my head, gripping my hair, and I moaned on his shaft. I was taking him in a little deeper with each plunge, but I'd reached the point where I couldn't fight the peak of my orgasm.

It was here.

Nearing so fast.

"Fuck, yeah, suck that fucking cock."

As I began to shudder, he twisted my nipple, squeezing it between his fingers, the pain only bringing me there quicker.

We were moving together in a rhythm, my hand matching my mouth, too full to form words, but my breaths were loud, my moans unmistakable.

"*Yesss*," he hissed. "I can almost feel you coming."

My release took over.

Part of that was what I was doing to myself, part was the control I had over his pleasure, and part was from the way he looked at me.

The thirst in his eyes.

It wasn't just erotic; it was consuming.

And it caused ripples to ignite through my navel.

When he pulled out, my lips made a pop, followed by, "Declan!"

In that moment, while my body was shuddering, his eyes lowered to my pussy, observing the way I fingered myself, the way I rubbed my clit.

"Goddamn it."

The intensity was almost like a fire, burning right through me, strengthening before it died.

When the stillness set in, he pulled out my fingers and brought them up to his mouth. "Fuck, you taste good."

He was licking my skin, savoring the wetness, rotating his tongue around my nail before he buried my entire finger in his mouth. And while he drank me in, he set down the condom and returned to that spot—the one I'd just left. Instead of using his palm, like I had, he used fingers and then added two inside me.

"Oh shit," I cried, my body just recovering, but his touch reminded me how easily I could get back to that place.

This time, it felt completely different because it was Declan's touch.

His control.

The only thing I could do was hold on, accept the tingles once they started to grow.

He'd moved off the table, and he stood in front of me, leaning into my ear.

I didn't know if he was going to bite my lobe. If he was going to lick the shell, breathing sounds of satisfaction into my skin.

But I wasn't surprised when I got, "I want you to come again. All over this table." The heat from his lips scorched me. "I want you to mark the wood with your cum."

I was already so close.

But his ruling reached all the way to my stomach. With it came this unexpected surge, tightening everything inside me.

"Fuck yes," he breathed. "I can feel it."

In and out.

Rubbing, circling.

Nonstop.

I could barely see.

The only thing I could do was focus on the throbbing that was moving through my body.

"Do you know how good you feel?" He picked up speed. "So wet, so fucking tight." He nipped my cheek. "I want you to come. Right now."

My head leaned back again, my toes grinding into the edge of the table, causing my legs to spread even wider.

But I wasn't in control of those movements.

I couldn't control anything.

The orgasm had taken over.

"Declan!" The shudders were in my stomach, my lips trembling, "Yes!"

He continued to finger me until I lifted my head, catching his eyes, my body completely still.

That was when he pulled out and licked me off his fingers. "So obedient." He swiped my pussy, gathering more wetness that he sucked off his skin. "You have no idea how badly I want to fuck you right now."

I'd gotten off twice in a matter of minutes.

Tiny sparks still lingered inside me, yet I wanted more.

"Then, fuck me." My teeth found my lip. Biting. "Make me come again."

His thumb pulled on that same lip. "That fucking mouth."

I thought he was going to kiss me. He neared in, aiming for my lips, but landed on my neck.

"Give me this pussy." He lifted my feet off the table and wrapped my legs around his waist. "Do I need to be easy on you?" He rolled on the condom. "Or do you think you can handle me?"

He strummed my clit, waking me up even though I hadn't even come close to falling asleep.

Before I had a chance to respond, he continued, "How about your ass, Hannah?" He left my neck, fixing our stares. "Are you going to give me that as well?"

My ass.

Something I'd never done before.

"That ..." I took in a breath.

"Let me guess." He went to that back entrance, his touch nothing like I'd ever felt. "I'd be your first."

I nodded, backing it up with, "Yes."

"Which means I'd have to be *really* easy on you." He licked across his mouth. "Something I can't promise right now." He pointed my face up to his, his thumb returning to my lip. "Because I want to fuck the naughtiness out of this mouth."

"Is that a punishment?"

Wasn't that what I should have been doing to him? For the way he had treated me?

"Yes." His grip strengthened on my chin. "But one you're going to like very much."

His eyes held no mercy.

His grasp full of strength.

But the weird thing was, I trusted him with my body.

I didn't know why.

How.

I just knew that with his touch came the most immense amount of pleasure.

And that proved to be true once again when I shouted, "Oh God, yes," as he slid inside me.

I wasn't sure how far he had gotten, but the depth came with an incredible fullness.

I spread to fit him in.

Pulsed.

"So fucking tight." He held my jaw, eyes devouring me. "Your cunt was built for me." He glided out and plunged back in. "Molded just for my cock."

Just for him.

A thought I could barely process.

He stilled, allowing me to get used to him, urging the pleasure to take over.

It came in through a steady stream.

Not just what he was doing between my legs. But the way he held me, the way he positioned me, the way he stared.

Dominance.

Authority.

I felt it all over my body.

An ownership that triggered more of my moans.

He didn't hit me with speed. What he used instead was power.

Long, rough strokes.

Filling me, emptying me.

"I can't get enough of you," he roared.

He released my face, and suddenly, it felt like a contest, how many parts of my body he could touch at once. I didn't know how it was possible with only two hands, but I felt him everywhere.

My nipples.

My clit.

My hips.

"Get on your knees."

His direction came out of nowhere, taking me a second to understand.

"You mean, on the table?"

"Yes."

He pulled out, and I ached for him, for that fullness I was just getting used to.

I lifted off the wood, earning myself a slap on the ass as I turned around along with the reminder, "On your knees. Now."

As my hands flattered on the wood, my knees pressed into the same hard surface, I glanced across the open space, where

146

there was a row of windows directly in front of me. I wondered if someone on the outside could see in or if the glass was tinted enough that they couldn't.

Were the residents of the high-rise next door watching the spectacle of Declan moving in behind me and thrusting into my pussy?

What I did know was that I could see our reflection in the glass.

Enough so that my eyes connected to his, like I was staring at us in a mirror.

"You like watching me fuck you."

The new angle allowed him to reach a spot that was deeper than before.

One so far in that I lost my breath.

I only had seconds to recover before he slapped the other cheek and barked, "Answer me."

My skin stung, and then the smarting turned into a heat that I found oddly enjoyable. "Yes." My lungs accepted the air I sucked in. "Watching ... is hot."

His exhales were moans. Not as loud as mine, but gritty and sexier. "You're so fucking wet." He pulled my hair, causing my neck to lean back. "Do you like getting fucked by your boss?" He swiveled his torso, his dick hitting every side of me. "That I can control how hard you come?"

He wasn't asking.

His tone told me he already knew the answer.

Still, I voiced, "*Yesss,*" and I said it again as he picked up speed.

But I knew the moment it came out of my mouth, that one word changed things between us. Regardless of what he assumed, now, he had confirmation.

My heart resented him for what he had done with Madison, but there was no denying that my body was completely obsessed with Declan Shaw.

Maybe, after tonight, he would regret what he'd done with her, and he would wish he had waited for me.

A smirk moved across his face, and he released my hair. "Look at yourself in the window." He slipped a finger to my clit, rubbing it, giving me that added pressure. "Look how fucking gorgeous you are when my cock is inside you."

With my ass high in the air, my braid fell against the side of my face, slapping against my mouth.

A look I barely recognized came through my eyes.

I was insatiable.

For him.

"Declan ..." Each muscle howled as the tingling returned. My body on the verge of bursting again. "This feels so good."

"Let me feel it, Hannah." His pumps turned hard, ruthless. "I want your cunt squeezing my dick." He rocked into me several more times before he panted, "That's it ... yes!"

Shudders completely took over, whipping through my stomach, my legs, even my face. They were so strong that I began to move with him, pounding myself against him, screaming through each wave.

I heard the slapping of his balls while he grunted, "You're tightening up on me." He flicked my clit, circling, rubbing. "Oh fuck, I can feel your cum."

I yelled out in pleasure, unconcerned with how loud and piercing my sounds were.

They were honest, pure.

And the second I turned silent, the crash quickly following the rise, he pulled out and turned me around, lifting me into the air like I was weightless.

My arms and legs wrapped around him as he carried me to the window.

"It sounds like you want an audience to hear you." He pressed my back against the glass and nodded toward the outside. "I'm going to give you one."

In one quick, easy push, he was inside me.

But this was different.

This position gave us a closeness that we hadn't had before.

Skin on skin.

Lips so near to mine.

There was emotion in the way he held me, the way he aimed me against the glass, driving into me while I smashed into the coldness behind me.

"I've watched you come three times tonight." He glanced down at my lips, like he was forcing himself not to kiss me. "I want to see what it looks like when we come together."

Four times.

Something I'd never thought was possible before Declan.

But I was there—again. Something I was sure he already knew.

One thing that would push me there even faster was the taste of him.

"Kiss me."

He arched his hips up and rammed into me. "You haven't earned my lips, Hannah."

"But—"

He took my nipple into his mouth instead, surrounding it with his teeth.

I yelped as he bit down, an explosion of pain moving through me, reverberating like an echo. I thought the hurt would pull me out of the moment. That it would be all I could focus on. But his bite caused a sizzle that only electrified the fervor.

He switched to my other breast, his eyes haunting as he stared into mine. "You get what I give you."

With that declaration came more speed.

More power.

He was igniting me.

And the second I opened my mouth, shouting, "Declan," the blaze was burning my entire body.

"Fuck yes," he roared against my nipple, his mouth rising, stopping inches above mine. "Give me that fucking orgasm."

He was pumping me so hard.

So fast.

I couldn't think.

I couldn't respond with words.

All I could do was scream.

Grip him.

And hold on while the spasms washed over me in layers.

"Your cunt is fucking milking me. It's begging for my cum," he growled. "Is that what you want, Hannah? You want me to fill you with my cum?"

A condom separated us, but the result wouldn't be any different.

I wanted him to feel the same thing I was.

"Yes," I urged. "Now." I pressed my nose to his. "Right now."

"Hannah." He didn't scream. His sounds were harsher than that. Deeper. "*Fuuuck.*"

His hands turned taut, his movements eventually slowing.

Satisfaction pooled in his eyes.

He kept our faces together, our bodies aligned until he caught his breath.

He said my name again, this time more of a whisper, and then he pulled me off the glass and walked me over to the table, where he set me on top.

The separation was like jumping into a winter lake.

My skin turned icy.

My lungs almost wheezed.

There was enough soreness in my pussy to make me stand.

While my feet had only just touched the carpet, he was already reaching for his clothes and shoes, walking it all toward the restroom in the back of the conference area.

"Get dressed," he said before the restroom door clicked shut behind him.

I reached for my yoga pants and pulled them up my legs, quickly putting on my sports bra and tank top and sneakers, trying not to get lost in my thoughts.

This time, I couldn't lie about sleeping with Declan.

I could smell us in the air.

The tenderness inside me was a feeling I couldn't ignore.

But underneath all the physical contentment, I had this raging uncertainty of how things were going to look between us.

He'd said this would never happen again.

But was that possible after *that*—the best sex of my entire life?

Even though I was his intern and he worked for my cousins?

Even though my feelings for him were so cloudy?

The door opened, and he walked out, dressed, polished, like he hadn't just been naked, inside me, ravishing my body only moments ago.

Now that I'd seen him undressed, I could picture what he looked like under that sharp, pristine suit, the ripples of muscles, the broadness of his shoulders, the inches of pure manliness that hung behind his zipper.

Somehow, I was hungry for him again.

But before I could even put my brain there, we needed to discuss something.

"Do you want to talk?"

His hand rested on the table, the same place where he'd made me come.

A mark of wetness just below his fingers.

His brows furrowed. "About?"

"Us."

"What about us?"

A few feet away, I leaned my butt against the edge of the wood. When that didn't feel comfortable enough, I gripped it with both hands. "You're my boss." I took a breath. "I'm your intern."

"How is that worthy of a conversation?"

"I just have to think that"—I pointed at the space between us—"what happened tonight is going to change things a bit."

My heart hammered, and I didn't know why.

"You mean, you think we're going to be together now?" He huffed, like he couldn't believe I was wasting his time. "Come on, Hannah. You just said it yourself; you're my intern. Your uncle signs my paychecks. When I have issues, I go to your cousin to resolve them. I thought we were on the same page about this. I didn't take you for a girl who caught feelings after a few orgasms." His eyes narrowed, the hardness returning, where just minutes ago, when he'd pressed me against the window, a softness had been in its place. "Didn't I make it clear that this was going to be a one-time thing?"

"You did." I swallowed.

"That this"—his eyes traveled down my body—"would never happen again?"

It pained me to nod, my feelings so messy and foggy that I couldn't even begin to sort them. "Yes."

"Then, there's nothing for us to discuss." He turned silent. "Are you going to have a problem with acting professional at work?" He looked at the wetness on his fingers before he crossed his arms. "Because if that's the case, you should have a conversation with your family and see if you can switch mentors. I've tried. Your cousins won't budge, but maybe you'll have better luck with them."

My hands were shaking. So badly that I hid my fingers behind my back.

Nothing had changed.

He was still the same dickhead as he had been before we had sex.

I didn't know why I'd thought that this could be the start of something or why I would even want that. The night at the bar had proven Declan wanted nothing more than my pussy.

Tonight had emphasized that.

He wouldn't even kiss me.

I meant that little to him.

"Professionalism isn't going to be a problem," I assured him. "In fact, I see no reason to find myself a new mentor." I shrugged. "It's not like anything special happened between us this evening."

Asshole.

If I'd thought I hated him before, it didn't even compare to the way I felt now. He'd triggered a new, heavier level of repulsion.

"Then, the next several months should be as smooth as *glass.*"

His eyes darkened.

I could tell we were sharing the same thought about the glass he'd just held me against.

"Exactly," I replied.

Men like Declan Shaw could walk away, unscathed, the intimacy meaning absolutely nothing to them. That was probably because he did this so often with girls like Madison—and now me—and the faces all started blending together.

God, that man was an asshole.

He was right about one thing: this would never happen again.

"We have to be in court in less than forty-eight hours," he said. "Tomorrow is going to be a very long day. Go home and get some sleep." He walked toward the door, stopping when he was halfway through it. When he turned around, I wasn't able to read his expression, but his lips slowly parted, stalling before he said, "I'll call Warren downstairs and have him escort you to your car. Good night, Hannah."

He didn't wait for a reply.

He just walked down the hallway, and I eventually heard the click of his office door, followed by the lock.

He wasn't just shutting me out.

He was making sure I couldn't get back in.

THIRTEEN

DECLAN

"To fucking winning," Dominick said, holding his glass high in the air.

I clinked my tumbler against his and then against Hannah's and Kendall's. "To winning," I repeated.

It had been a long, hard week, but the Kennedy trial was finally over. Dominick's client was extremely pleased with the result, as was the entire Dalton Group. The congratulatory texts had been flooding my phone since the second I'd stepped out of the courtroom.

My team had given me everything I needed. As for Hannah, she had stayed in the background during the trial, providing support whenever she was asked, seemingly unfazed by what had happened in the conference room, not even bringing it up once.

As I took a drink, looking around the table, sitting in one of the most popular bars in LA, it looked like we were on a goddamn double date.

The rest of my team was supposed to join us, but each member had sent me a text before we even arrived at the bar, choosing sleep over cocktails. They'd been working their asses off, so I didn't blame them. But, Jesus, this semi-alone time with Hannah wasn't helping my hard-on.

"I told you we had this case by the balls," I said to Dominick, setting down my glass, a sip in and already ready for a refill.

"Thanks to my cousin." He nodded toward Hannah. "Let's not forget her contribution. The precedent she found was one of the main points of your defense."

My growl was too quiet for him to hear.

Did he think that was going to earn her a goddamn trophy? I was the one who had finessed the jury. I was the one who had built an impenetrable defense.

If anyone was going to get a trophy here, it was me.

And when the semester ended, I would earn myself another one for surviving this fucking internship.

Hannah's stare tested me.

Did she actually think I was going to agree with Dominick?

The thought made me fucking laugh.

"Let's face it," I started. "There isn't another litigator in the state who would have stood in that courtroom and demolished the opposition like I did."

"I'm not denying that fact," Dominick said. "I'm just giving credit where credit is due, my friend."

Everywhere I turned, I was surrounded by Hannah.

At the office.

In the courtroom.

At the bar.

Now, she was getting credit for winning the trial.

As though she could read my thoughts, her expression switched to a smile.

One that goaded me.

Jesus fucking Christ.

I was done with this conversation.

"With the Kennedy trial over, what else do you have for me?" I asked Dominick. "One of your clients must be neck deep in some shit, no?"

"Things are unprecedentedly"—he grinned—"quiet at the moment." He swished his scotch around in its glass. "Jenner's been grumbling about some issues that have popped up in his world, so there's a chance he's going to be keeping you very busy."

I rubbed my hands together. "I'm ready."

Silence settled across the table, and Kendall stood from her seat. "Excuse me, guys. I need to go to the ladies' room."

"I'll join you," Hannah said.

Hannah got up from her chair, linking arms with Kendall, her black pants tightening across her perfect ass as she walked through the bar.

This was my chance to be free of her, yet my eyes were still on her.

Watching.

Dreaming.

Fuck me.

When my stare returned to Dominick, he was looking at me.

"What?" I asked.

He rested his forearms on the table, his hands now surrounding his tumbler. "I'm trying to figure out what the fuck is going on with you."

"You do realize you're a broken record at this point, right?" I shifted in my seat. "Nothing was wrong the last time you asked, and nothing is wrong now."

"I've been sensing that something is off, and I just can't shake that feeling."

"I'm all good, man."

His eyes narrowed. "Are you really?"

I adjusted my tie, loosening it at my throat. "Don't I look good?" I gave him that winning smile I'd used today in the courtroom. "I crushed the Kennedy trial. My team at work is solid. I'm enjoying my job—mostly." I chuckled. "What the hell could be wrong?"

He combed the side of his beard with his fingers. "I don't know. I can't quite put my finger on it."

He was lawyering me, trying to see below the surface, analyzing my movements, my expression, looking for cracks in my exterior.

He continued, "But I can tell you one thing, Declan: I'm going to figure it out."

I just hoped that didn't involve testing the conference room table for DNA.

"Listen to me. Things are perfect," I said. "There's no need to waste any energy on something that doesn't exist."

"Well"—he stopped to take a drink—"I can see that things with Hannah haven't improved."

I sighed. "If her performance improved, maybe my attitude would. However, at the moment, she's like a fucking wart on my team."

He was quiet for a moment. "For real, do you think you're being a little tough on her?" He raised his hand before I could chime in. "I'm not saying you should give her any special treatment. I've made it clear that I'm dead set against that kind of behavior, but is she really as bad as you're saying?" He waited for a response. When I didn't give him one, he added, "She's young. Fresh. I assume she requires a bit of extra patience and attention, which we've compensated for by giving you an additional clerk. But finding that precedent? Come on, man. That's not your average intern accomplishment, especially not on an intern's first couple of days on the job."

Where the fuck were the girls?

How goddamn long did it take to pee?

"Are you as invested in your other interns' careers as you are with Hannah's?"

"I put her in your hands. At this point, I can stop pretending it was a random selection—not that you ever believed that anyway. I did that because you're the best, Declan, and that's whom I wanted Hannah to learn from. I think she has what it takes to be the top in her field one day, and I can't wait to watch her climb." He leaned in, emphasizing, "Not because she's a Dalton, but because she's earned it. So, yes, I have a vested interest, but what I can't understand is why you don't."

I didn't know how to address that statement.

Shit.

I should have been flattered he'd chosen me to mentor his brightest, most promising intern. And, of course, I wanted the best for Hannah. But, fuck, this situation was messy as hell.

Rather than feeding him a lie, I said, "Says the man who preached so hard about favoritism. Bending the rules for your own flesh and blood? Doesn't surprise me one bit."

"You want to talk about surprise?" He fingered his cuff links. First his right sleeve, then his left. "When I asked Hannah how her internship is going, she sang your praises. Bragged about how much she's learned from you. Said this experience has been better than she could have imagined."

"So?"

"So ..." His hands folded together, stilling. "I'm looking at two very different sides of the same coin."

"I don't know what you're getting at."

"I've been trying to get to the root of what's bothering you. Originally, I thought it was because you were getting an intern. On the day you were hired, that made sense. But as time has gone on, I just can't buy that theory. Then, I thought, is it really because she's my cousin and future partner—an argument you used when you tried to pass her off to a different team? But I know you, and if anything, that would challenge you more. Which leads me to my final conclusion."

I took a deep breath. "Which is what?"

"You're more interested in her than you want to be."

My brows rose, my heart beating in my throat. "Interested how?"

"You know exactly how."

Sweat slicked across my palm as I barked, "What the fuck, Dominick?"

"Tell me I'm wrong."

"You're wrong. So fucking wrong."

He leaned back in his chair, his arms crossing. "We'll see about that."

Anger pulsed through me.

Had I not hidden my feelings well enough?

Had I gotten soft?

I set my arms on the table, moving closer to him, locking our stares. "What exactly are you going to see?"

"Something has crawled up your ass since the day Hannah walked into your office. Men like you show rage when they're trying to fight an attraction. I know how you work. How? Because it takes one to know one." His hand lifted to his chin. "Here's what I'm going to say about that. Hannah has about as much experience with men as she does with law. She's innocent. Wholesome. What she doesn't need is a man who fucks a different woman every night, who's going to toss her the second he conquers her." When his hand dropped, he brought his drink up to his mouth. "Like her brother, I've protected her my whole life, and that's never going to stop."

"You're reading this all wrong."

"Am I?" He set down the scotch, his eyes now challenging me. "If so, then just consider this a warning. But if I'm right about this, then also consider this a warning."

What had happened with Hannah in the alley was a mistake. A night I had misjudged, and it shouldn't have happened due to how much she had apparently drunk.

But the conference room?

The table. The window.

That piece of heaven between her legs.

That was ... everything I'd wanted.

And it had been just as hot as the alley.

But it couldn't happen a third time even though it shouldn't have even happened a second time.

"The last thing she needs right now is a distraction." He took a drink and freed up his hand, sticking it in the fold of his crossed arms. "She needs to finish out this internship, pass the bar, and then come take her place at our firm. I don't want anything derailing that plan. Understood?"

"You're wasting your breath."

His face turned hard, edgy. "I'm glad we're on the same page."

The moment he finished speaking, the girls returned to our table, the scent of Hannah immediately filling my nose as she sat beside me.

The same scent that I'd sucked off my fingers after they were inside her cunt.

The same scent I'd smelled all day in court while she sat directly behind me.

As she laughed at something Dominick had said, I took a quick glance at her profile. Her smooth, beautiful cheek, etched with a faint line from her stunning smile. Penny-shaped eyes, lips that were so perfectly pouty.

She was a vision, almost impossible to look away from.

But I forced myself to and instantly caught Dominick's stare.

Ah hell.

That motherfucker was no fool. Somehow, he'd seen right through me.

Our conversation was a warning all right.

I needed to fight these feelings. These urges. The thoughts of her that were consuming me more and more each day.

"Let's go grab a refill," Kendall said to Dominick, wrapping her arm around his. "Our waitress is slammed; it's going to take her forever to return." She looked at me and then at Hannah. "Refills?"

"Yes," I replied.

Hannah nodded.

"Be right back," Kendall said, and the couple left.

Once we were alone, I felt Hannah's stare.

But I didn't look at her. I focused on my drink, which was almost empty.

"I haven't had a chance to congratulate you," she said. "What you did at that trial was nothing short of amazing."

I had to give it to her. She could certainly separate business from pleasure.

"It's what I'm good at."

I finally looked at her, instantly knowing it was a mistake.

I shoved my hands into my lap, squeezing my fingers together so I didn't reach out and grab her.

"No, Declan ... there are many things you're good at." She licked her lips. "I need to ask you something. Something that's been eating at me." She quieted, as though Dominick were still at the table. "Why wouldn't you kiss me?"

She was going there?

Now?

After a week had passed and I hadn't so much as tucked a piece of her hair behind her ear.

"Hannah, it doesn't matter."

Because it wasn't going to happen again.

Yet all I could think about was grabbing her face and slamming our mouths together.

I needed to control myself.

I needed to get this girl out of my fucking head.

She traced the rim of her glass. "If you're not going to give me anything, at least give me that."

I tried not to read into the words she'd chosen.

How her desire to have something between us had clearly been spelled out in that single sentence.

"It's too intimate," I blurted out. "It's just not something I do."

That was a lie.

Hannah had been the exception.

Of course, she didn't remember.

Thank fucking God.

"You mean, you've never put your lips on a woman's mouth? And there's no exception to that?"

She looked confused.

I didn't know why.

What I had said was simple to understand.

"No exceptions. Not ever."

"Not even with me?"

I drained the rest of my scotch. "What would make you think you were any different, Hannah?" I checked Dominick's placement, and he was still standing at the bar. "Because you're a Dalton? My intern? Because you happen to be more than just a pretty face?" I paused. "None of that earns you a pass."

It was like a bee had landed on her arm and stung her, the pain in her face getting sharper by the second.

"You're nothing to me. Just another number."

I wanted her angry.

Disgusted.

I wanted to make sure she stayed the fuck away from me.

I wanted to be the most hated man in her world.

"I see." She huffed out an exhale of air. "I just wish I had known you were this much of an asshole before I made the biggest mistake of my life."

"That's why they're called mistakes, Hannah." I lowered my voice, almost roaring, "They're things we learn from."

Dominick could see through me, but I had the same capabilities when it came to Hannah.

I didn't believe a thing she was saying because, even now, as she stared at me with a cuff of betrayal wrapped around her throat, I could see how badly she wanted me. How she would do anything to have me fucking her pussy again.

"They're things we never do again ... like coming a fourth time against the window in the conference room."

I'd slipped in the reminder, just to see if there was a change in her eyes.

The flame was there.

One that smoldered as low as her cheeks before she made it disappear.

I leaned into her ear, watching her chest freeze, hearing her breath hitch. "How many days were you sore? Can you still feel me, or is that ache long gone?"

God, I was a mean motherfucker.

She pulled away, putting several inches between us.

But that didn't stop me from saying, "What a feeling it must be to know you've had the best and there isn't another man out there who will ever make you feel like me."

She shook her head. "You're vile and so full of yourself."

"And?"

"And I'm repulsed by you."

I smiled. "Good. Then, we can both agree that we just need to survive this internship. You stay the fuck out of my hair, out of my office, and off my tip." I pushed my back against the seat, grabbing her dirty martini and shooting back what was left of it. "Do we have an understanding?"

"Oh"—she ground her teeth together—"we absolutely do."

FOURTEEN

HANNAH

"I appreciate you coming over to babysit tonight," Ford said as I sifted flour into a huge bowl.

Little Miss Eve was standing next to me, kneeling on a stool, holding a wooden spoon, ready to mix the food dye I was going to drop in next.

Not only were we dyeing the vanilla-based cupcakes pink, but we were also going to decorate them with rainbow frosting.

I planned to eat at least a dozen, so I'd tripled the normal recipe—that way, they'd have leftovers.

"Yeah, well, I appreciate that you hired a nanny," I replied, glancing up from the bowl.

Watching Eve was oftentimes one of the best parts of my day, but I just couldn't do it anymore. I needed to dedicate the hours I spent here to school and bar prep. Even though I still didn't require as much sleep, the tiredness was beginning to creep in.

"Pink!" Eve shouted as I swirled in the dye. "Whoa, it's *sooo* pretty." She dipped her finger into the bowl and quickly licked the batter before I could stop her. "*Mmm.* Vanilla." She swallowed. "Daddy, Hannah even got pink sprinkles. It's gonna be a pink explosion."

"Hannah spoils you, you lucky girl." He kissed the top of her head. "Baby, I need you to do something before I leave."

"Daddy, I'm very busy right now."

I hid my laugh.

I swore she took after me, not her father.

"This isn't negotiable," he told her.

She stomped her knees on the stool in response.

"I need you to go pick up your room. When I walked by a few minutes ago, your books and stuffed animals were everywhere. It's your job to clean it up, not Hannah's or mine."

"But, Daddy—"

He pointed to the ceiling. "March those buns upstairs now, please."

When she looked at me with melancholy eyes, I said, "Don't worry, bestie. I'm not going to bake these cupcakes without you. The second you're done, we'll pick up right where we left off. Okay?"

"*Okaaay.*" She stuck out her hand. "But pinkie promise."

I locked my finger with hers. "I pinkie promise."

She wiggled off the stool and took off for the stairs. "I'll be back!" she shouted as she climbed the large floating staircase.

Ford never had a problem with me picking up his daughter's room, something that occurred every time I babysat; therefore, I knew he wanted to talk to me.

Once Everly was halfway to the second story, I wiped my hands on a dishrag. "What's up?"

He grabbed a beer from the fridge, twisting off the cap as he returned to the island, where I was standing. "Just making sure things are good at work. Dominick mentioned Declan has been a little spicier than normal."

I snorted. "I never said that to Dominick."

He tossed the metal cap in the trash. "You didn't need to. We've noticed that on our own."

By we, I assumed he meant him and his brothers.

"Listen, we all know Declan isn't the warm and fuzzy kind. He's crass and moody and—"

"Dickish," I chimed in.

He said, "*Mmhmm*," as he took a drink. "That too." He wiped his mouth. "The other night, when you were watching Eve, I met the guys at the bar, and Declan was there. I gave him one of the chocolate chip cookies that you had made."

I knew what night he was talking about; it was the same evening that Ford had met Sydney, his new nanny.

Since this story was about Declan, I rolled my eyes. "He texted me from the bar, asking if I'd poisoned the cookie." I winced, not sure if I wanted to hear the rest of what had happened, but I knew Ford would tell me the truth. "What did he say to you?"

"Well, he was more than pleased with the cookie. He even moaned while he was chewing."

"God, he's an asshole." I held my breath. "But that's it? That's really all that was said?"

He rested his arm on my shoulder, a move that was so fatherly. "Aside from some bitching, yes." He studied my face. "I need to know how you're feeling about this internship. You haven't really said much about it to me. Are you hanging in there? Learning? Or are you on the verge of quitting and telling us all to fuck off?"

Whatever I told him, he would never repeat. That was the kind of relationship I had with Ford.

We'd always been the closest. Maybe because he was the youngest and there were only six years between us. Maybe because he was the softest of the three brothers.

Still, this was difficult territory.

Ford and Declan were friends, and Ford was also Declan's boss.

"I'm loving it. The passion and knowledge I'm gaining from Declan's team is addictive. They've welcomed me in, and I couldn't be more excited about my future and the opportunities I'll have once I pass the bar."

"And Declan?"

Ford had left the question rather ambiguous.

I wondered if he'd done that on purpose.

"He's challenging." I exhaled loudly. "In lots of ways."

Ford leaned his upper body against the counter, cupping his beer. "Talk to me."

I went over to the fridge and grabbed myself a beer, taking a long sip before I straddled one of the stools. "I'm going to paint you a scenario."

"All right."

Why was my brain conjuring up these questions when Declan had been such a bastard to me?

Why, when his words had sliced me open, the wound still fresh and raw, did I want more from him?

Why, when I had proof that he'd been with Madison, was I somehow able to see past that?

I didn't know.

But what I did know was my knowledge of men was limited, and I didn't understand the opposite sex at all. Not the way they thought, how they reacted, or how they processed. I couldn't work through this on my own. I needed help, someone on the inside, and Oaklyn wasn't that person. Since I couldn't have this conversation with my brother, that left Ford.

"There's this girl and guy who meet one random night. Things happen between them. Physically, I mean. Think sparks, like the Fourth of July, loads of chemistry, breaking down barriers like they never existed." I paused, my pulse spiking as I thought of the way we'd kissed. "The night ends, and so do they. But fast-forward a tiny bit, and the girl and guy now work together—a partnership that neither of them knew was coming." I was tempted to put the beer on my forehead just to cool myself down, but I didn't. "Now, the guy is her boss, and since her first day of employment, they've hooked up again. You'd think the setting would be perfect for dating, for more evenings together, for anything"—I pressed my cold hand against my chest instead—"but no. He wants nothing to do with her. Actually, that's not true. He's a total dickhead to her."

"Jesus, Hannah. I wasn't expecting that."

My head fell, focusing on my beer. "Yeah ..."

"I mean, I had a feeling something happened by the way he's been acting, but that's not what I assumed had gone down."

I looked up. "Elaborate."

"Whenever your name gets brought up, he loses his shit—that's not normal behavior." He swiped some of the frosting from the edge of the bowl and licked it off his finger, the same way his daughter had. "There are two reasons why a guy would act that way. One, he doesn't want anyone to know how he's really feeling, so that's his way of masking his emotions. Two, he has zero respect for women in general, and that's his true personality. Declan is type one." He took another fingerful of frosting. "But I figured he was still in the thinking phase, not in the acting-on-it phase."

"Ford," I groaned, "what the fuck have I gotten myself into?" I drained the rest of my beer. If I wasn't watching his daughter, I'd go for a second one, but I needed to be responsible for Eve. "When we met at the bar, I had no idea he worked for The Dalton Group, and when I walked into his office that first day, finding out I was his intern"—I shook my head—"things got interesting."

There was a vital piece of information I was leaving out of this story.

But Ford didn't need to know that I'd lied to Declan about blacking out.

"I'm trying to piece this together, but I'm getting the sense that you want to be with him."

I shrugged. "Yes. No. Maybe." I set down the bottle and my hands thrust into my hair, pulling the strands back into a ponytail. "I don't even know. He's mean. Cocky. Arrogant as hell. He's ... my enemy at this point."

"Listen, I've known Declan for a long time. He's a tough nut to crack, and he isn't one to ever get into relationships. But once you break through all his bullshit, he's a great guy."

"How do I break through?"

He was quiet for a moment. "Guys like Declan want what they can't have. It drives them fucking crazy; it makes them want it more. So, you need to act unaffected by him. Uninterested." He washed down the frosting with the rest of his beer. "Make him believe he can't have you."

Ford wasn't judging me. He wasn't lecturing me about making poor decisions and crossing a line in the office.

That wasn't the kind of guy he was, and I loved him for that.

"It sounds like you're actually encouraging this," I said softly.

"You need to be careful with your heart—I can't emphasize that enough." He let another second pass. "If this is what you want, then, yes, I'm for it."

That was a bold statement.

One I heard very clearly.

"Understood."

"Remember this, Hannah: even the dominant falls at some point, but that doesn't always come without a war. And with every war, there are casualties, and sometimes, those wounds are irreparable."

Every word vibrated through me, especially *the dominant*.

Like the kind who didn't kiss women and never made exceptions to that rule.

But Declan had made one with me on the first night we met. Before he knew who I was. Before we barely even spent any time together. He'd kissed me against the wall between the two restrooms prior to even taking me into the alley, and then his lips had been all over mine once we reached that spot behind the bar.

Why?

Because I was different and he'd immediately sensed that?

Because he'd wanted to give everything to me?

But what didn't make sense was that for someone who was so willing to give me his mouth, why had he run off with Madison? Why had he kissed her as well?

"Did I help?"

His voice dragged me out of a Declan cave.

"I think I'm more confused now than ever."

"That's a good place to be."

"It is?"

He pushed himself off the counter and began to twirl his keys. "It means you care." He walked out of the kitchen and headed for the stairs. "Just so you know, if you have another popcorn fight in my bed tonight, the both of you are dead." He winked before he ascended the first step.

"How about a cupcake fight? The rainbow frosting would look fab on your black comforter."

He leaned over the floating banister and looked at me. "You know ... I think Declan Shaw has met his perfect match."

"Ford!"

He laughed and continued up the flight. "Don't deny it, Hannah. You know I'm right."

I was in the middle of sorting through one of Declan's files when the phone on my desk rang. When a call came from an interoffice line, it showed who the caller was. In this instance, it was from the office directly behind me, the door closed, the dickhead tucked inside his dark chamber.

I sucked in a deep breath and picked up the receiver. "This is Hannah—"

"I need you." Declan's voice was rough, deep. A mix between a lion and a Rottweiler. At first, I was semi-excited by his choice of greeting until he said, "Get in my office now," and I knew I was about to face a rabid pack leader.

He hung up before I could respond.

I placed the receiver back in the cradle and pushed myself out of my chair, finding a steadiness on my heels before I hurried to his door. I didn't bother to knock—it would only waste more time—and I found myself no longer breathing the second our eyes connected.

Since it was nearing the end of the day, his tie was slightly loosened, and his jacket was off. The sleeves of his shirt were rolled up to his elbows, revealing muscular, veiny, dark-haired forearms.

Oh God.

Rather than waiting for his order, I sat in a seat in front of his desk. "Hi. What's—"

"I had a meeting with Jenner."

I knew that. Monitoring his schedule was one of my job duties.

"Walter Spade, the owner of Spade Hotels, is in some hot

water over a land dispute. The conflict has gone into litigation, and the case will now be going to court, which means I'll be taking over from here."

Walter was Jenner's future father-in-law, which meant this wasn't just a business matter for Jenner; it was a personal one too. Jo, Jenner's fiancée, also worked for her father, so the layers of this story just kept adding up.

"I need you to pull county records and titles and—" He zoomed in on my hands. "Where's your little pad, Hannah? Shouldn't you be writing this all down?"

I was so frazzled by Declan's phone call that I'd forgotten to grab something to write on.

Of course, he was calling me out over a minor slipup.

"I'll remember," I told him. "Keep going."

"I doubt that."

As I recalled my conversation with Ford, I gave Declan a smile. "Don't believe me? Then, quiz me after."

He leaned on his desk, the dark hair on his arms drawing my attention.

The guys I'd dated, mostly during my undergrad years, hardly had any chest hair; it was never something I'd really found attractive.

Until Declan.

His wasn't extreme, but the dusting across the top of his chest and the line that ran down the center of his abs, dipping below his waist, were an incredibly sexy sight.

As were his arms.

He was all man.

Every bit of him.

"An associate at my other firm had a mouth just like yours, and you know what happened to her?"

I shook my head.

"She became unemployed."

I made my voice nonchalant as I said, "If you don't want to deal with me anymore, then I'm happy to communicate through your paralegal." I recrossed my legs, like this conversation was boring me. "Feel free to reiterate the things you need to her, and I'll make sure you get them." I shrugged. "Whatever works, just tell me what you decide."

It was time the dominant fell.

But inside, I was screaming at how much of a dick he was, how he shouldn't have been blessed with good looks because he didn't deserve them.

His fingers clenched into fists.

His mask had broken, but only for a second as he instantly straightened his fingers and flattened them on the desk.

I tilted my head. "Is that it? Are you done?" I waited. "Should I get to work?"

With eyes that were boring through me, he handed me a folder. "The paperwork on the Spade case. Read every word. Don't leave this building until you've finished."

I was supposed to leave in an hour.

The folder was at least a hundred pages thick.

He was punishing me.

"I want your findings on my desk before sunrise."

The dick had upped the ante.

I smiled. "Anything else?"

He opened his mouth to respond and got interrupted by a knock at the door.

"Come in," he said through gritted teeth.

Declan's assistant opened the door, a bouquet of flowers in her hands. "Hannah, I was hoping to find you in here. These just arrived for you. My goodness, girl, someone certainly loves you. These are positively gorgeous." The flowers were so tall and thick that I could barely see her face through the blooms. "Would you like them—"

"Put them on her desk," Declan snapped.

The door shut, and we were alone again.

If I'd thought he was angry before, his expression was now boiling. "You have a lot of work to do." He nodded toward the door. "You can leave now."

I wondered if my smart mouth was what had set him off this round or if it had anything to do with the flowers—a delivery I hadn't expected. I recalled the way he'd acted when he overheard the phone call I had with Oaklyn, telling her I loved her.

Is this Declan's jealous side that I'm seeing?

"Would you like the door open or closed?" I asked once I reached the doorway, turning around to face him.

I was surprised to find him still looking at me rather than at his computer screen. I assumed that meant he'd also watched me get up and walk here, taking in my ass with each step.

Everything I wanted.

"Open." His lips were tight, his eyes narrow slits.

I smiled. Fluffy and extra-large this time. "No problem."

I returned to my desk, putting my back toward Declan, and knowing he could see everything I was doing, I grabbed the card that was tucked into the bouquet. What I wasn't letting him see was the way he had worked me up, the slight tremble in my fingers, the way it was impossibly difficult for me to take a deep breath.

My grin grew as I read the inscription.

HANNAH,
YOU'RE THE BEST BABYSITTER IN THE WHOOOLE WORLD. I'M GONNA MISS YOU TONS AND TONS NOW THAT I HAVE A NANNY. YOU'D BETTER COME BY OFTEN TO MAKE CUPCAKES. DADDY SAYS HE'S PROUD OF YOU FOR KICKING BUTT AT THE TRIAL.

LOVE YOU,
EVE

The warmth on my face was as honest as ever as I held the card against my chest. I would certainly miss seeing Everly as often as I had been, but this decision was best for the both of us.

I set the card inside my purse and took out my phone.

Me: *The flowers are absolutely gorgeous. Thank you. That was such a thoughtful gift, Ford.*
Ford: *Eve also picked you out a purse, but she wants to give you that in person. My daughter already has extremely expensive taste—Lord help me. She took me straight into Gucci and told the sales associate exactly what she wanted.*
Me: *LOL. I swear she's my child—in a non-creepy way, of course.*
Ford: *I don't disagree. How are things going today?*

I felt a heat burning across my back and glanced over my shoulder.

Declan hadn't moved, his hands still flat on the desk, his eyes narrow while he stared at me. "If you're done swooning over your flowers, you can get back to work."

So, this was what jealousy looked like on him.

Man, did I love it.

Instead of replying to him, I looked back at my phone, practically giggling as I typed.

Me: *Have I told you that you give the best advice ever? Because you do.*

FIFTEEN

DECLAN

As I stared at Hannah, I was frozen at my desk like a goddamn block of ice with my hands flat on the wood, feet pressed against the floor, right leg bouncing in anticipation.

The woman was fucking consuming me.

And while I sat here, obsessing about her, her smile was aimed at the vase of flowers, worth at least several hundred dollars, and at the screen of her phone, assuming she was texting her gratitude to whoever had sent them.

It wasn't just any kind of smile. This was one that tugged at her full lips, causing a slight wrinkle at the corner of her eye, a rosy circle forming in her cheek.

I wanted to see the goddamn words that were written on the card.

I wanted to know who had this kind of power to cause such a reaction from her.

Was this a woman in lust?

Or worse, a woman in love?

Those questions didn't break through the ice. Instead, they made the glacier even thicker.

I wanted Hannah Dalton to be mine.

The fact that she wasn't just made me angry.

Angry that she was my intern and I knew it wasn't appropriate to have a relationship with someone at work, especially with her being a subordinate. Angry that she was a Dalton and I had already been warned by Dominick. Angry that our first time together had been an evening she didn't remember and, with that, came a heavy layer of guilt.

Angry that the first woman I wanted more with was off-limits.

I didn't know how to make this right.

And I didn't know how to make her mine.

I just knew that her presence had become too much to resist.

Whenever she stepped into my office, I wanted to bend her over my desk. Whenever a moment of silence passed between us, I wanted to pull her into my arms and bury my tongue in her mouth.

Rather than doing any of those things, I barked. I treated her like shit. I took my frustration and resentment out on her.

I'd never had a Hannah in my life.

I didn't know how to do this.

I fucked women and then immediately left them. No one had ever occupied my mind this long.

Fuck.

I needed an escape, a deep breath that wasn't monopolized by thoughts of her.

I walked out of my office and went into the kitchen. I didn't know what I was doing in here. It was just a space that didn't reek of her, a room I didn't frequent often since Hannah got me coffee and food whenever I wanted. But the Daltons paid for an in-house caterer, and today, she was setting up a dessert station in the corner.

I grabbed a cookie and a cup of coffee and took a seat at one of the tables.

A group of three male interns walked in, hovering by the cupcakes.

One of them, after swallowing his bite of chocolate frosting, said, "Did you see the skirt she has on today?" to the other two.

I had no interest in making conversation. I also didn't give a fuck about what they were discussing, so I was scanning emails on my phone; it was just impossible not to overhear.

"Fuck, man, she has the most beautiful legs I've ever seen, and her nipples have been hard and poking through that white shirt every time I walk by her desk," another one said.

Hannah had on a white shirt. I'd noticed her nipples every time she came into my office today.

Hell, there wasn't a part of her I didn't notice.

But I was sure the mention of the white shirt was just a coincidence. There were hundreds of women who worked at this firm; they could have been talking about any of them.

"You know we went to undergrad together," the first guy said. "Studied together, sometimes partied together. She had such a tight little body, and, fuck, it's even better now." Just as I glanced over at the group, he added, "Dude, Hannah Dalton was the hottest girl in my prelaw classes by a fucking mile."

Out of all people, they were talking about Hannah.

My Hannah.

A little of the black coffee spilled onto the table; the cookie crumbled in my palm.

"I've got that beat," another one said. "We go to the same law school, and we've been in most of the same classes. There's a study group next week, and I'm going to ask her out. I've been trying to since the start of the semester, but the second class is over, she darts out, and I never get the chance."

That earned him a fist pound from his other two buddies.

"Man, if you hit that, I need details," one of them replied.

"Dude, you lucky bastard," the other one voiced. "She's fucking smoking. I'd kill for a chance with her."

"Get in line, motherfucker."

Jesus Christ.

Every person in this fucking building who had a cock was noticing Hannah.

She was getting flowers. She got hit on wherever she went.

Guys would do anything to have a taste of her.

She was worth it; I could understand it, as the girl was gorgeous.

But that didn't help the rage erupting in my body.

Nor did these three fools.

I tossed the pieces of cookie into the trash—it wasn't nearly as good as anything Hannah baked—and went over to their small group. "Shouldn't you be working?"

They turned silent with a bit of shock on their faces.

"What I'm looking at right now is a bunch of fuckoffs, gossiping like some fucking hens, clucking about shit you shouldn't be talking about." I took a final drink of my coffee and threw the paper cup in the trash. "I'm sure the Dalton brothers would be pissed to hear that you're wasting the firm's billable hours, talking about how badly you want to fuck their younger cousin." I nodded toward the door. "Get to work. Now."

They said nothing.

They just filed out, one by one, until I was left alone with the caterer.

I thought the quietness would be a relief. I thought I'd find some satisfaction in putting those boys in their place.

I didn't.

I just got angrier.

I left the kitchen, and as I made my way down the hallway, one of the clucking hens was parked at Hannah's desk, a smile now covering his face.

I was positive I was going to lose my shit.

She was supposed to be working on the Spade case, reading the notes, putting together a report that I wanted on my desk before she left.

Instead, she was basking in his attention, just like when she'd admired the flowers and worshipped the card and cherished the text exchange that followed.

Sweat covered my clenched palms, as if I'd just taken off a set of boxing gloves, and as I neared the doorway to my office, about to tell the motherfucker to get lost, I heard, "Declan …"

The voice was familiar enough to know it had come from one of the Daltons, but I was too worked up, seeing far too much red, to identify which brother it was.

The clucking hen was using everything in his inventory to charm her. His efforts earned him laughter—a carefree, sweet sound that I didn't hear often enough. That was probably because all I did was upset her. But it didn't end there. She was also smiling at him, a sight so genuine that it made my fucking chest hurt.

"You all right, buddy?"

I turned toward the voice, Jenner now less than a yard away.

Am I all right?

The fury moved into my throat when I hissed, "Yeah."

"I've been calling your name. Didn't you hear me?"

I took another glance at Hannah. She was running her fingers across the bottom of her mouth, back and forth, drawing the hen's attention to that spot.

My favorite spot.

A spot that would make him think about her perfect lips

wrapped around his dick. But the thoughts wouldn't end there; they'd spiral, bloom into questions, like how hard she could suck, if she would swallow, if she was the kind of girl who would enjoy it.

The hen was lost in a goddamn hard-on, and Hannah thought she was just brushing something off her mouth.

I was going to kill someone.

Jenner patted my back like he was burping a fucking baby. "Declan?"

I swallowed, trying to calm myself before I exploded on my friend. "What do you need, Jenner?"

He leaned his shoulder against the wall, the small section of space between my office and the one next door. "I had a thought I wanted to run by you."

"I'm listening."

"You're planning on going to Wyoming to view the land that's in dispute, am I right?"

Walter's land. The pictures showed the property was in Jackson Hole, several acres that sat directly in front of the Grand Teton. A place that, for years, had been on my list to visit. I'd just never made it there to vacation.

"Yes." I cleared my throat, forcing myself not to look at Hannah. "Of course."

"Then, I think you should bring Hannah with you."

I followed his gaze to her desk, and when I reached the back of her chair, I wouldn't look any further.

"It's not customary for our interns to travel, but I think it would help her connect the visual dots of the case and give her some hands-on experience. Besides, she has a personal connection to Walter, so if she has questions and wants to lead any discussions, he'll be patient with her."

I'd planned on going at the end of this week. I was going to

MARNI MANN

take the corporate jet to Wyoming, spend a night, possibly two, while the rest of my team stayed here.

Traveling with Hannah hadn't even crossed my mind.

But I didn't hate this idea at all. In fact, I fucking loved it.

I just didn't want her cousin to know that, not when I'd begged the brothers to reassign her. I needed him to think I was against it. I needed to show as much resistance as he was expecting.

"Jenner, are you sure? I don't know if she's ready for something so hands-on, in your face. I'd prefer to go alone and—"

"She's more than ready," he countered. "I realize you do things a bit solo. I'm the same way, to be honest, but Hannah isn't just any team member. She's a Dalton."

A point I couldn't forget. I didn't need the reminder.

If she wasn't a Dalton, we wouldn't even be having this conversation.

A trip together meant time on the private plane.

Two rooms in the same hotel.

Dinners.

"Understood," I said.

When he touched me this time, it was on my shoulder, praising me like a goddamn dog. "I knew you would."

He disappeared down the hallway, and I finally glanced at Hannah again, the hen still at her desk.

I couldn't take another second of this.

"Hannah!"

The hen was startled by my sound, his back going erect, his eyes immediately flitting to me.

Hannah slowly swung her chair around, giving me her full face.

"You"—I pointed at him—"get to work. This is your last warning. I'm not going to tell you again, and you"—I nodded toward Hannah—"get in my office."

I took a seat at my desk, and within a few seconds, she walked in with a notebook in her hand.

"I thought you wanted to be quizzed?" I waited for her to sit. "Or did that little boy get you so frazzled that you're afraid you won't remember what I'm about to say?"

She set the notebook on the chair beside her, placed the pen on top, and crossed her arms. "What do you need to tell me, Declan?"

Oh, this fucking girl.

She tested me at every opportunity.

Challenged me.

Her attitude was so nonchalant that I wanted to tie her hands behind her back and show her what submissive really looked like.

"I know you've been so fucking busy flirting your ass off, but if you happened to read any of the information in the file that I gave you, then you'd know Walter's case is regarding a piece of land in Wyoming. I plan to visit that location at the end of this week, and you're coming with me."

Her brows rose. "Oh?"

"For the record, this wasn't my choice. Jenner insisted."

"How long will we be gone for?"

I pressed my hands together, holding them close to my face. "Is your calendar so full that you don't know if you can fit it in?"

"Actually, it is." She recrossed her legs, switching sides. "I'm in law school, Declan. I'm bar prepping. I'm working here more hours than I can even keep track of. I need to make arrangements if I'm going to miss class."

Things I hadn't considered. My mind had been somewhere else.

"We'll plan the trip around your schedule since you insist that you're the busiest person on this floor."

Her head leaned back, and the most lighthearted sound came out of her.

Laughter.

But it wasn't the sound I found myself drawn to as much as the beautiful arch of her neck. The way her throat bobbed as she took in a breath. The way her cheeks flushed as her neck resumed its normal position, her eyes catching with mine again.

"You"—her tongue swiped my favorite lip—"are too much."

I felt the same way about her.

Consumed.

Over-fucking-whelmed.

I was in competition with the clucking hen and the flower dude, and it seemed like every other motherfucker.

I needed to claim what was mine.

Mark her.

Make sure she knew, without a question in her mind, whose cock belonged inside her.

I couldn't wait until after hours, when everyone was gone from the building.

This was risky, dangerous. I didn't care.

Nor did I care that I'd promised myself I was never going to touch Hannah again, that the night in the conference room would be the last time.

Even then I had known I was lying to myself.

And now, all rational thoughts were gone from my mind.

I needed her.

Now.

"Go lock the door, Hannah."

Her head cocked to the side as she analyzed me. "For what reason?"

"Because I ordered you to do so."

She set her arms on my desk, leaning on the hard edge.

"And you think, just because you gave me that order, I'm going to listen?" Her voice was serene.

She was trying to gain the upper hand.

"Yes," I growled. "Now, go."

"For the record," she said, using my own words, "I'm locking the door because I'm interested to see where this is going, not because you told me to."

I didn't care what her reasoning was as long as she moved quickly.

And she did, turning the lock with those delicate fingers once she reached the door.

From there, she didn't move. She stayed put, flattening her palms against the door like she was being arrested.

The reason was because she'd heard me get up and follow her, stopping directly behind her. "Hannah ..." My hands moved above hers, closing our bodies together, inhaling the scent of her hair as I buried my face in her locks. "Tell me to stop."

"You've been such a dick to me."

My eyes closed as I got lost in the scent. "You're making me fucking wild."

She pushed back, rubbing against my erection. "I know ... I can feel it."

I wrapped an arm across her chest, holding her neck. "Why do you do this to me?" I strengthened my grip. "Why do you make me hurt for you?" I traced the cartilage with my lips. "Why do you make me ache for you?"

She leaned the back of her head against my chest, her hair splayed across my suit, like I was a pillow. "Make me forget how much of an asshole you are."

My fingers moved to her chin, tilting her face toward mine. "I want to make something very clear." In the back of my mind, the flower dude, the hen, they had only confirmed what I had already known. "When you're in this building, this is mine." I pushed my hips forward and ground my cock into her ass. "All mine." I lowered my face until our lips were almost touching. "Say it." I waited, listening. "Say it, Hannah. Make me believe it."

Still flat-fisting the door, she released it to wrap her arms around my neck. She fingered the back of my hair, pulling my face to the same position it had been in before. Breaths separated us as she exhaled, "Kiss me."

She was making demands.

Because this girl, this goddamn unicorn, knew she held all the power.

And she knew what a kiss meant to me.

I didn't question it.

I didn't even attempt to fight it.

I smashed our lips together.

Our mouths instantly melded, my tongue sliding in to circle hers. I held her face so she couldn't pull away and breathed her in, remembering the last time we had kissed and the attraction I had felt.

This was stronger.

The intensity even more commanding.

I separated us, and she took her time opening her eyes, filling her lungs.

"Say it," I reminded her.

Her teeth grazed both lips, like she was sucking me off them. "Make me yours, Declan."

An invitation.

One that she backed up with the loosening of my belt buckle and the lowering of my zipper. She reached inside the hole of my boxer briefs and fisted my cock.

I panted through my nose, the air hot and fierce, like a bull. "Your uncle and aunt and cousins have offices right outside my door." I continued to hold her face, pressing into her cheeks. "I need you to remember that."

"You're not good at keeping me quiet."

"Hence the warning."

She leaned up on her toes and kissed me. Slow. Steady. Almost like she was memorizing my lips. "I'll try."

"You need to do better than that."

My fingers slid down her chest, unbuttoning the white shirt so I could cup her tit. She moaned as I rubbed across her nipple and then lowered to the flatness of her navel, halting at the top of her skirt. It was too tight to slip under the waist, so I reached behind and unzipped it, the material falling down her legs.

"Keep your heels on." I discovered a pair of lace panties and dropped those too. "How wet are you ..." My voice trailed off as I got my answer. "God-fucking-damn it." My fingers dripped as I dipped inside her pussy, using my thumb to graze her clit. "What made you so wet, Hannah?" I made sure she felt each of my exhales across her face along with the hum of my tongue. "When I told you that you were coming to Wyoming with me?" I added a second finger, heading toward her G-spot. "When I told you to lock the door?" I kissed her hard. "Or when I told you that you were mine."

The walls of her pussy clenched my fingers, a narrowness that was going to feel fucking incredible on my dick.

"When you got jealous of Ford sending me flowers and of Travis talking to me at my desk."

I growled, and it wasn't because my dick was fucking throbbing even though it was.

So, Ford was the flower dude, and Travis, the clucking hen, was a name I didn't care to remember.

The important part of this equation was that Hannah could see right through me.

I plunged deeper inside her, turning my wrist, aiming upward.

"Are you going to tell me I'm wrong?" She smiled. "That the attention, the fear of me slipping away, doesn't turn you into a roaring bear?" She grasped the back of my neck like she was about to fall. "Declan"—she sucked in a breath—"oh my God."

"You know how to set me off."

"That's it?" She moaned again. "That's what you're going to call it?"

I gave her my face, allowing her to stare at it. To read me. To see the words that I wasn't saying. "What do you want from me, Hannah?"

"The truth."

"That I want to be able to do this"—I pulled out of her pussy, rubbing those wet fingers across her lips—"whenever I please? That I can't stop thinking about you? Us? What that could even look like?" I narrowed my gaze to her mouth, her lips now wet. "If that's what you want to hear, then there you go." It didn't change the fact that she worked for me, that her cousin didn't want us together. But I wasn't going to get into that now. Now, I was on a much different mission. "Taste yourself."

She licked across both lips before she took my fingers into her mouth, holding my stare the entire time, licking up and down and around my knuckles.

"Fuck me," I hissed as she bobbed before sucking the tips. "You want my cock?"

She nodded. "Please. Now."

I'd never heard such a sexy demand.

"You have one job, Declan."

I returned to her ear, tasting the vanilla on her skin, and whispered, "To make you come as many times as possible."

"That's always the answer, but there's something else too."

"And that is?"

"To make me forget how much of an asshole you are."

I chuckled as I returned to her pussy. "You want me to fuck the hate out of you?"

"Yes." She got even wetter. "Relentlessly."

SIXTEEN

HANNAH

The words had only just left my mouth, and I was already in the air, Declan carrying me to his desk, where he set me on the edge. He spread my legs and stood between them, lowering his face until he was eye-level with my waist.

"This view ..." He gazed up at me with such an animalistic level of hunger. "This scent ..." He pressed his nose against my clit. "You have the most beautiful cunt I've ever seen."

I ran my hand through his hair. "Are you teasing me?"

"Savoring ... not teasing." His tongue swiped me and then stilled. "I've thought about doing this all fucking day. I want to take my time."

I tugged on his hair until he gave me his eyes. "Maybe if you were a little nicer to me, I'd give it to you more often."

There was a pattern to Declan's behavior. When he felt challenged and threatened, he became even more of a dick. When he wanted something he believed he couldn't have, he fought with his words. But one thing was obvious: he was acting this way because I mattered. Because he wanted me.

Because, for some reason or another, he believed we couldn't be together.

I needed to change that.

He circled my clit and stopped. "You know I'm not good at that."

"Try." My hips bucked as he sank his finger inside me.

"Try to be sweeter? Or try to constantly give you my face to ride?"

"Try to whisper instead of roar." I pulled on his hair to urge him closer. "But I still can't get enough of you."

He sucked my clit into his mouth, flicking the end, releasing it to say, "Of my tongue."

"That. Yes." My eyes closed; my mouth stayed open. "But there's more, Declan. I think about you." I gradually connected our stares. "Fantasize about you."

He licked the entire length of me. "You want this to be mine."

I'd wanted that since the night at the bar.

He was the one who had been battling this, who had been causing my thoughts to be such a tangled mess.

"Yes," I replied.

"But there's more."

I was grateful he could see right through me, so what I was about to say wouldn't come as such a surprise.

I bit my lip, preparing. "There's something so sexy about a dominant alpha." I fisted his hair, ruining the gel he'd put in this morning. "A man who's angry all the time, except when I'm feeding him what's between my legs. That's when he softens. When his vulnerable side comes through."

He huffed air, like a brief, deep laugh.

"But I need more, and I need you to think about that." This wasn't the right time to get answers out of him. This was the time to sprinkle crumbles that he could inhale later when he was ready. When he was alone. When he was reflecting about today. "I want to be the girl whose pussy you eat on top of your desk, but I also want to be the girl you cuddle on Sunday mornings."

He stared, unblinking, his tongue slack against me.

"Now, are you going to kiss me with that wet mouth?"

"Or?"

"Are you just going to make me come?"

He flattened his tongue, gently dragging it up and down my clit before he moved on to his fingers, licking me off them as he stood. From inside his wallet, he pulled out a condom and set it beside me. His pants then dropped, his boxer briefs next, exposing that beautiful, massive cock. With his teeth, he tore off the corner of the foil packet and aimed the latex at his tip, rolling it down his shaft.

"Declan ..."

Once he finished, he pumped himself several times and looked up at me. "Yes?"

My chest rose and fell as my gaze dropped to his dick. "I don't know if I'll be able to be quiet." I licked across my lips. "Not when I know what you're about to do to me."

"I know just how to solve that problem."

He loosened his tie and slipped it over his head. I had no idea where he was going with this, but as soon as he placed it over my head and positioned the knot in front of my mouth, I knew.

"Open." He inserted the knot between my teeth. "Bite down." I followed his order, earning me a, "Fuck. You're so hot."

The tie was one of the sexiest I'd ever seen him wear. The same color red as the day I'd met him, but this one was smoother. Almost silk. No texture or pattern. Just buttery, like his skin.

He held both of my cheeks. "I know this won't completely silence you, but at least your sounds will be muffled. If I had another tie, I'd shackle your wrists ..." His voice trailed off as his fingers went to my shirt, unbuttoning what was left. "I have another idea." Once the shirt was fully open, he positioned my arms behind my back and slid the material down to my elbows. Although I couldn't see what he was doing, it seemed that he was tying both sides together, creating his own version of a straitjacket. He stepped back to admire his work. "Gorgeous."

And submissive.

He'd taken away my voice and hands, and I was completely at his mercy.

I couldn't reciprocate.

I couldn't communicate what I wanted, needed.

I could only take.

And by the looks of it, that was about to start now as his hand returned to the spot between my legs.

The motion he used was circular, like he was spreading my wetness from my clit to my pussy, and my hips slid back and forth in anticipation.

"Do you feel the difference?" His mouth was near my neck, his words hitting my skin, like rocks thrown into a pond, the ripples causing more goose bumps to rise. "When you can't touch or vocalize, there's a different type of intensity."

As he captured my earlobe and kissed down to my shoulder, he replaced his fingers with his crown. The wideness caressed my entrance, glided up to my clit, and back down. He did that over and over. Each time, I held in my breath, biting the tie, waiting for the fullness to take over. But each time, he was merely just passing by.

"Do you feel it, Hannah? The wanting? The longing?"

I nodded.

I sure did.

There was fire.

Awareness.

Every inch mattered, every breath.

I could feel the air he took into his body, as though I were on the inside, watching his lungs fill.

"You're about to feel more."

He slid in with zero hesitation. A move that was full of power and need, and he continued with deep, full strokes.

My eyes bulged; my breath got caught in my throat.

"Fuck me, Hannah. You're so tight."

With Declan, the beginning was always the most overwhelming. The stretching, the reacclimating. But once my body remembered him, the pleasure owned me.

"So fucking wet."

I surrounded him with my legs, digging my heels into the back of his thighs. Since my arms were bound behind me, that was the only way I knew how to hold on.

"You like that ..."

My mouth was stretched so thin that my lips absorbed his words like sponges.

"You want more ..."

I wasn't sure what he was referring to; there were so many parts to this—to us—but I easily liked it all, and I wanted everything.

He licked across my mouth, and the sound I released was quiet but clear, especially as his finger landed on my clit. This didn't feel like any of the previous times he'd touched me.

This was an explosion.

A sensory overload.

I pulled at the shirt cuffed at my wrists. I didn't want to be released. The straitjacket was strangely arousing. I just wanted to share the passion with something.

"You got there fast."

If I could, I'd be screaming.

"I can feel it coming on. You're getting tighter, wetter." He nipped my cheek. "Should I take your orgasm away from you too?" His thumb paused on my clit.

What?

No!

I stabbed the heels even deeper into his thighs.

"Easy there."

I didn't lighten up.

"All right, all right." His thumb picked up speed. "I'll give you exactly what you want."

And suddenly, out of nowhere, there was a slap across my clit.

It wasn't hard. It didn't make me yelp. It was just unexpected.

But with it came tingles, igniting through my body, causing everything inside me to become electric.

He did it again.

And again.

The swish of air, the slight sting from contact, was just enough to make me shudder.

Oh God.

"How fucking good does that feel?"

He growled into my throat as my head was back, my hair tickling the bare skin on my arms.

"There's nothing better in this world than watching you come."

The bursts were taking over, traveling throughout my body, turning me completely sensitive.

But he didn't stop.

He didn't even slow.

He just ground his hips and drove through my wetness, his thumb returning to my clit as I breathed out the moans.

"Am I still an asshole?"

It took a second to process, to clear my head of all this paralyzing satisfaction.

Once I could make sense of his question, I nodded.

It took an asshole to think he could make me come by slapping my clit. Even if the move had been successful. Even if I would have screamed so loud if I could.

Even if I fucking loved it.

"Looks like I have a lot more work to do."

He lifted me off the desk, creating a whole new balancing act since I couldn't wrap my arms around his neck. He stayed inside me, thrusting. And at first, I was so stimulated that I couldn't accept this new rhythm. But Declan was extremely good at reading my body, knowing what I needed. Knowing how to bring me back to that place.

"Fuck, you're wet."

There was a ledge in front of one of the windows, and that was where he set me, my hands pressed against the cold glass, my legs spread around him. He exhaled into my face, these quiet, gritty, masculine moans that got breathier, the harder he plunged. Now that he wasn't holding me, his hands were free to roam. They were on my breasts, my clit.

Giving.

Tugging.

Massaging.

My lips weren't in a position where I could kiss, but that didn't stop him from pressing soft pecks against my mouth, a gentleness so unlike everything else he was doing to me.

"I need you to come again." He widened my legs, arching my hips upward, hitting a whole different angle. "Yes, that's it."

I panted through the knot in my mouth. My eyelids squeezed shut. My muscles began to shake.

He was on my G-spot.

And it only took a few more blows across that touchy place before I began to shudder.

"*Mmm!*"

That was the sound that left me because, within a second, I was silent, lost in the waves.

In the rush.

In the shivers.

They darted through me like a slow-moving storm, melting me in the wake.

I felt his lips on my neck.

I felt his breath across my chest.

I felt his cock diving in and out.

And then I felt a moment of stillness before he peeled me off the ledge and carried me to his chair, where he set me on top of his lap.

"Ride me, Hannah." His kiss was much longer this time. "Fuck the asshole out of me."

I'd never been on top of him, nor had he ever given me this much control.

But in this position, he felt even larger, enough so that I felt myself open wider, having to push past the lingering orgasm still consuming me to find my own beat.

"Show me what your cunt can do."

As I lowered, his thumb returned.

Swiping, brushing.

The pressure had been there before I even heard his command.

His eyes only added to that feeling, the way they dipped down me, the way they inhaled me. His other hand moved back and forth between my nipples. The lace of my bra did very little to hide them, and it was like nothing was covering them at all by the way he was pulling them.

Each flick, I inhaled.

Each pinch, I exhaled.

Each inch that filled me, I tightened around him, squeezing again as I rose.

"Yes," he hissed. "Fuck me."

I kept myself low and rocked against him. It felt like he was twisting inside me, hitting walls and edges, creating friction from every corner.

"Oh fuck."

His fingers bit into me, his teeth took ahold of my earlobe, and he gnawed the small flap of skin. "You're fucking naughty, you know that?" He bit harder. "You're fucking me like you want me to come."

My speed increased.

I panted through the knot.

I wanted to give him something to remember.

Something that would make him hard every time he thought about this moment.

I switched things up, bobbing over him, and then I swayed my hips forward and back, narrowing when he was in the deepest. When that became too repetitive, I quickened the pace, pumping, circling.

"Now, you're really going to make me come."

He tried to slow me down, but I wouldn't. There was no stopping me at this point.

I wanted him to lose himself inside me.

I wanted him breathless.

I wanted him to be mine.

"Hannah ..." My name sounded like a moan. "Goddamn it, you're fucking milking me."

I wanted to scream out my release.

I wanted the entire building to know how good this felt.

But all I could do was breathe, my nostrils flaring as the hot air escaped them.

"Fuck yes," he roared against my face. "*Fuuuck*."

As he took over the movements, blasting hard, relentless strokes into my pussy, the tingles returned to my body.

"Hannah ..." He pulled the tie off and slammed our lips together, taking my tongue into his mouth. "Fuck, Hannah!"

My body trembled from each quake, from the peak, from the aftermath.

Pleasure began to drain as the slowness changed to a stillness.

I lowered my body down and rested against his chest. "Declan ..."

I was a beating pile of wetness, just trying to find my breath.

"You ..." His emerald eyes gazed back at me. They didn't just stare; they hugged me. "Jesus, Hannah, you know how to ride some serious cock."

His compliment made me laugh. "Thank you—I think that's what I'm supposed to say."

He wrapped his arms around me, loosening the shirt, freeing my wrists. Once they were clear, I rested my hands on his shoulders.

"I'm surprised you didn't ask when you can do it again."

I wanted to.

He was still inside me, and all I could think about was when we were going to do this again.

If things were going to change.

If ...

"Declan—"

"Don't." He grabbed my face, holding me steady. "You

know this isn't going to be easy. There are so many circum-stances that make our situation different."

He always knew what I was thinking.

I said quietly, "I know."

"Just give this time."

They weren't the words I'd wanted to hear.

They weren't the words that would fill my heart.

They weren't the words that would make me pull him toward me, locking us together.

"Can you do that?" he asked.

I didn't trust my voice—there was too much emotion pulsing through me—so I nodded.

He brought me close and kissed me.

His embrace didn't have the same passion he'd given me before.

Still, I was getting his lips, and I knew what that meant.

As he pulled away, the Declan I was beginning to know so well returned. I could see him getting inside his own head, weighing the complications of our situation.

Pushing me away.

Any second, he would turn into a raging asshole.

"I have to get back to work." He scanned my eyes. "So do you."

The statement wasn't as harsh as I'd expected, but it wasn't cuddly either.

I lifted myself off his lap, and we both got dressed.

"I'll be back," he said, heading for his private bathroom, where I assumed he was going to dispose of the condom.

I fixed myself as best as I could, and I went to my desk.

He didn't see me leave. He didn't see me take a seat at my desk.

He didn't see me wipe my eyes and catch my breath.

Because I was already gone when he came out of the restroom.

And when he took a seat in his chair, attempting to look at me while I sat in mine, he wasn't able to.

I'd closed his door.

I'd shut him out.

I'd pushed right back ...

SEVENTEEN

DECLAN

Hannah made any outfit she put on look incredible, whether that be workout clothes or jeans. She knew her body, how to dress it, and accentuate her features. She always looked gorgeous.

Today, she took it one step further and looked absolutely magnificent.

She had on a black dress with hints of red that blended across her waist and chest, as though the designer had taken the faintest paintbrush and traced the sexiest parts of her body. Her heels were sky-high, like the ones she had dug into my legs several days ago. She wore her hair in long curls, her makeup highlighting her eyes and lips, both sparkling from the sunlight that came into the plane.

She sat across from me, running the toe of her shoe across her opposite shin, her black nails clicking on the keys of her laptop.

One thing had become extremely clear since I'd bound her hands in my office. Hell, maybe it had become clear since I'd kissed her outside the bar's restroom.

Hannah Dalton was going to be the end of me.

The fear of losing her had gotten in my head.

I'd shown weakness.

I'd kissed her.

Fuck, I couldn't help it.

It didn't matter how hard I tried to fight it; this girl won every time.

I wanted her.

But it went beyond that.

My need wasn't just physical, and that was the part I struggled with.

I wanted ... more.

Except Hannah wasn't just a normal girl and this wasn't a typical circumstance.

With her being a Dalton and the cousin of my friends, there were certain expectations of me—and that was assuming Dominick didn't fucking destroy me when I confessed the truth to him. Those brothers knew my reputation. If I was going to date their cousin, I needed to be sure what we had was going to last. Not only because I was going after my intern and that could jeopardize my job and the chance at being a partner, but also because she was a woman they loved, and that made all the difference.

I couldn't dabble.

I couldn't sway back and forth.

It was either us or nothing.

I had assumed this trip to Wyoming was going to answer many of the questions that had been haunting me. I would leave LA behind, and the mountains and nature would give me a chance to clear my head and provide some resolution. Shit, I'd even planned to do some horseback riding and hiking while I was there. But that plan got derailed when I was told Hannah would be coming along. Even then, I'd adjusted my outlook. I would see her in a different environment, away from The Dalton Group and her family, and we could enjoy some time together in Jackson Hole.

But those plans changed again.

We got a chaperone.

At the last minute, Jenner decided to come as well. Given that Walter Spade was one of his largest clients and future father-in-law, it made sense.

But his presence prevented me from having any alone time with her.

All I'd thought about as I stepped into the shower this morning, my fucking dick hard as I stood under the scalding spray, was how I was going to take her into the private bedroom at the back of the plane. The different positions I was going to bend her in, the way I would eat her pussy if we hit turbulence.

Maybe having Jenner here was for the best. Maybe what I needed were these thoughts of Hannah to evaporate from my head, so I could focus on Walter and my upcoming cases and the fast-track plan to making partner.

A woman had never been part of my long-term goals anyway.

And things had been fucking perfect before I walked into Professor Ward's classroom.

I didn't know a goddamn thing about relationships or how to be in one.

Who the hell was I kidding? I wasn't the boyfriend type.

But had I ever thought about a woman as much as Hannah? Had I ever shown this level of jealousy and rage over a woman? Had I ever had to force myself not to kiss, not to eat a woman's cunt? No, because women didn't tempt me that way.

Not like her.

"Fucking jet lag," Jenner said, tearing me from my thoughts, reminding me that I was in a plane since the only thing I could apparently focus on was Hannah. "It's winning; my ass is toast. I need a nap."

He was sitting beside me and closing his laptop, stuffing it into his briefcase.

"I don't recommend flying to Australia, spending twelve hours there, and flying right back." He yawned as he closed the top of the briefcase.

"It sucks that you didn't have time to do anything but work while you were there," Hannah said.

"Tell me about it," he agreed. "Especially since Australia is one of my favorite places to visit."

"I feel that way about this trip to Jackson Hole," I admitted. "I've wanted to visit this area for a while, but we're just in and out with almost no time to do anything."

"Don't laugh, guys, but I was really looking forward to going horseback riding." Hannah had this dreamy expression on her face. "I had this whole plan to live out my *Yellowstone* fantasy and buy myself a cowgirl hat and boots and ride off into the—I don't know—sunset or something."

Hannah, on the back of a horse—a sight I definitely wanted to see.

Hell, I was even impressed that she was interested in doing something like that.

Something we certainly had in common.

"You mean, *Yellowstone* the TV show or the park?" Jenner asked.

"I know Jo makes you watch it, so don't even try to act like you don't know what I'm talking about. Jo and I have had endless conversations about you impersonating Rip."

"Jesus Christ," Jenner groaned.

"I don't watch it," I confessed.

Both of their heads turned toward me.

"Now, that's just silly," Hannah said. "You need to. That show is everything."

"Do you agree with her?" I asked Jenner.

He laughed. "It's good. I don't know that it's *everything*."

"That's such a guy response," Hannah teased, rolling her eyes. "Anyway, I'm bummed we won't have time for horseback riding or to even head into Yellowstone National Park. I've been reading up about the geysers and all the animals that live there. They have moose and bears—I'd love to see those in the wild."

So would I.

Heading into Yellowstone was something I really wanted to do during this trip.

I liked hearing that Hannah was down for the same experience.

"You know, Hannah, I heard about this rafting excursion through the Grand Teton," I began. "It's not far from where we're staying. It's a ten-mile—"

"Scenic tour down Snake River," she finished excitedly, her eyes lighting up. "I found the same one. It looks amazing, doesn't it?"

I nodded. "It does."

"You know what I think?" Jenner asked. "That all of that sounds extremely exhausting." He yawned again. "I'm going to go get some rest." He looked at me and added, "Do you need anything from me before I go?"

"Nah. Sleep well, buddy."

As he left, I turned around, watching the flight attendant in the galley prepare us breakfast. I was gazing at the biscuits she was placing on our trays when I felt Hannah's eyes on me. And as I faced forward, our stares locked.

"I didn't know you were so into nature and the outdoors," she said. "I wouldn't have thought that."

I chuckled. "I wouldn't have thought that about you either."

She moved all her hair to one shoulder, running her fingers through the curls. "I take Everly hiking almost every time I watch her. She's really the one who got me to love nature as much as I do." She smiled. "What's your excuse?"

"My excuse ..." I huffed. "Don't know. I just want to see the world. How's that for an answer?"

"It's a perfect one."

Some silence ticked by, and I knew she wanted to bring up the conversation we'd had in my office the moment I unbound her hands. What we were and where we were going—something I'd been thinking about nonstop since she'd said the words. She hadn't brought up the topic in the days that had passed. But even now, I could see the urge on her face, in the way she was breathing, how her fingers were flicking the ends of her hair.

"So, are you prepared for today's meeting?" I asked, needing a subject change before the subject was even broached.

Even though she'd written a report on the Spade case, each day more details came in, and I needed her to know all the information.

Knowing Walter personally didn't give her a pass.

If he had a question during today's meeting, I wanted her to be able to answer. If he wanted to discuss certain aspects of the land, I needed her prepared.

She shifted in her seat, crossing her legs to the other side.

They were perfect, toned and tanned.

The only way they'd look better was if my face was buried between them.

"I stayed up most of the night, reading over the material again."

"Yeah?" I questioned. "Well, I can't have you tired and yawning, like Jenner, during the meeting."

She cocked her head to the side. "Are you really questioning my professionalism? I think I'm far past proving that to you."

Her spicy side had come out to play.

"I'm not questioning, Hannah. I'm just warning—that's all."

"Well, I don't need a warning."

My eyes narrowed as I took her in. "As long as you're my intern, you're going to get one."

She pulled the laptop against her chest like it was a shield. "Would you treat any intern this way? Or just me?"

There had been a shift.

I didn't know where it had come from.

But I didn't like it.

"What the fuck is that supposed to mean?" I demanded.

"I get that you're in charge. I get that you're the one who gets to make all the decisions here regardless of what I want. I don't need the reminder."

I laughed, taken aback by her reaction, but now, I knew where the attitude was coming from. "That's not what I was doing."

"Then, what are you doing, Declan?"

We weren't talking about Walter anymore.

We were talking about us.

"Why don't you just tell me what's bothering you, so we can skip the theatrics and get to the point?"

She licked across her lips.

I didn't think, in this moment, she'd intentionally tried to make that look sexy, but Hannah looked sexy when she was simply breathing.

"It's upsetting and quite honestly disappointing that what's happened between us means nothing to you."

"Who said that?" My brows pulled together. "Because those words never left my mouth."

"They didn't have to. Your actions have done all the talking for you."

If we had been alone without a flight attendant and Jenner in the back bedroom, my voice would have risen. I was doing everything in my goddamn power to keep it low, but the anger was certainly coming through.

"I've treated you like an employee these past couple of days. Have I mentioned what happened between us? No. Have I hauled you into my office to fuck you? No, I haven't done that either. So, what actions are you talking about?"

"That's the whole thing—you've done nothing. How do you think that makes me feel?"

I'd told her to give this time. When I'd asked if she could do that, she'd nodded.

Now, she was changing her opinion?

"Hannah, this isn't easy—"

"You keep saying that." She leaned forward in her seat, as though she were trying to get closer. "And you said to give this time." When she paused, I swore she could see right into my thoughts. "But, Declan, why isn't this easy? What the hell are you going to do with more time?" She moved the laptop to the seat next to her, her free hands now holding her knees. "Are you going to contemplate whether you like me? Whether I'm worth it? Whether you can handle—"

"Whether I'm willing to risk it all to be with you."

Her face scrunched up, like I'd just taken all the air out of her lungs. "Then, why do you keep trying to fuck me? Is that all I'm good for? A body, nothing else. You know I won't say anything to my cousins, so you're safe. You can have your cake —or brownies—and eat it too."

"It's not like that."

"What's it like, then, Declan?"

Fuck, she was going to make a strong litigator.

She had more power in her voice now than when I'd mentored her in the classroom.

"I've more or less been single for thirty-two years, Hannah. Relationships aren't something I'm good at. I was warned by Dominick to basically stay the fuck away from you. I have a very serious position at your family's firm, and it wouldn't bode well for me if they found out I was fucking my intern— someone who shares the same last name as them. I'm trying to become partner, not get my ass fired. Like I said before, this isn't easy."

"Dominick warned you?"

I glanced out the window as the plane hit a patch of rough air. "Yes."

"What did he say?"

"He wants you to be successful, and he doesn't want anything or anyone to wreck those plans."

"Interesting." She sat back in her seat, her posture erect. "That doesn't change anything. What my cousin wants and what I want don't have to align."

"When he's my boss, it absolutely does."

"So, you're going to let Dominick dictate where we stand?"

My hand went to my hair, and I didn't know if I should slide my fingers through it or tear it from the fucking roots. "No, I'm not. But when I told you this needs time, I need you to respect that. So, this drama"—I pointed between us—"doesn't need to happen."

She bared her teeth. "Show me some respect, then. Stop being an asshole."

"That's who I am. You, us, work—nothing will change that."

She crossed her arms over her stomach. "When I heard you in Dominick's office, pleading with him, Ford, and Jenner to assign me to a different mentor, I should have pushed them for it. There are more important things than learning from the best."

She had overheard me in their office, fucking begging to get rid of her. I'd asked her how long she'd been standing outside the door, and she had made me believe she hadn't eavesdropped.

She'd lied.

What she didn't know was why I had asked them to reassign her, how the guilt of fucking her that night at the bar was too much for me to stomach.

And, goddamn it, I still wasn't ready to tell her the truth.

We were both lying.

But instead of admitting that, I said, "What would be more important?"

She was quiet for a moment. "Protecting my heart."

We sat around the large dining table in Jenner's suite. Each of us, including Walter, had a folder in front of us that my team had put together. A heavy stack of paperwork, which included blueprints and land surveys and permits along with aerial photographs of the land in question.

Walter had remained silent as I went through the presentation, flipping through the tabs of notes my team had left me, covering each of the major points.

I had just reached the end when he asked, "What do you think? Have I wasted far too many millions on a piece of land where a hotel will never come to fruition, or should I fly out the architect while I'm here?"

"I think—" Hannah cut herself off as she looked at me and then added, "May I, Declan?"

If any other intern were sitting at this table, this scenario wouldn't play out. A client didn't give a fuck what an intern thought—someone with no law degree, no authority to practice, and more importantly, no experience to back up their opinion.

Any other intern would have sat there silently.

But Hannah was using her personal connection to Walter to her advantage, and Jenner's expression told me he was all for it.

As soon as she received my nod, she continued, "From what I've seen during my research, the land in question is yours. The previous owner had nothing more than a gentleman's agreement with the neighboring owner"—she held up a piece of evidence that was included in the folder, confirming this—"and the agreement isn't registered with the county or the state. It wasn't even notarized. When the sale of your property went through, this piece of land—from what I can tell—was included. Now, the neighboring owner is saying he paid the taxes and can prove that with receipts, but that doesn't define ownership. In addition, I've reviewed the entire contract you signed when you purchased the land, and the piece in question was included in the survey; therefore, it's part of the sale. That tells me that the seller either forgot about the gentleman's agreement or didn't care enough to resolve it prior to closing. Either way, a verbal agreement—or in this case, a poorly executed written one with two illegible signatures—doesn't define ownership." She glanced at me and then back at Walter. "In my opinion, again, without a proper piece of documentation, the land is legally yours, and you can do with it whatever you see fit."

She was right.

And, fuck, I was impressed.

Walter processed her conclusion, allowing several seconds to pass before he said, "Is there a chance the neighboring owner will surprise us with more documents when we go to court? Can he provide more evidence, proof, whatever that he hasn't already shown?"

Hannah looked at me, waiting for approval. When I gave it to her, she replied, "Sure, that's always a possibility. But my gut tells me that if the neighboring owner had more documentation, he would have provided it. No one wants to go to court and incur the expense of hiring an attorney unless they absolutely have to."

"She's right," I confirmed. "In addition, my team has scoured through all the available evidence, digging through fifty years' worth of land ownership, deeds, and county records. I can't imagine the neighboring owner has resources that are better than ours."

Walter exhaled loudly. "You know how these small towns work. It's all whom you know, who can do you favors, who has more cattle, who has a bigger horse—you get my drift."

"Walter, Declan is going to do everything in his power to win this case." She leaned her chest against the table. "Please don't worry."

She was confident without being overbearing. Patient and charming.

On top of it all, she'd done her research, and she knew what she was talking about.

"The only thing I can add to what Hannah said is that the neighboring owner might want a credit for any money or taxes that he's invested into the property since you've taken ownership. But we're talking thousands of dollars versus the millions he's suing you for."

"I can live with that," he said to me. He then crossed his hands over the top of the folder, his eyes softening as he looked at Hannah. "I remember the last time I was at Jenner's for dinner. We were all sitting around the dining room table, and you were telling us about law school and your hope to intern at The Dalton Group. Never then did I think we would be here, working together. Or, if the opportunity did arise, that you would be this impressive." He reached across the table and rested his hand on hers. "I should have never doubted you. You remind me so much of my daughter, and like her, you're going to have a bright future ahead of you, young lady. I can see it, I can feel it, and quite honestly, I'm blown away."

"Take every word of that compliment and run with it," Jenner said, smiling at his cousin. "Walter isn't known for handing out praise."

"He's right," Walter agreed. "But you've earned it, Hannah."

"Thank you," she whispered.

The truth was, I was just as blown away as Walter.

At Hannah's ambition, at the respect she had shown me before answering any of his questions, at how well she had processed the hundreds of pages of information in Walter's case file.

I'd heard several of the other lawyers at the firm speak about their interns. Many were book smart, but didn't know how to apply their knowledge. Some could barely handle more than pushing paperwork around their desk.

Hannah was the exception.

And I had no doubt that she was soon going to become a brilliant litigator.

"I'd like to take you to the property," Walter said, pulling his hand back. "Give you a chance to see the land in person, take some of your own pictures."

"I'd like that," I replied.

"Then, we're going to my second-favorite restaurant in Jackson Hole."

"And why not your first favorite?" Jenner questioned.

"Come on, son. You know the best restaurant in this town will be the one that's in my hotel." He looked at Hannah and me. "The hotel that you two are going to ensure gets built."

"You can count on it." I chuckled.

"I'm going to grab us another round," Hannah said, jumping down from the stool as we sat around the high-top in the corner of the bar, where we'd come after dinner. "Does everyone want the same drinks?"

Walter, Jenner, and I nodded.

As Hannah left the table, I watched her disappear into the crowd of dancers, a much different setup than the spots we frequented in LA. There was a bluegrass band on a small stage in the front, and people of all ages were line dancing. With all the cowboy hats and thick belt buckles and boots in this room, I felt extremely out of place in my navy suit and gold tie.

The Wild West wasn't just in movies, but never had I visited a town quite like Jackson Hole.

And never had I seen so many cowboys outside the rodeo.

"You've got a firecracker on your hands," Walter said to me.

"You think so?" I looked toward Hannah, and one of the cowboys was standing just a little too close to her, the two of them talking.

Goddamn it. It didn't matter where she was; she attracted attention.

I didn't fucking like it.

Not one bit.

"She's so much like my Joanna," Walter said to Jenner, referencing his daughter for the second time today. "Eager, energetic. A girl who goes after what she wants and doesn't settle. You know, I wasn't sold on hiring Joanna right out of college. She was too young; she had no experience. I wanted her to prove herself, get a few years under her belt. But she fought hard, and by God, she won a position at Spade Hotels." He shook his head. "I saw the same fight in Hannah today."

The cowboy was now turned toward Hannah, smiling. His fingers were running through his beard and around his lips. He was flirting. Eye-fucking the hell out of her.

Why was the bartender taking so long to make her drinks?

Why was she even giving that cowboy the time of day?

I looked at Walter and said, "I'm not denying the fact that she's going to be good—we can all see that. But the courtroom is a lethal environment. A place that can destroy the weak."

"You're saying she's weak?"

"No." I drained the rest of my drink. "I'm saying, I want her as prepared as possible, so when it comes time to fight, she'll be ready."

Walter's eyes narrowed as he gazed at me. "I'm old and wise, young man. I've seen it all in my day, and I've probably experienced it in some form or another. That's why I'm confident in what I'm seeing right now."

The cowboy moved a pace closer to Hannah and set his hand on her shoulder.

If I didn't know better, I'd think the bastard was going to lean down and kiss her.

But before his lips got anywhere near hers, I'd fly off this fucking stool and demolish his mouth.

"Wouldn't you agree with me, Jenner?"

"Yes," Jenner said, laughing. "I'm in full agreement."

I turned toward the guys. "What are you talking about?"

Walter lifted his tumbler off the table and held it against his chest. "You."

"What about me?"

Walter laughed. "Kids these days. They think us old folks are so out of the loop, except we see everything." He nodded toward Jenner. "That one was no different, you know. He thought I was clueless, thought I had no idea what was happening between him and my daughter."

Jenner sighed. "Turns out, what happens in Vegas doesn't really stay in Vegas, especially if you're sleeping in one of Walter's hotels." He smiled. "But, you know, us kids—as you call us—aren't so blind either, Walter."

Walter's brows rose. "Oh yeah? How so?"

Jenner wrapped his hand around his drink. "You think we can't see what's happening between you and Gloria."

"I'm lost," I admitted.

Jenner looked at me. "Brett's mother is Gloria Young. My parents represented her in her divorce. The second the ink dried, Gloria and Walter started spending a lot of time together."

"Merely speculation," Walter said. "We're just friends."

"Bullshit," Jenner bit back. "According to Jo, she's never seen you happier since Gloria's divorce became final."

Walter tipped his head at me. "A coincidence of timing. Nothing more."

Jenner shrugged. "Maybe. But isn't it ironic that Gloria found someone to run her bakery in Miami and now divides her time between LA and Park City, but hasn't rented or purchased a home in either location? So, that makes me wonder, where is she staying when she's in those cities, Walter?" Jenner addressed me and said, "I need to mention that Gloria has now opened a bakery in LA in addition to the one she has in Walter's Park City hotel."

Walter smiled and glanced at his hands. "Well, looks like you have things all figured out, don't you?"

"Tell me I'm wrong."

Walter was quiet, finally saying, "All right, all right. I'll admit, things are moving along quite nicely between us." He paused. "But this conversation is about Declan, not me."

Fuck.

I had hoped things weren't going to circle back. The two of them had been on such a roll.

"No, no, we're not discussing me." I stretched my arms out above my head. "And no disrespect to you, Walter, but you have it all wrong."

"Are you sure about that?" Jenner asked.

I ground my teeth together. "Yes."

"Then, why does it look like you're about to pummel the cowboy Hannah's talking to right now?" Walter asked.

My jaw unclenched as I turned toward her, grinding right back together when I saw that the cowboy hadn't removed his hand from her shoulder.

"You have something you want to tell me?" Jenner said.

My stare returned to him. "No."

"Are you sure about that?"

Fuck me.

"Listen ..." I had to force myself not to look at Hannah, so I didn't give off any more signs. But as I stared at Jenner, his expression was demanding the truth. As my friend, did he deserve that? As my boss, was I thinking like a fucking fool? "Goddamn it ... I don't know what to say."

"You don't have to say anything, son. It's clear as day." Walter gripped my arm. "Women are the best things that have ever happened to us, wouldn't you agree?"

I didn't dare nod my head.

Jenner crossed his arms over his chest. "Has something happened between you and Hannah?"

The second Walter's hand left my arm, my fingers went to my hair, running through both sides. "Jesus Christ, how did this get turned on me?" I lifted the glass up to my lips, realizing there was nothing in there but ice. "I'm done with this conversation."

"Oh, no," Jenner said, "we're only just beginning."

I released a long, deep breath. "What do you want me to say, Jenner?"

"How about you start with the truth?"

My head dropped, his gaze far too strong. But if I was going to come clean, he deserved to be looked in the eyes, so I glanced up and said, "Yes, things have happened between us, but"—my hand went up as his eyes widened—"in my defense, I didn't know she was your cousin at the time. I didn't know she was a Dalton until she walked into my office the day she became my intern. Why do you think I was so persistent in trying to reassign her?" I waited for Jenner to respond, and when he didn't, I added, "Your brother warned me, more or less telling me to stay the fuck away from her. I'm trying, man. I'm fucking trying."

Had I really been trying?

Hell, I didn't know.

"Which brother?" Jenner asked.

What kind of question was that?

"Does it matter?"

"Yes, Declan, it matters."

"It was Dominick. Why?"

His stare shifted to Hannah before he replied, "She's the closest to Ford. If he were the one who had warned you, I would look at this a little differently."

Now, I knew Ford's opinion was the strongest of the three. I wondered if she had confided in him about what had happened between us. Ford had given me no indication that he knew anything, but would he?

This was all getting in my head far too much.

"Differently how?" I asked.

His head tipped back and forth like a pendulum. "Dominick takes the fatherly approach. I'm not surprised he warned your ass. But Ford's approach is more like the best-friend role, and you know girls and their best friends and how much weight they hold."

"Let me see if I have this straight." I licked my lips, craving another drink. "You're saying if Ford didn't approve, then you'd agree with Dominick, and you'd want me to back off?"

"Basically."

"Fuck, I'm not a dog, Jenner."

His brows rose. "You're not?"

I looked at Walter, and he laughed. "So, I might have a reputation when it comes to women but ..." My thoughts were all over the place. I needed to reel this in, stay neutral, and not let a single emotion escape. "I respect you three far too much to play her."

But, goddamn it, isn't that what I've been doing?

Taking what I want and kicking her out.

Not out of my office, but out of my fucking heart.

"I can't believe I'm having this conversation about my baby cousin," Jenner said.

"Jenner, I recall a similar conversation when you finally admitted to me that you loved my daughter. Do you think that was easy for me?"

Was Walter really on my side?

Never in a million fucking years had I thought that would happen.

But more importantly, the things I was feeling for Hannah, was that love?

Jesus, I couldn't wrap my head around any of this.

"I'm about to marry your daughter," Jenner said. "Let's keep you on this side of the fence, Walter."

"Look, I'm not the relationship type," I quickly voiced. "Marriage, kids—those aren't words in my vocabulary. Jenner knows that. So, there's no reason we should even be discussing this."

Walter set his glass down. "I'm not so sure about that."

The cowboy moved his arm, gaining my attention, and I saw him take out his wallet. Hannah shook her head like she was turning down his offer.

"What would you do if we weren't here?" Walter asked. "Or at least, if Jenner wasn't here."

He wanted honesty.

The anger in my chest was making that an easy question. So were the three scotches I'd had at dinner and the vodka rocks I'd polished off at this table.

"I'd probably walk up to the cowboy and threaten his life if he didn't take his hand off her and walk the hell away."

"What's stopping you, Declan?"

I looked at Jenner. "You."

"I say, threaten the bastard's life," Walter said.

"Fuck," I groaned.

The table turned quiet.

"I love that girl like a sister," Jenner admitted. "I don't want her future jeopardized in any way. I don't want her to lose focus. Law school is hard enough. When you add in an internship and bar prepping and then taking the bar, it takes a toll on a person."

"I know," I told him. "Don't forget; I went through it too."

He clasped his hands, his thumbs circling, finally stilling. "My dream for her is to be with a nice guy. Someone who's not going to treat her like shit. Who's going to be patient and

223

understanding. Who hasn't dated all of LA—like the two of us."

"Don't you think I wanted that for my daughter, Jenner?"

I was starting to really love that man.

Jenner rolled his eyes at Walter. "Jesus."

"Son, wouldn't you say most of your friends are like you and Declan? Men who have slept their way through Hollywood until they found the one—"

"I didn't say I found the one," I interrupted. "Let's not get ahead of ourselves."

"You didn't," Walter agreed. "But something tells me you know it's true, whether you'll admit it or not."

Hannah was unlike any woman I'd ever met. I had known that the moment she started speaking at the mock trial. So different, so unique, so fucking irresistible that I'd kissed her at the bar.

I craved her body.

I yearned for her attention.

I made up fake scenarios to haul her ass into the office just so I could spend more time with her.

But was I looking for a commitment?

Did I even know what that meant?

What that would look like?

Communication wasn't a strength. I didn't know how the hell to be a boyfriend.

What I knew, what I was absolutely positive of, was that I couldn't stand the thought of another man taking what was mine.

Of losing her.

Of not being with her again.

There was no question; I wanted her.

And I knew, even if I wanted to admit it to Walter or not, that those emotions went deeper.

Far deeper.

I looked at Walter. "You might have a point."

Jenner's expression changed. "What does Hannah want?"

I took a breath before I said, "Me."

"Then, my friend"—he clasped my shoulder—"you've got some work cut out for you, and you know what a hothead Dominick can be at times, so good fucking luck with that."

"Don't worry, Jenner's been in your shoes. He has plenty of tips to give you," Walter said.

"Again? Really?" Jenner challenged his soon-to-be father-in-law.

As Hannah carried our drinks to the table, Walter looked at me and winked. "It's a good thing he knows that I love him like a son." He twirled the ice around in his glass. "Declan, Dominick might be hotheaded, but I assure you, he's not a hard-ass, like me. That one"—he nodded toward Jenner—"had it much worse than you will."

EIGHTEEN

HANNAH

Ford: How's it going?
Me: I think I impressed Walter. He actually gave me a compliment, and according to Jenner, that's a miracle.
Ford: Jenner's right. Walter's not the kind of guy to give a single word of praise. That means you killed it. Proud of you.
Ford: Do I dare ask how things are going with Declan?
Me: Ugh. One minute I think he loves-ish me, and the next, I think he wants to murder me. Like tonight, when I was talking to a cowboy at the bar.
Ford: Trying to make him jealous?
Me: LOL.
Me: Maaaybe.
Ford: The love-hate thing is called a relationship, by the way.
Me: If he heard you say that, he'd probably die.
Ford: Then, change his opinion ... if you want to, that is.
Me: I do. I just don't know how.
Ford: By being you—the girl Declan is wild about.
Me: You don't know that. Besides, the more time I spend with

him, the more lost I become. I don't speak man language—you
guys are beyond confusing—and he's giving me whiplash.
Ford: Hannah, you speak Declan.
Me: Ugh, I'm going to bed. Maybe some of this will make sense
in the morning.

I set the phone on the nightstand and climbed into bed, trying to find the energy to text Oaklyn, knowing we'd have the same conversation I'd just had with Ford, except it would be far more detailed. But with each second that passed, I sank farther into the bed, my head buried in the fluffy pillows, losing my motivation.

Today had been a long day, starting with the early morning flight that caused nothing but tension between Declan and me, followed by meetings and food and lots of drinks.

I just wanted sleep.

I wanted to be able to shut off my brain and not see him every time I closed my eyes. Not hear his voice. Not question his uncertainty.

But I had a continuous loop in my mind, thinking about what had gone wrong, replaying so many conversations, contemplating our future, analyzing his reactions. It was exhausting.

I needed a Declan manual.

I needed him to help me make sense of this.

Of ... us.

But he wasn't here.

He wanted time.

He wanted to figure out if I was worth the risk.

That thought made me feel sick.

I pulled the blanket up to my neck, and as I reached for my phone, there was a knock at the door. I had no idea who it could be. I hadn't called housekeeping or ordered room service. I didn't think Walter or Jenner would stop by, unannounced.

Unless the knocker had mistakenly gone to the wrong room, that left only one other person.

Oh God.

I climbed out of bed and stopped by the closet, putting on a bathrobe to hide the tank top and panties I had on, and when I got to the door, I looked through the peephole.

Declan was on the other side.

He was still in his suit, hands flat against the door. With his arms extended, his head fell between them, facing the ground, like he was having a hard time holding himself up.

Was he ... drunk?

Was he fighting with himself over being here?

The same way I had fought with myself to open the door?

Whenever we spoke, nothing got resolved.

My emotions would just explode, and I'd get angrier, more confused.

And then I'd find myself falling deeper.

"Declan ... go to bed." I rested my forehead on the door, my hand clutching the thick gold chain that kept the room locked, my other palm pressed against the wood in the same place as his but on the opposite side.

"I need to talk to you."

My eyes squinted together, a knot as big as a boulder moving into my throat. "You can wait until the morning."

"I can't. Hannah ... let me in. Please."

There was something about the tone of his voice, the rawness of each word, the way his plea wrapped around my chest that caused me to unlock the chain, lift my face off the door, and open it.

His hands didn't drop; they just moved to the frame, his body now leaning through the doorway. "You told me there's something more important than learning from the best. You said that's protecting your heart."

It took a second for his words to register. "Yes, I did."

"Because you think I'm going to break it."

I couldn't tell where he was going with this. If I needed to put up a shield or unzip my skin, allowing him to see right inside.

But I squeezed both sides of the robe together and replied, "I have to protect myself, Declan."

"What if I want to be the one who protects you?"

I stared into his eyes, my hands shaking, the mountain in my throat now pressing against the back of my tongue. "What are you saying?"

His hand dropped from the frame, and he reached forward. I was about to move away, but his fingers caught me. At first, they grazed my cheek so softly, his touch like a whisper, and then he cupped the same spot, ensuring I didn't move.

"I've told you, I don't know how to do this. I don't know how to be a boyfriend. I don't know how to give you all the things you need." He looked down, the intensity fully exposed on his face. The lines deep in his forehead and the sides of his mouth. His knuckles white as he gripped the molding. He looked up as he added, "That doesn't mean I don't want to try."

A wave shot across my chest, like a crack in a frozen lake, a web spidering across the entire surface. "What are you telling me, Declan?"

His fingers fastened a bit harder on my cheek. "I want us."

Us.

In my eyes, those two letters were as powerful as the ones that spelled *love*.

Still, I wasn't sure he knew the magnitude of what he was saying.

What this actually meant.

It was one thing to want me, but it was a whole different thing to want us.

"Do you know what you're telling me?" I searched his eyes, digging, assessing like I'd done in this room only minutes ago, a loop starting all over again. "Because I know you've had a lot to drink tonight, and by the way you stared me down when I returned to our table, you weren't happy I was talking to the cowboy, and I'm sure that has something to do with this."

"This has nothing to do with the booze, Hannah. It's long worn off. I'm dead sober." His stare expanded, and I felt it the second it entered me. "It has nothing to do with the cowboy either." He stepped closer, his other hand now on my face, tilting my chin upward. "I need you to hear me. I need you to understand this."

When I nodded, his fingers didn't move.

"Okay."

His gaze lowered to my mouth and lifted to my eyes. A pattern. And during each dip, my mind spun to every place imaginable.

"I can't promise I'm never going to hurt you. I can't promise I'm going to be perfect. I can't promise I'm going to know how to navigate this or that my decisions will always align with yours. I can't promise you're not going to hate me at times"—he lowered his mouth, pressing our noses together—"or that I won't lose my patience, making you want to kill me." As he pulled away a few inches, his thumb brushed my bottom lip. "But here's what I can promise you. You're going to get all of me. I'll be honest with you even if the words I speak aren't the ones you want to hear."

His eyes closed, and when they slowly opened, a pang moved straight into my heart.

"I'm going to try like hell to be the man you need me to be, Hannah."

"Why?" I swallowed, needing to make sure this was real. Needing to make sure I wasn't dreaming. "Why now? Because this morning, on the plane, you said this wasn't easy and you were deciding whether you were willing to risk it all to be with me." The sting from that conversation was present in my eyes. "Do you understand how confusing this is when you go from cold to hot—"

"This morning, I was being an asshole. I was being selfish. I was avoiding what I knew I needed to do because I didn't know how to do it." He exhaled. "I shouldn't have acted that way. You didn't deserve that, and I'm sorry."

"That doesn't change what you said and what you meant."

His eyes dropped from mine for only a second, and I knew he was so far outside his comfort zone, this discussion so unlike anything he normally had.

"You're right; it doesn't. But for what it's worth, my feelings for you this morning were as strong as they are now."

I wanted to get to the bottom of this, so I said, "Something's changed. What was it?"

He shifted, and the brief movement sent me his cologne. "While you were at the bar with the cowboy, I was talking to Walter and Jenner about you."

"Really?"

His expression softened. "Walter saw right through me. He immediately knew I had feelings for you, which came as a surprise to Jenner. What I learned from that chat was that Jenner had gone through the same thing with Jo. Jenner didn't want to tell Walter that he was in love with his daughter, the same way I haven't wanted to tell my bosses and friends how I feel about you."

My lip started to tremble, and I pulled it into my mouth.

Is this really happening?

"The job, I can replace," he continued. "The friendships,

those will be much harder, if it even comes to that, but I won't let that stop me." His thumb stroked my cheek. "I can't lose you, Hannah. Everywhere I turn, someone is trying to steal you. If I wait any longer, you'll be gone forever." He brought our faces closer. "I'm not going to let that happen."

A tingling moved through my body. Not the kind I was used to when it came to Declan. This was more of a warmth that reminded me of campfires and the glow from a sunset. The feeling increased as I took in more of his eyes.

"You're choosing us ..." The admission came out of me softly, my heart catching up, as though it were a step behind my voice.

Because even though I was witnessing this moment, I was present for it, I still couldn't believe it was happening. I hadn't been sure if Declan was ever going to come around, if he was capable of giving me what I wanted.

But he stood in this doorway, not even inside my room, like he hadn't been able to wait to get this out, and he was speaking the words I'd dreamed of hearing.

His fingers pressed down harder on my face, and his lips moved closer, hovering above mine. "I am," he whispered. "That is, if you'll still have me ..."

NINETEEN

DECLAN

"*That is, if you'll still have me ...*"

I heard the words I'd spoken to Hannah repeat again and again in my head as I stared at her beautiful face.

Before I stood at her door, pouring my fucking heart out, I'd gone for a walk around Jackson Hole's tiny downtown, aimlessly wandering up and down the streets, trying to sort through my thoughts. I passed cowboys and couples, music filtering out to the sidewalk every time a bar door opened. When I didn't feel like walking anymore, I found myself in a small park, the entrance an arch of antlers.

While I sat on that bench, I thought about Hannah. She was such a good girl, goddamn it. Considerate, caring. Almost every day, she brought some kind of dessert into the office, most of them apple-flavored after she found out that was my favorite. I remembered the morning, several weeks back, when I'd looked out my office window and saw her outside with my lunch in her hands, stopping to place money in a homeless man's cup. My team always spoke about how appreciative they were that Hannah would stay long past normal office hours to help them with every assignment.

Time was something Hannah had very little of, but it seemed that was what she gave out the most—to Ford, when-ever he needed her to watch his daughter; to my team, when even the slightest hiccup arose; and even to me, never saying no regardless of what I asked.

The truth was, I didn't deserve her.

But at least I'd poured my heart out to her.

At least I'd finally told her how I felt.

And now, what gazed back at me were eyes so shocked and emotional that I could have told her she'd won the lottery.

When she'd returned to the hotel after the bar, washed the makeup off her face, and climbed into bed, she obviously hadn't expected me to come to her door.

I hadn't either.

Not during this trip, not while she was still my intern.

But here I was.

"Declan ..." she started after taking several moments to gather herself. She filled her lungs with some deep breaths before she continued, "I know there's a chance you're going to hurt me. You're human. I'm probably going to hurt you as well at some point." She released the sides of her robe to put her hands on my shoulders. "And I don't want you to be perfect. Perfect is boring." She scrunched her nose in the most adorable way. "To be honest, I don't really know how to navigate this either. I don't have a ton of experience with relationships, so we can figure this out our way." She slid her hands up to the back of my head. "I don't want your opinion to always align with mine. How boring would it be if we couldn't have hate sex after an epic debate?" She lowered her voice as she added, "I can promise, there are going to be times when you'll want to kill me,

234

too, like when I accidentally use your toothbrush or leave a wet towel on the bed."

I rubbed my nose against hers, breathing her in. "You can use my toothbrush anytime you want."

"I'm choosing us, Declan." Her hands left my head, and they pressed against the back of my palms, holding us together. "The answer is yes. I'll still have you."

I couldn't wait a second longer.

I closed the tiny space between us and slammed my mouth to hers, my entire body lighting on fire the second I tasted her.

Fuck.

This girl could kiss, and it didn't matter how much I was savoring her mouth or taking my time with her tongue; it still wouldn't be enough. I needed more. As I backed her up into the room, she moaned with each exhale, running her fingers through my hair.

I didn't want to hurry.

I didn't want tonight to be over.

I wanted to feel.

I wanted to devour.

I wanted her to know she'd made the right decision.

When we were halfway inside, the door shutting behind us, I lifted her into my arms. Her legs circled my waist, her arms hugging me, and I brought her to the edge of the bed, the mattress hitting my knees.

"You don't have to be quiet," I whispered against her mouth. "Jenner is on a different floor. You can scream as loud as you want."

"*Mmm.*" She gnawed her lower lip, grinning. "Hotel sex might just become my favorite for that reason."

"You think it'll be better than the conference room table?" I kissed down her neck, tasting the vanilla on her skin. "Better than the top of my desk?"

She let out several quick breaths. "You do realize this will be the first time we've had sex in a bed. Table, office wall, window, chair, a desk. But never a bed."

I chuckled. "You know what that means, don't you?"

I rested her against the mattress and climbed on top of her, opening the robe with my teeth. Once the fabric was moved to each side, I found a sexy tank and a pair of lace boy shorts underneath.

"No," she sighed. "What?"

"I'm going to have to make sure you never forget it." I lifted the bottom of the tank and kissed her navel, licking around her belly button, making my way to her pussy.

"Declan, it would be impossible to forget any of the times you've touched me."

I pulled the lace boy shorts off, so there was nothing separating me from her clit. "Not like this time. Trust me."

Smelling her had become a tradition, something I needed to do first.

A need to have her scent covering me was as strong as my desire to fuck her. Because Hannah's cunt was a perfume I couldn't get enough of.

My nose rubbed the outer shell of her pussy, running through her slit and stopping at the top to inhale her.

Goddamn it.

This was perfection.

Even more so as I gazed up into those gorgeous sapphire eyes, seeing how feral she looked as she stared back, keeping them locked while I flattened my tongue and licked her clit.

"Oh fuck!"

That scream.

I couldn't get enough of it, so I licked harder, the taste even more delicious as it got thicker, coating my tongue. I wrapped my hands around her thighs and buried my face even deeper.

"Declan ..." Her head pushed against the mattress, tilting back, exposing her throat. "Oh God."

My tongue went faster, her back now lifting off the bed while she pulled the strands of my hair.

The rush happened fast. I could see the way her body was reaching, arching, pushing toward that peak.

I added to it by inserting a finger, and that was when she started to lose it.

The orgasm taking control.

"Declan!"

I gave her another finger, plunging, twisting.

I licked even harder.

"Fuck!" she shouted.

I wanted to eat the sensations right out of her, making sure she felt every swipe of my tongue, the heat from my mouth, even my spit.

Her moaning turned louder as her stomach rippled, her hips rocking with me, churning out each wave of pleasure until there was only stillness.

And breaths.

"Fuck, Hannah." I didn't wipe my mouth. I sucked the wetness off my lips instead, drinking her in. "You're incredible."

"No." She shook her head, her hair already wild. "That's you." Her back rose off the bed and tore at my tie, loosening it enough to slip it off, and began working on the buttons of my shirt.

Since I was kneeling on the carpet, she couldn't reach my pants, so I stood and let her strip me. The sight of her fervently peeling my clothes away was so fucking hot, each piece falling off me, her hands not stopping until I was naked.

I cuffed my palm around my shaft and pumped it a few

times while I admired her pussy. "Are you on the pill, Hannah?"

There was so much weight behind that question, one that I'd never asked another woman before.

I had a feeling she knew that.

And she responded, "Yes."

I met her eyes. "Do you want me to use a condom?"

She shook her head. "No."

The first thought that came to me was how good this was going to feel when I wasn't covered in thick latex. But just to be extra cautious, I said, "You're sure?"

"Unless you see a reason to, then, yes, I'm absolutely sure."

I growled as I grabbed her ankles and pulled her ass to the very end of the bed. Once I had her in position, I placed her legs over my shoulders and thrust inside her.

"*Fuuuck*," I roared.

I tried to be gentle.

I tried to move slowly.

I tried to give her time to spread and get used to me again, but I fucking couldn't.

She felt too good.

And it didn't seem that she minded as her hands moved to her nipples, pulling them through the tank top, her moans so loud that they were all I could hear.

"You're so fucking wet." I dropped my thumb onto her clit, rubbing circles across it. "Damn it, you feel amazing."

In a way that I'd never felt before.

And when combined with her tightness, I could easily come.

But that wasn't happening anytime soon.

"More," she cried. "Declan ... more."

Her voice whipped across me, the vibrations causing me to fuck her harder.

"Hannah," I hissed, the demand almost a challenge because she felt unbelievable. "Shit."

Her hands moved to the blanket, and she bunched it in her fists, her heels digging into my shoulders.

Those weren't the only signs.

I could also feel what was happening inside her—the narrowing, the extra dampness—and barked, "Don't you dare come."

I pulled out and flipped her onto her stomach, arching her ass up, and instantly dived back in.

"Goddamn," I groaned. "You just keep getting better."

There was something about this position. Maybe it was having her ass face me—a part of her body I was obsessed with. Maybe it was just an angle that caused her to be even tighter. Maybe it was because I could reach her G-spot and it felt like I was hitting the end of her.

But with Hannah, doggy style was my favorite.

I swiveled the tip of my cock around the sensitive spot every time I dived in. Each time, I felt her getting closer, pulsing harder, until she screamed, "I'm going to come!"

I was dangerously nearing that place, too, so I switched up my pattern, grinding my hips, roaming my hands down her back, around her ass, across her clit.

"Oh God!" she gasped. "Declan!"

She couldn't stop the shudders—she was too far gone.

I didn't want her to.

The feeling of her coming on my dick was indescribable.

So, I increased my speed, her screams matching my strokes, her ass hitting me as we moved together.

Because I knew she was on that edge, because I knew what this would do to her, I clamped her clit between my fingers, brushing the top of it with my thumb.

The movement earned me the loudest moan of them all and an explosion of trembles right on my dick.

"*Ahhh!*" She reared back and forward. "Yes!"

My head fell backward, and I gradually slowed until all the energy left her body. That was when I rested on top of her, clasping us together, kissing her shoulder blades.

"God, that was sexy." My teeth moved across the skin I'd just pecked, biting the same spots. "Hannah, I need to know ... do you trust me?"

I knew she was in that empty space where thoughts weren't processing, where every part of her was extremely sensitive, so I waited, listening to her pant, taking in the heat from her flesh.

"Of course I do."

I took my time pulling out, earning myself a whimper when I was no longer inside her, and I rolled her onto her back. With my lips above hers, I said softly, "If I give you pain, will you trust that it will eventually lead to pleasure?"

She scanned my eyes. "I don't know what you mean."

She'd experienced my pain before.

The times I'd bitten her, even when I'd slapped her clit.

But none of that was this extreme.

"What I want to do to you is going to hurt, and with that comes a lot of trust in me. Trust when I say, it's going to feel worse before it feels incredible."

Her eyes darkened. "You mean ... anal?"

Just the sound of that word made my dick fucking throb. "Yes."

Her chest rose, like she was ending a sprint. "Declan—"

"Trust me." I widened her legs, bending her knees to give me more access. "All I want is your pleasure, Hannah. If I knew it wasn't going to eventually lead there, I wouldn't do this."

Given that she had just come, her body was hyperaware of

every touch, and the second my finger landed on her pussy, she sucked in a mouthful of air.

"Do I have your trust?"

She glanced from my face to my finger and back. "Yes."

For many reasons, that response was one of the best things I'd ever heard.

I lowered my hand, taking her wetness with me. "I don't have any lube. I'm going to have to make do with what I have."

"Which is what?"

"You." I dragged her cum down to that forbidden place, and as soon as I got close, her breathing changed again. I traced the same route over and over, bringing more with me each time. Satisfied, I added my own spit and said, "Along with this," and when she was primed and ready, I prodded her with the tip of my finger. "A virgin hole." If she'd never told me, I would have known by her reaction, by her loud inhales, by the way her entire body froze every time I came in contact with that area. "That means your ass is going to mold and hug my cock just like your pussy does." Fuck, that excited me, but her eyes told me she didn't feel the same way. "Don't worry, Hannah; I'm not going to break you."

"You're just so big."

I had known that was what concerned her, and the same was true for my strength and power, the combination inducing enough fear that she was probably regretting her decision.

I dipped my finger in a little further. "I'll fit." I could tell she wasn't so sure. "And if you can't handle it, I'll stop. I know you have your reservations about this, but I can't say this enough: you have to trust me." I moved her legs around me, and I leaned over her, aligning our mouths. "Get out of your head. In a few minutes, you're going to be coming harder than you ever thought was possible." I held her cheek, taking in her face. "What am I going to say?"

"To trust you."

I smiled. "No, I was going to tell you how fucking beautiful you are."

Sex gave Hannah a rosy glow, like she was staring at Christmas lights next to a fire.

She dragged her teeth across her lip before connecting our mouths. I gave her my tongue, trying to shift her focus to me, giving her something else to concentrate on.

When I finally pulled away, I whispered, "I need you to touch yourself." I nuzzled my nose over her cheek. "Rub your clit for me. Show me how you would get yourself off if I wasn't here."

I felt her slip into place, her hand lifting enough that it grazed my lower stomach.

"That's it, Hannah." I reached down and added more spit to her ass, making sure she was wet enough there.

"Oh fuck," she exhaled.

"Kiss me."

I kept my lips against her cheek. "Does that feel good, baby?" My finger was back in her ass, deep as it would go. I glanced down her body, needing to see what she was doing to her clit. "Yes, Hannah. Fuck, that's so sexy."

I added a second finger, needing to spread her more. But I didn't take my eyes off her face, assessing where she was at, what she needed, and the second she began to get used to it, I plunged faster.

"God, yes," she gasped.

Her body was teetering on the edge of an orgasm, and right before my teeth sank into her cheek, I growled, "Don't you come yet." I nipped and released her skin. "Slow your hand down."

She did.

And I could tell it hadn't been easy for her. She wanted to come.

She wanted more.

I moved down her body and removed her tank, my mouth flicking the center of her tit the moment it was no longer covered, and then I sucked her other nipple before I knelt at the end of the bed. From down here, I had the perfect view, allowing me to see the look on her face, the pressure she was giving to her clit, the head of my cock aimed at her ass.

"Remember ..."

Her stare didn't move from mine. "I trust you."

I pulled my finger out and inserted just the tip of my cock. Her legs were straining to stay open, her chest not moving at all.

"Hannah, I need you to breathe. This is going to hurt, but once I'm in and you're used to me, it's going to feel so different." I waited for her chest to rise a few times before I slid in any further. "You're doing great."

I held her gaze, the discomfort obvious in her eyes. But she wasn't saying a word. She wasn't wincing. She wasn't even making a face. And I knew, because I was in even deeper now, that there was burning and stretching, but she rallied right through it.

"Breathe, Hannah." I went in another two inches before I asked, "Do you want me to stop?"

"No." She shook her head over the mattress. "I'm okay."

Damn it, this girl was tough.

My fingers took over the rubbing, and I rotated the back side of each one around her clit. Every time I shifted forward, I added more friction, making sure I compensated for the pain.

"You have no idea how fucking tight you are." Air hissed from my mouth. "Fuck."

I wanted to plunge into her, swing my hips back and rock straight in. It took every bit of restraint I had to stay at this pace.

When her head tilted away from me and her hands fisted the blanket, I ordered, "Look at me."

We locked eyes.

"Breathe." I continued in, and once my balls were pressed against her, I stopped. "I'm all the way in." And, fuck, I could come right now. I lifted my fingers off her and only used my thumb, strumming her back and forth. "Your ass is pulsing around me." I took some of the wetness from her pussy and added it to her clit. "Tell me when you're ready."

Without her approval, I wasn't going to start thrusting. But what I did was give her a bounce, a gentle shift to prepare her even more, my thumb never stopping its rotation.

"I'm ready."

I wasn't sure how much time had passed; with how intense this felt, seconds were like hours.

But I took her admission, and I carefully pulled out, adding more spit before I dived in. Within a few pumps, there was a change in her eyes. An expression so tameless that I had to control myself.

I rubbed her harder. "I was right, wasn't I?" I arched back and sank in, repeating that motion several more times.

"*Yesss.*"

That sound, that snake hiss, couldn't have made me happier.

She was getting used to the fullness, the ache now turning to pleasure, and—*my fucking God*—did it look stunning on her face.

I placed her hand where mine was, and I leaned over her body again, taking her nipple into my mouth, releasing it long enough to say, "You trusted me, but you didn't believe me."

She moaned, "Declan," as I blew across the peak of her breast.

"I should punish you for that."

"You're already in my ass." She bit her lip. "What more can you do to me?"

I laughed, my air spreading across her chest. "Don't say that to me, Hannah. The opportunities are fucking endless." I moved to the other side and blew against that nipple, her body lifting as I slid out and glided back. "And now"—I bit down on her nipple and let it go—"you're enjoying this as much as I am."

"Oh God," she moaned.

My stroke wasn't as sharp as when I was in her pussy.

This was a slower sail.

Almost ... romantic.

To the point where she started to move with me.

"Someone likes my fucking cock in her ass." I spoke against her tit, glancing up as I did while she cinched around my shaft. "Wait until you come. When the orgasm not only takes over your pussy, but your ass too." I felt her get wetter. "When you're tightening so hard that it causes me to come."

"I want that."

And as much as I wanted this to last forever, I wouldn't do that to her. Not during her first time.

"Is that what you want, Hannah? To come?"

"Please." She was begging, her eyes pleading.

"Tell me." I replaced her hand with mine, her clit hardening as I rubbed. "Tell me you want to fucking come."

I could tell she was already there; she was just trying to figure out where all the sensations were originating. Especially since there was a new one. A fullness that I hadn't given to her until now, my finger sliding into her pussy.

"Fuck!"

I growled, "You like that, don't you?"

245

She swallowed and breathed. "Declan ..."

"I'm filling every part of you, Hannah, and you're taking it." I increased my speed just a little. "You're fucking taking it, baby."

I wanted the orgasm to pound through her, so while I kept my thumb on her clit, I added a second finger to her pussy. I was only a few dunks in when she began to tighten.

"Yes," I roared. "Your ass is milking me."

She didn't need to tell me; I felt what was happening inside her. I saw the shudders move across her stomach. My ears filled with her screams.

"That's it," I demanded. "Now, make me fucking come."

I couldn't slow. I couldn't even maintain the same speed.

My hips started to pound into her, urging the orgasm through her body.

"I'm going to fucking fill you," I threatened as the burst rose through my balls and into my cock, shooting my first load into her ass. "Fuck yes!" There was a raging intensity that exploded through me a second and third time, each resulting in another stream of cum, emptying myself inside her.

"Declan!"

Ripples broke out across her body, the wetness in her pussy thickening as I softened my movements, dying off the second we both stilled.

"My God"—she shook her head over the mattress—"that was ..." She paused. "I don't even know what that was."

I chuckled. "One of the best things I've ever felt."

"Yes." She swallowed. "That."

Gently, with as little pressure as possible, I pulled out. My fingers were next, exiting each spot, leaving her a quivering mess. She attempted to close her legs, but I wouldn't let her, staying between them and kneeling back for a better view.

"I want to watch the cum pour out of your ass."

It took a few seconds before the white drip worked its way down to the bed.

"Hannah ..." I gazed up at her face. "That was so fucking hot." I placed a soft kiss on her clit and then pecked my way up her navel until I reached her mouth. "I was going to grab a towel to clean you off, but I have a better idea."

I wrapped my arms around her and lifted her off the bed. Carrying her into the bathroom, I set her on the bench inside the shower. I waited for the water to warm before I guided her under the steam, holding her against my body.

As I gripped the sides of her head, the water pouring over us, I realized how different she tasted. Still sweet. But there was also a saltiness on her tongue that I couldn't get enough of.

It tasted like ... us.

When I pulled away, her eyes bore into mine.

"I love this side of you." Her arms wrapped around my waist. "I don't know that I've ever seen it. Maybe hints here and there. But I could certainly get used to it."

I couldn't deny that there was a difference.

I didn't know if it was just tonight, if this side would still exist tomorrow.

If this was a completely new version of me.

But I felt it too.

I cupped her cheeks and aimed her face up to mine. "I told you, I'm giving you all of me."

"I want it. Every bit."

With that came a pang of emotion that I'd been avoiding.

Followed by another.

And then another.

The first for needing to admit to Hannah that we'd slept together before her internship.

The second for needing to talk to Dominick about my relationship with his cousin.

The third for this wedge of guilt in my fucking chest.

Nothing was simple when it came to Hannah Dalton.

But I knew one thing to be true.

"What's going to make this a little easier is that you're only going to be my intern for another month."

The weeks had gone by so fast, probably because I'd spent them so fucking irritated that I couldn't tell Monday from Saturday.

"That means graduation." She sighed. "And full-force bar prepping." Her hands flattened on my back, her brows rising. "Will that change things ... between us?"

"I think we need to play it cool in the office—out of respect for your family and our jobs."

She nodded. "Of course."

"But, no, I can't see it changing anything."

Unless, when I eventually found the balls to tell her the truth about the night in the alley, she fucking hated me for it.

That could change a lot of things.

"Good." She leaned up and kissed me. "Because I'm really starting to get used to this."

My hands left her face and took hold of her ass, squeezing that perfect roundness. "Is this what you're talking about?"

She laughed. "No, silly." She brought my face closer, and right before she kissed me, she whispered, "This."

TWENTY

HANNAH

A date. That was the way Declan had described our upcoming plans for Saturday night before I left the office on Friday. He told me to wear something nice-ish and that he'd pick me up at seven. When I'd tried to ask for more details, he'd shut me down and told me he wanted the evening to be a surprise.

There was something so incredibly sexy at the thought of Declan surprising me, about giving me such little information that my imagination wandered. That he actually put something together he thought I would like.

Once I woke up Saturday morning, every time my brain fast-forwarded to seven o'clock, I would get anxious. Excited. I could barely sit all day. And when the time finally came, I hurried downstairs to the lobby of my building and found him double-parked along the curb.

Since he wasn't able to park, he reached across the front seat and opened my door as I arrived.

I barely needed to pull the handle before I climbed in. "Hi."

His eyes dipped down my dress before they came back up to settle on my face. "Gorgeous." He watched me position the seat belt across my chest and click it into the holder. "Really fucking gorgeous."

A heat moved across my cheeks, and I brushed the hair out of my eyes to keep my hands busy. "Thank you."

He didn't move. Neither did the car. He stayed facing me, taking me in, his gaze now warming every part of my body.

"Hannah ... I need your lips."

A demand that I'd never get tired of hearing.

I leaned across the center armrest and placed my mouth on his. He didn't care that mine was covered in gloss, that I would probably get it all over him. That our lips were slippery because of it.

When I pulled away, our eyes slowly opened, and his mouth had the glow that I had been afraid of.

I wiped off as much as I could and said, "Are you going to tell me where we're going?"

He pulled into traffic, weaving in and out of cars.

One thing I'd learned in the two weeks since we'd been back from Jackson Hole was that Declan liked to drive fast. Regardless of which car we were in—and he had several—he ignored speed limits and traffic signals.

The man wanted to be fully in control, no matter what he was doing.

As he slowed for a light with several cars in front of him, giving him no choice, he looked at me. "A place where we're not going to run into any other Daltons."

Something we'd been very careful about since we'd gotten back.

Declan wanted to tell them on his terms, when he was ready, and I didn't blame him.

What he didn't know and what he'd never asked was if I'd mentioned anything to them myself.

Aside from Oaklyn, Ford was the only person I'd told, and he pretty much knew everything—at least the important parts. But if and when Declan brought it up to him, Ford had assured me that he wouldn't out me.

"That doesn't narrow down the options," I told him, paying attention to the turns he was taking, trying to figure out what was in the area based on the direction we were going.

"No ideas?"

I shook my head. "I mean, I assume we're starting with food or at least a drink. It's dinnertime, and you're always hungry."

He laughed. "Always?"

"For me, yes." I winked as he looked at me. "And for food, also yes."

His hand landed on my thigh. "I'm not going to deny either claim." He turned again. "Tell me about your day."

"I took Everly hiking this morning. I wasn't babysitting; I just like to take her, and I knew Ford and Sydney could use the alone time since they rarely get any."

I had been the one to orchestrate Sydney becoming Ford's nanny. Now that the two of them were dating, I couldn't be happier.

"And then Oaklyn and I went for pedicures and manicures. We stopped by my parents' house on the way home to help them with graduation planning." He looked at me as I added, "A joint party—that's what happens when you're a twin and you're both graduating law school a week apart. Once I got back to the apartment, I bar prepped. Now, I'm here." I smiled before he glanced away. "This is my favorite part of today."

He squeezed my leg. "Are your parents having a big party?"

This was the first time I'd mentioned the party even though it had been in the works for months. I didn't want to put any pressure on him to attend, considering we weren't openly dating and everyone at the office assumed he couldn't stand me. But I'd mailed his invite this morning. If he came or didn't, I would understand either way.

"Less than a wedding, but more than your average graduation party." I shrugged. "We're Daltons. We don't know how to do anything small."

He chuckled as he turned into a parking lot. Once I saw the sign, I immediately knew where we were. Although I'd never eaten here, the restaurant was LA famous. My father had even taken my mother here for their anniversary.

"The food here is supposed to be the best," I said as he parked.

"I happen to be friends with the owner."

He got out of the car, and as I was about to follow, he came to my side and opened my door, holding out his hand. "Miss Dalton ..."

I grabbed his fingers, smiling as he pulled me to my feet. He continued to hold my hand as he led me past the front entrance, around the side, and to the back, where he knocked on an unmarked door.

I didn't ask.

Of course, I wanted to know.

But something about the way this was all unfolding was so interesting to me.

Within a few seconds, the door opened, and a man dressed in a suit with slicked-back gray hair greeted us. "Declan, my man, it's great to see you."

He reached his arms out, and they man-hugged, slapping shoulders before they separated.

Declan turned to me. "Freddy, this is my girlfriend, Hannah. Hannah, this is Freddy, the owner."

I heard nothing after *girlfriend*.

A word we'd never used between us in the two weeks we'd been hanging out since Jackson Hole. We hadn't given us a label—*us* just seemed to be working. But I couldn't deny the sensations he had just drawn from my body, how those simple letters had caused a burst of tingles to hit my chest.

Over and over.

Freddy held out his hand, shaking mine. "Hannah, it's wonderful to meet you. I've heard lots of things about your eating habits." He smiled.

I glanced at Declan. "My eating habits, huh?"

"Let's get you inside and set up," Freddy said, pressing his back against the door to give us enough room to step in.

Since I was unsure of where to go, I stopped a few feet into the hallway, Declan directly behind me, and we let Freddy pass.

As we made our way down the narrow hallway and through another door at the end, Declan's hand went to my lower back. It stayed there, even when I stopped walking, taking in this new space we had stepped into. It was a kitchen. Not a busy one that ran the entire restaurant. This was an intimate, private room with a cooking station in the center and a large cooler in the back, a table set up along the side that I had a feeling was for us.

A woman dressed in chef's attire stepped out of the cooler with a mixing bowl in her hand, smiling as she walked toward the island.

"Hannah, Declan, I'd like you to meet Alex," Freddy said as he brought us over to her. "Alex is our pastry chef."

She shook Declan's hand and then extended her hand to me. "It's very nice to meet you both." Her grin was so warm as her eyes met mine. "Hannah, I understand you love to bake."

My heart was pounding as I nodded. "I do."

"Then, you're in the right place." She rubbed her hands

together. "I'm going to be doing lots of that for you tonight. In fact, a little later, I'd really like for you to join me in preparing a course, if that's something you'd be interested in doing?"

"Are you kidding?" I felt my fingers on my chest, but I didn't remember putting them there. "That would be so fun. Thank you." I turned to Declan as he stood behind me, his eyes already on mine. "You did this?"

He held my cheek, like two other people weren't in the room. "Dessert is much more important to you than dinner." He gave me a quick but passionate kiss, his hand staying on my face longer than his lips had.

"I'm going to leave you guys to it," Freddy said. "Enjoy yourselves and please let me know if you need anything."

We thanked him, and Alex brought us over to our table. It was set for two, a black tablecloth covering the top with rose petals and tea lights between the plates.

"I've paired all six dessert courses with wines," Alex said. "Ones with notes that I believe will work well with the flavors I've chosen."

She went to the cooler, returning with a bottle. "The first is going to be a prosecco from a vineyard near Valdobbiadene, Italy. It's a full body with hints of apple and orange." She opened the bottle, pouring some into each of our glasses. "I'm going to serve this with an apple and orange sponge cake that has a cinnamon glaze with toasted, sliced almonds." She set the bottle in an ice bath and went to the counter she'd previously been working at, bringing over two plates. "I garnished the cake with a bit of spiced pear jam. I know it sounds heavy on the fruit, but the cinnamon will provide the needed balance, and the nuts add a really great texture to the delicate sponge." She paused, allowing us to soak in her description. "*Bon appétit.*"

I waited for her to return to the island before I looked at

Declan and whispered, "I literally don't even know what to say right now, but I'm in absolute heaven."

Even the table had carefully constructed details, like the napkin that had been folded into a fan, a jeweled ring around it that had my initials engraved on it. The votives were red, matching the rose petals. There were even edible flowers frozen in the ice that floated on top of our waters.

Declan had done this; he'd made sure everything would be perfect.

Because he knew how much this would mean to me.

Because he knew how much I would love this.

Tears wanted to prick my eyes, but I wouldn't let them. If I started to get emotional, I didn't know if I'd stop.

He held up his glass. "How about you just say cheers?"

I clinked my drink against his. "To us."

"Us." He took a sip.

I lifted my fork and pierced the end of the sponge. "I cannot wait to try this." I broke off a piece, dipping it into the cinnamon glaze along with the pear jam that had been swirled around the exterior of the plate. The moment the cake touched my tongue, I moaned, "My God."

The flavor wasn't as light as I had expected. It wasn't rich either. It was tart and bold, the cinnamon toning it down.

I glanced at the chef, waiting for her eyes to meet mine. "Incredible. I'm in awe of you."

She grinned. "I'm so glad you like it."

Declan was smiling when my stare returned to him.

Since I'd taken another bite, I covered my mouth with my hand and said, "What?"

"Not everyone shows happiness as beautifully as you do."

I swallowed, wiping the corners of my lips. "I've always worn my emotions on my sleeve."

"It's not just that, Hannah. It's like I can feel your happiness. It's in your eyes. Your cheeks. Your lips." He lowered his voice, growling, "Those fucking lips."

"Later," I promised, knowing exactly what this was going to lead to and how tonight was going to end. "Tell me something." I slid my fork around my plate, capturing the juices of the different flavors. "What is one thing that makes you the happiest?"

He stared down at his dessert, like he was contemplating. "How about a few things?"

"The more, the better."

"A well-aged, say thirty years or so, single malt scotch makes me extremely happy. I like watching it swirl around the glass before feeling it slide over my tongue. The slight burn when it goes down my throat. I also really enjoy experiencing something for the first time—whether that be seeing a gorgeous landscape or going on a unique adventure or even developing a new friendship. I like the idea that I've never done it before, whatever *it* happens to be."

"Sounds like you need a future trip to Yellowstone, then."

"Yes." He took a bite. "But I also like to read, as you've seen since you've been in my home library, and I like to run and work out. There's also nothing wrong with a memorable meal, like this one."

"What about sports?" I refreshed my mouth with some prosecco, the water almost too pretty to drink. "What's your favorite team?"

"Lakers. All the way."

"So, basketball over ..."

"Baseball." He licked his lips. "Hockey over football."

"Really? Now, that shocks me."

"Don't get me wrong; you won't find me passing a football game if it's on TV. I just prefer the ice." His eyes narrowed. "Do you like sports?"

"Camden played lacrosse in high school, and I swam. So, those sports I love." I winced. "But I'm kind of a big Dodgers fan."

His head tilted to the side. "Tell me more."

"I love going to the games and eating oniony hot dogs with extra ketchup and beer. I love baseball beer. It's nothing like other beer. It just tastes different when you're there."

"All right, I can hang with that. Maybe hold the onions."

I shook my head. "Nope. Can't. Onions on stadium dogs are a requirement. Just like I can't leave without getting cotton candy."

"So, as long as it comes in the form of sugar, you're into it?"

"No." I took another bite, licking the glaze off the back of the fork. "The way you feel about onions, I feel about raisins." I scrunched my nose. "I despise them. So, desserts like bread pudding are a huge no for me."

"Fair enough."

I got quiet as I weighed the importance of my next question. "What's your biggest fear?"

"Losing."

He hadn't even taken a second to think, his response so ready on his tongue.

"Losing what?" I asked. "A case?"

He set down his fork. "Anything—a person, possession, and, yes, a case. I don't want to ever feel loss."

I focused on his gaze, trying to read it. "Where does that come from?"

He laughed, but I could tell he didn't find this funny. That was how Declan handled uncomfortable moments. "It took until late high school for me to grow into my body. I was a super-smart kid, but I was awkward, and I didn't excel in athletics until my junior year, so I didn't have that in my arsenal either." He paused. "Kids weren't nice."

I couldn't believe what I was hearing. I'd envisioned Declan as this hot and cocky teenager who could get any cheer-leader he wanted.

"I remember you telling me that you grew up with boys who didn't want to listen to you," he said. "To make them hear, you had to be better. I think you said something about fighting and clawing to outsmart them." His stare turned deeper. "I used my own methods, but we're not all that different, Hannah."

"You beat them with your words."

"My fists weren't strong back then like they are now." He rubbed across his knuckles, and then he did the same to the other hand. "I was fueled by rage. I still am. It'll never go away. I'll never allow them—or anyone—to beat me again." The corner of his lip lifted. "Not even a cowboy at a bar in Jackson Hole who's trying to steal my girl."

It was all making sense.

His demeanor.

His reactions.

The way he fought and how it never felt like it was fair.

"I get it," I whispered.

"I knew you would."

Alex appeared at the side of our table, dragging our attention away from each other. "I'd ask how it was, but you both cleaned your plates, so I'll take that as a good sign."

"That apple flavor?" Declan shook his head. "Amazing."

"Don't worry; there's more apple to come." She lifted the plates away. "For your second course, I went with something a bit more powerful—chocolate."

"*Yesss*," I moaned.

Alex laughed. "I'll be right back with a heavy cabernet sauvignon that's going to pair so well."

Once we were alone again, I reached across the table, my

fingers folding over his. Squeezing. "I love this. Every part of it."

"I know."

I took a deep breath. "I don't know how to thank you, Declan."

As he scanned my eyes back and forth, I felt him inside me, just like that first night in the bar.

"The way you're looking at me right now, Hannah ..." His voice trailed off. "It's stronger than any words."

TWENTY-ONE

DECLAN

"I had dinner with Walter last night," Jenner said as he stood in the doorway to my office, his shoulder leaning against the frame.

My hands froze on my keyboard as I looked up, waiting for him to continue.

Three weeks had passed since we'd returned from Wyoming. In that time, I'd learned a lot about Walter Spade. One of the more prominent things was that he was a hard-ass, like me, and I could never predict what he was going to do or the words that were going to come out of his mouth.

"Yeah?" I inquired. "And?"

"He's pleased."

That wasn't what I had expected to hear.

My team had been hard at work, building his case. In return, Walter had sent daily messages, showing his plans for the Jackson Hole hotel and his team's internal progress—all not-so-subtle hints that he expected a victory.

That wasn't something I could ever promise, but I sure as hell was going to try.

I crossed my arms over my chest and leaned back in my chair. "Is that so?"

"He's disappointed that Hannah's internship will be ending so soon. He likes the weekly reports she's been sending him and requested that once she's gone, someone will still maintain those reports and email them to him."

The reports were just filler; they were of little importance. What really mattered was that I had a sound, experienced staff who was handling Walter's case. Walter needed to stop focusing on the insignificant details, like the eye-pleasing intern I had on my team, and focus on the fucking trial.

I'd be lying if I said I wasn't relieved there was only a week left of her internship. Her working for me wasn't sitting right, her position preventing me from really diving into our relationship.

That didn't stop us from hanging out. We'd been on plenty of dates since we'd been back. Numerous overnights.

But still, something inside me wasn't meshing.

I glanced past Jenner to where Hannah was seated at her desk. With her profile aimed in my direction, I watched her tug my favorite lip. Jesus, all I could think about was that lip bobbing over my crown, sucking the cum out of me.

"Declan?"

I cleared my throat. "There isn't a goddamn thing we can do about Hannah's internship ending. The girl has to graduate and study for the bar. What, does he want her to put that on hold for him?"

Jenner laughed, rubbing his hand over the side of his beard. "I don't think he's saying that at all."

Really, neither was I. Something far larger was eating at me, but it was much easier to channel my anger to Walter.

Jenner stepped inside my office, his back now against the wall. "You want to talk about the elephant in the room?"

Hannah, *goddamn it.*

I was sure he was curious about why I hadn't spoken to Dominick and why he hadn't heard anything more about our relationship—if there even was one or if we'd fizzled out.

The reason he'd heard nothing was because I was dragging my fucking ass and because I didn't think it was a good idea to discuss our relationship with Dominick while Hannah still worked for me.

And because I still hadn't told Hannah the truth about the night at the bar.

I knew Jenner was just trying to be a good friend, but this wasn't some random chick we were discussing. This was his cousin. And that made this conversation extra fucking messy.

"Nah, man. That's a topic we can just glaze over for the moment."

He turned his head, really staring me down. "Are you sure? You look ... off."

"You're saying I don't look good?" I glanced down at the light-gray suit I had on, the navy tie, the cuff links that had been hand-cut with my initials, piercing my perfectly starched shirt. "I think I look sharp as hell."

"Asshole, I wasn't talking about your fucking suit."

I leaned over the top of my desk. "Then, what are you trying to say, Jenner?"

He shut my office door and took a seat in front of me. "Listen, in less than a week, you're going to be sent an extremely detailed questionnaire that's going to ask some invasive questions about Hannah's internship. I need you to be honest. I need you to be unbiased. It's an exit interview that's going to HR. At the bottom of that document, there's a question with two boxes. Would you hire the intern for a full-time position or not?"

Goddamn it.

"Why are you telling me this?"

"You've done nothing but bitch about Hannah since the moment she was assigned to you. You've begged Dominick how many times to relocate her? You've even talked shit to her fucking twin brother." He crossed his shoe over his knee, his foot bouncing. "I know what your intentions were, but Dominick doesn't. So, don't you think it's going to be a little odd when you're discussing the questionnaire with him and he asks why you gave her such a stellar review?"

When the brothers had told me about this internship, they'd said nothing about a goddamn exit interview. Still, I knew better, and I should have assumed there would be one.

"I don't have an issue with whatever is going down between you and Hannah—it's your business, not mine. But I need to make sure things stay solid at work. Do you understand me?"

I didn't know what the hell to say.

Up until a few weeks ago, I would have ripped her apart in that questionnaire because I was a bitter asshole who couldn't fucking deal with his emotions.

I ground my teeth together. "I hear you."

"Good." He stood from the chair. "This is her dream, Declan. This is all she's ever wanted to do."

My eyes followed him to the door. "I know."

With his hand on the knob, he turned to me and replied, "Then, don't fuck this up."

He opened the door and walked out, and my gaze instantly fell on Hannah.

Have I fucked this up?

Would it have been easier if I'd come clean at the very beginning, telling the guys what had happened, so I wouldn't be in this situation?

And was the same true for Hannah and the alley?

Fuck.

My hands tore through my hair just as Hannah turned around and faced me. Within a few seconds of staring at me, she got up and came into my office, standing in the center. Not satisfied with that position, she walked closer, sitting in the same seat Jenner had just left.

"What's wrong? What happened?" She was getting too good at reading me. "Is it Walter that's bothering you? Is he becoming intolerable? I can see how that could happen."

For so long, her presence had been the biggest cocktease. The only thing I could focus on while she moved around my office, bending over to file or leaning down to drop off coffee and food, had been where I wanted to stick my dick. But during those moments, I'd missed some of Hannah's best qualities. The way she brought a sense of calm wherever she went. The way she cared about how I was feeling. The way she wanted to fix whatever was causing me to be angry.

This office was going to be an interesting place without her.

"No." I mashed my lips together. "It's not Walter."

She lifted my coffee mug, seeing that it was empty, and set it against her lap. "I heard Jenner in the doorway, talking about him."

"He was."

I took a deep breath, focusing on my hands.

I couldn't put this off any longer. I needed to be a fucking man about this. I needed to get the situation handled with Hannah and Dominick before things spiraled further out of control.

"Declan, what's wrong?"

As I glanced up, there was concern all over her face. "What are you doing tonight?"

She shook her head back and forth. "Oaklyn's out of town for the week. I didn't plan on doing much. Baking, maybe some laundry, definitely some bar prep. Why?"

"How about I come to your place?"

"Is this a date? Or something else?" Her brows pushed together. "I'm not really getting the best vibe from you right now."

There was no reason to hide my intentions. She wanted me to communicate more, and she wanted my honesty; she was about to get both.

"I'm coming over to talk."

"Okay ... about what?"

My computer dinged, and an email from Walter appeared on my screen. Even though I was working on several other cases, he wasn't just my most needy client; he was also my highest paying. No matter what time or day he reached out, I made myself available.

Like now.

I clicked on the email, reading his list of questions, the demandingness of his tone prickling my nerves.

"Declan?"

I finished reviewing his list of needs, each one adding to this nagging feeling in my chest, one that made me gnaw my lip. "What?" I looked over at her, realizing I was snapping at the wrong person. "Jesus."

"Don't even tell me you're going to turn into an asshole right now."

God, that fucking mouth.

I wanted to remind her that I was still her boss.

But I held in my breath instead, working the anger through my body so it wouldn't erupt. "I'll meet you at your place tonight. I'll be there whenever I'm able to drag my ass out of this office." I attempted to lighten my tone as I added, "Now, I'd be really grateful if you could grab me a coffee."

"This will be your fourth today."

When I got to her place, I wanted nothing more than to tie

her wrists to her headboard. To tie her ankles to her bedframe and keep her legs spread far apart.

To make her scream so fucking loud that we would worry her neighbors might call the police.

But tonight was about talking.

And I had no idea what that was going to look like or what the results would be.

"I know." My head dropped, and I stared at my hands again, my thumbs rubbing together as I continued, "And, Hannah, please keep the coffee coming. I'm going to need a hell of a lot more."

TWENTY-TWO

HANNAH

A mix of emotions was bolting through me as I waited for Declan to show up at my apartment after work. I'd even poured myself a glass of wine to help settle my nerves. Something had set him off today at the office, and he wouldn't tell me what it was, but he was reverting to his old ways.

Shutting me out.

Shutting down.

Fueling himself with endless coffee to ... *fight?*

I didn't know, but I couldn't imagine what he wanted to talk to me about.

Things had been going so well.

Too well maybe?

I weighed every possibility as I paced my apartment.

At first, I wondered if he was going to ask if we could continue keeping us a secret. I had no problem with that. I hadn't asked him to air our relationship; I hadn't tried to persuade him to speak to my cousins. Time wasn't something we were running out of, so I had no issue with the way things stood.

In fact, things had just started to feel normal between us—a description I could never use before when referring to our relationship. The push and pull had been so rapid, so intense, that I had whiplash for a long time. But since Jackson Hole, I'd found myself loving him much more often than hating him.

Love.

A word that frequently came to my mind as we spent more time together.

A word I'd never said to another man.

A word that I could see myself saying to him.

But maybe he couldn't. Maybe that was something he was having a hard time dealing with.

Or maybe he had concerns about the next several months, post-graduation, when I'd be studying for the bar and not able to hang out nearly as much.

I had no idea. I couldn't even make a prediction.

So, I sipped my wine, and I tried to control my brain from spiraling. I waited until the tablet by the door buzzed, a notification from our doorman letting me know Declan had arrived. I gave him enough time to make it up the elevator and down the hallway before I opened the door.

He was just approaching, looking as hard and irritated as he had at the office. His tie was loosened a bit at his throat, and the gel had worn off in his hair—probably from how many times he'd run his hands through his locks.

This wasn't the first time he'd been to my apartment.

But this time felt different than the others.

I sucked in a breath. "Hi."

"Hannah ..."

He leaned down to kiss me.

It was soft.

Short.

But enough.

"Do you want a drink?"

He nodded, and while he walked in, I went to the kitchen and grabbed a beer, taking off the cap before I met him in the living room. He was already sitting on the couch when I handed him the bottle. He took a sip and then held the beer between his legs.

I curled up in the chair across from him, wanting to give him space to speak. "Talk to me."

He gradually looked up, not immediately answering. "There's something I've wanted to tell you for a while."

I still had no idea where this was going.

But I saw emotion in his eyes.

I saw fight.

"I should have told you this from the beginning." He set the beer on the floor, and he folded his hands together. They didn't last there, almost instantly unclasping, and they dived into the sides of his hair. "Fuck, I've been putting this off for too long. I need to tell you the truth."

I shook my head, trying to make sense of this. "About what?"

"The night we met."

I repeated his statement out loud, and when the last syllable left my lips, my hands started to shake.

The alley.

The lie.

It was staring me right in the face.

I set down my wine on the small table beside me. "Declan—"

"When you came into my office on the first day of your internship, we briefly spoke about the night at the bar, and you asked me if you did anything inappropriate. I wasn't honest with you, Hannah. I should have been." His eyes were pleading with mine. "Fuck, I should have been. I didn't want to lie to you … but I did."

My heart began to pound.

The knot in my throat was moving into my chest. I couldn't stop it; I couldn't slow it down.

I knew exactly what he was going to say, and the anxiety was paralyzing me.

"Declan—"

"No, I need to get this out." He stood, bringing the beer with him, and he walked over to the windows just to the left of me, leaning his back against the ledge.

"We were flirting with each other at the bar. I swear, you were giving me every sign that you wanted something to happen between us. Damn it, I could even feel the fire coming off your body." He lifted his beer to his mouth but looked at the rim and lowered it.

"I didn't want to wait to have you. I asked if you lived nearby and you said that you lived as far from campus as I did."

There was pain in his eyes as he gazed at me. "We were by the restrooms, and we were kissing, and I asked if you were adventurous. Your hand was on my dick. You were circling my fucking tip." He exhaled so loudly. "I brought you into the alley behind the bar, and we had sex." He put his hand up, stopping me from saying anything. "I wore a condom, Hannah. I took every precaution. But I didn't know you were that wasted. We had all been drinking, yeah. But I didn't think you were at the blackout stage."

His hand, still up in the air, rose to his face, where he brushed it over his scruff. "If there had been any indication that you were that far gone, I wouldn't have touched you. I'm not the kind of guy who seeks out women who are intoxicated. I'm not a scumbag. Anyone I sleep with, I want them to remember it. I want them to be a participant."

He set his beer down, his hands clenching. "Jesus, the thought of *that* makes me fucking sick."

He glanced all around my apartment, but his stare finally returned to me. What I saw made me breathless.

"I didn't know how to tell you. I didn't know how you'd react. And then time passed, and it got away from me, but the guilt still ate at me." He paused. "I couldn't let another second go by without you knowing the truth."

He slowly walked over, kneeling in front of my chair, his hands staying in front of him, not touching me. "You have to believe me, Hannah."

In his mind, this entire time, he'd felt guilty.

Because if I hadn't been conscious that night, then he blamed himself for taking advantage of me.

For being that kind of man.

Oh God.

The spit burned as I swallowed it down my throat.

My heart was splitting in half.

Everything inside me shook.

"Declan ..." I shoved my hands under my thighs to stop the tremors and tried again. "Declan ..."

I hated myself.

I hated myself more in that moment than I'd ever hated Declan in the past.

I didn't know how to say this.

I didn't know what this was going to mean for us.

I didn't know how he was going to respond.

But it didn't matter.

He'd voiced his truth, and now, it was my turn.

My lips parted, my head slowly turning to the right and then lifting before I locked eyes with him. "I wasn't that drunk."

Small wrinkles formed at the corners of his eyes as he stared at me. "But you said—"

"I know what I said."

He knew what was going to come next.

I saw the recognition come across his face.

Immediately in his eyes, followed by his lips.

His jaw tensed. "Hannah ..."

"I remember it," I whispered. "I remember every second of it."

TWENTY-THREE

DECLAN

She remembered ... *everything.*

How I'd kissed her in the hallway.

How I'd led her outside.

How I'd fucked her against the side of the building.

She'd been lying to me since the conversation we'd had in my office on the first day of her internship.

And the lies hadn't ended there.

Because when we'd had sex in the conference room, she'd acted like that was our first time together. When we had spoken about kissing, she had known I'd laid my lips on her outside the restroom and again in the alley.

This whole time, in my head, I'd been this giant asshole who'd had sex with a woman who was too drunk to remember.

And this whole time—almost an entire semester later—she had fucking known.

She had known, and she had let me live with this tremendous amount of guilt.

I was still staring into her eyes, still kneeling in front of her, still keeping my hands at my sides because I didn't dare touch her.

Then, I stood and backed up.

And I rested against the window's edge, my teeth grinding together, my hands clenching the air. "Explain yourself, Hannah. Right fucking now."

Emotion dripped down her cheeks, a stream so perfectly lined that it was as though her eyes were faucets.

Every drop that fell from her chin, I saw a little more remorse.

I didn't fucking care.

I had zero patience.

I wanted honesty, and I had wanted that from the goddamn beginning.

"When I walked into your office," she started, flattening her hand against her chest, the spot just below her throat, "I wanted to die. I never expected to see you again—maybe in the courtroom, but definitely not at my family's law firm.

"You have no idea what it's like to start a job you've wanted your whole life, only to find out your boss is someone you've slept with. Someone who's going to be teaching you, mentoring you, spending countless hours with you. And what made that feeling even worse"—she stopped to fill her lungs, appearing like she was pushing against her chest to make that happen—"was that after the alley, you had stood me up. You had just left, and you'd made me feel like I wasn't even worthy of a good-bye."

She wiped her eyes with the back of her sleeve. "When I walked in, expecting to see Christopher as my boss but finding you, I panicked. I didn't have the courage to tell you—my new boss—how shitty you had made me feel that night. I definitely didn't have the courage to tell you how much it had hurt to see the picture of you and Madison. With your faces pressed together and her lipstick all over your mouth, I knew you'd kissed her right after we had sex in the alley. Honestly, it was like you'd punched me in the gut. I had felt disgusted and embarrassed at how little you thought of me. So, yeah, I lied. It felt like the only option at the time."

I needed to do something with my hands, so I gripped the cold ledge of the window. "And you did that without considering the repercussions of your lie? What it could do to me? How it could make me feel?" I saw the beer that I'd deserted and grabbed it, chugging what was left.

"We're going to get back to that, but first, I need to address one of your points—that you think I stood you up, that you weren't worthy of a good-bye, that my mouth was covered in Madison's lipstick. Who the fuck is Madison, Hannah?"

She looked at me like she didn't recognize me, and then she leaned to one side, retrieving her phone from her back pocket. She scrolled until she found what she wanted and pointed the screen at me. "That's Madison, and that's her lipstick all over your mouth."

I stared at the selfie of myself and some chick, the memory from that moment coming back to me. "You're fucking kidding, right?"

I laughed, the anger erupting, and I went into the kitchen and grabbed another beer from the fridge, returning to the couch I'd originally sat on. The beer hissed as I twisted off the cap, the cold liquid not nearly enough to take this feeling away.

"You *think* I abandoned you at the bar? You *think* I left you for Madison?" My voice growled as I added, "You *think* I fucking kissed her?"

Her head gave a slight nod.

"That's not what happened, Hannah." I sighed so loud that my goddamn chest vibrated. "Not even close."

She looked at me like a fucking deer in headlights, her hands covering her mouth. "Then, what happened?"

"I stood in that goddamn alley, waiting for you, Hannah. After ten minutes, I didn't think you were coming back. Maybe you had gotten sidetracked, maybe you had run into someone—something had happened. So, I went to the parking lot and got into my car, and I drove around to the front of the bar, where I waited another ten minutes for you. But even then, I didn't give up. You know what I did?"

I moved to the end of the couch, set the beer on the floor, and crossed my arms over my chest, clenching my fingers together. "I left my car and went into the bar and looked for you. And when I couldn't find you, I went to the bar next door to look for you there since I'd overheard some of your class-mates saying they were going there. That's where I ran into your little friend. I wasn't even two steps through the fucking door when she pounced on me, wanting to buy me a drink and take a picture together. The picture happened; the drink did not. I searched that entire bar, too, and when I didn't find you, I left and drove home."

My hand rubbed across my lips as I recalled the night in question, when I'd gone into my bathroom to brush my teeth and ended up scrubbing my mouth with a towel to get the color off my lips. "The lipstick you saw, that was yours, Hannah. Not Madison's."

"Declan ..." Her voice wasn't any louder than a whisper. "I ..." With her elbows resting on her knees, her hands clasped between them, her head fell. "I'm sorry. I ..."

"You're sorry about what? That you misjudged the situation? That you jumped to conclusions? That you created a scenario that hadn't fucking occurred? For what? To make your life easier? To avoid addressing the truth? Please tell me. I'm dying to hear."

She pressed her palms together, resting the tips of her fingers against the center of her chin. "I called Oaklyn as soon as I left the alley and went inside the bar. When we finally hung up, I looked for you everywhere. I thought you'd left." She shook her head, recounting the events of that night the same way I had. "I couldn't find you, Declan."

"I was there."

"I'm so sorry—"

"And then you lied to me." My arms dropped, my hands holding the leather cushion. "You looked me in the fucking eyes, and you lied."

She covered her face for a brief second, but it did nothing to stop the flow of tears. "I'm not proud of that. I wish I hadn't lied. I wish I could go back." She wiped her cheeks. "I wish so many things right now."

"Were you ever going to tell me?"

She took several seconds to answer. "I don't know." She swallowed.

I picked up the beer, pushed myself off the couch, and walked to the table, holding the back of one of the chairs. "Hannah—"

"Listen to me, Declan. Things haven't been easy between us, and I'm not using that as an excuse. I'm just speaking the truth. You went from hating me, yelling at me, to trying to sleep with me. I didn't—"

"Just stop, Hannah. I'm so fucking angry right now; I can't even see straight." I was squeezing the wooden frame of the chair so hard that I couldn't believe it hadn't splintered.

"What happened between us after you lied is irrelevant. It's completely dismissible. You were selfish. You acted like a jealous teenager. You didn't give a fuck about how your lie could affect me. But you know what surprises me most about this conversation? That you want to be a litigator, and a massive

277

part of your job is studying evidence and drawing a factual conclusion. You know what you did the moment after you walked out of the alley? You assumed a bunch of bullshit." I dragged my teeth across my lip. Again and again. "And not a word of that bullshit was correct."

She drew in some air, her chin quivering. "Madison sent a photo to our law group, and your lips were covered in the same color lipstick she was wearing. Madison has a reputation for sleeping with everyone. She's been with professors, mentors—hell, she even slept with Dominick at one point. When I looked for you, you were gone, nowhere to be found. That's the evidence I had, that's the way I pieced it all together, and that's the conclusion I drew. Maybe I got it all wrong, but it felt like I was right at the time."

Every point she had made only caused me to be more furious.

Because she was thinking like a litigator.

Because she was quick with her words, coming right back at me with that fucking mouth.

"You still fucking lied."

She paced to the windows and back to the chair. "What was I supposed to say when I walked through your door? *Oh, hi, Declan. Remember me, the girl you fucked in the alley right before you left me to go take selfies with a whore?* And was I supposed to say that to my new boss? On my first day of work?" She stopped walking and looked at me. "You know, you're so quick to point your finger at me, but what about you?"

"I can't wait to hear this. What about me, Hannah?"

"When I asked you if I'd done anything inappropriate, you said no. You had plenty of opportunities to tell me we'd had sex. But you didn't. You said nothing about it. You withheld your own evidence." She lowered her voice as she said, "What's your excuse, Declan?"

My brows rose so fucking high. "You're saying I lied?"

"I'm saying we're both at fault here, so don't stand there and look at me like I'm the only one who's guilty."

She had some fucking nerve.

I downed the rest of the beer and set the empty on the table. "I didn't lie."

"I'm not saying you did."

I didn't want to fucking admit it, but she had a point.

I could have said something.

I could have told her what had happened.

Fuck.

I tore at my hair, pulling it from both sides. "This is a goddamn mess."

"Declan ..."

I heard my name.

Her pleading.

Her emotion.

"Declan, please look at me."

I looked at the ceiling, like the answer was written across the blades of the circulating fan. "I need time, Hannah."

Time to figure this shit out.

Time to come to terms with everything I'd heard tonight.

Time to get my fucking head straight.

"You've said that to me before."

I fixed our stares. "And I'm saying it again."

She moved through the living room and didn't stop until she was a foot away from me. "What does that mean? What does that even look like? That we're—" Her voice cut off as a cry came through her throat. "That we're over before we even really got started?"

I'd never seen her cry before today.

It killed me to see the tears start up again, soaking her cheeks, running over her lips.

I wanted to wipe them away.

And I wanted to scream that this never would have happened if she hadn't lied.

"It means, I need a minute to think about this," I barked. I just wasn't able to control my tone anymore. "I don't have an answer right now. I'm pissed as hell, and I need to cool off before I say something I'll regret."

"Declan ..." she begged as I turned around and headed for the door. "Please, just hear me out."

I halted and faced her.

"I care about you. You have to believe that. You have to feel that. I want to make this right." She hugged her chest, giving herself the comfort that I wouldn't. "No one has ever made me as happy as you have over these last few weeks. I don't want to lose that." Her lips quivered as she said, "I don't want to lose you."

"Hannah ..." I raked my fingers through my hair, taking in the intensity of her stare. "I feel the same way, but I've been carrying around this guilt, thinking I had sex with a girl who was too drunk to remember and then finding out she was my intern and the cousin of one of my best friends." I hissed air through my mouth. "It's just too fucking much for one night. I need time to sort this out."

If I stayed, we would only go around in circles—a shape that wouldn't help our situation.

This situation needed an end ... whatever that end looked like.

"I'll see you at work tomorrow, Hannah."

As I gripped the doorknob, she released a sob. "That's it? You're just going to leave? Don't you realize I'm not fighting you, Declan? I'm fighting for you."

Her words echoed through my chest.

Through my throat.

Through my head.

I stayed there, holding the handle, frozen.

Debating.

Weighing each side.

And then I twisted the knob to open the door, I walked into the hallway, and I let the door slam behind me.

There was always a fierceness in my body after I delivered my closing statement to the jury and left the courtroom.

A lightness in my step.

An emptiness in my chest from having purged every thought, every bit of research, making room for my next case.

I didn't feel that way now as I stood with my back to the door, hearing her sob before I walked to the elevator.

In fact, I felt even more fucked up than before we talked.

As I got into her lobby, I pulled up Dominick's number and held the phone to my ear while it rang.

"Declan," he answered, "can I call you back? I'm in the middle of something and—"

"No need to," I replied. I was going to pour myself some scotch when I got home, and I needed to be of sound mind when I had this conversation with him. "Just make room in your schedule for me tomorrow morning. First thing. I need to talk to you."

"Are you all right, buddy?"

I got into my car and started the engine. "I'll see you at eight tomorrow."

I hung up and placed my phone in the cupholder and pulled onto the street, weaving my way through the cars. I wasn't more than a hundred yards from Hannah's building when a text came across my screen.

Hannah: Nothing has hurt me more than seeing you walk out that door ...

TWENTY-FOUR

HANNAH

I sat in the chair across from Dominick's desk and crossed my legs, holding the to-go coffee mug in my lap even though I was leery about whether my stomach could handle the strong brew. "Thanks for coming in early to see me, Dominick."

Long after Declan had left my apartment, I'd texted my cousin, asking if we could talk in the morning. He'd told me to meet him in his office at seven thirty.

"Declan called me about an hour before you did last night and also requested a meeting," Dominick said. "Tell me, does one have to do with the other, or is this merely a coincidence?"

My chest hurt.

It had been hurting since Declan had told me his side of what had happened at the bar. That was twelve hours ago, and he hadn't replied to my text. He hadn't called. But he'd phoned Dominick and requested a meeting. There were only a few days left of my internship; Declan wouldn't try to reassign me at this point.

Would he?

"I don't know why Declan asked to speak to you," I said. I

set the coffee on the edge of his desk. I couldn't hold it; I couldn't even look at it anymore. "But I did come in here to talk to you about Declan."

He leaned back in his chair, folding his hands together. "Go ahead. I'm listening."

I'd gotten no more than an hour of sleep last night, so I'd had plenty of time to prepare myself for this conversation. I'd rehearsed it—out loud and in my head.

But as I hugged myself in this chair, I couldn't remember a damn word.

"I want to start off by saying Declan has been an incredible mentor. I've learned a tremendous amount over this last semester, things the classroom never taught me. Working with him, watching the way he conducts business, how he practices —it's given me a foundation that I'm extremely grateful for. But even beyond that, he'd given me chances to apply what I've learned. Like a few weeks ago, when we met with Walter in Wyoming, he allowed me to lead that discussion and present the results I'd found during my research. I even gave Walter my opinion on what I thought the outcome would be in his case."

Dominick's hand moved to his chin, combing the whiskers of his beard. "Interesting."

That response caused me to pause. "Why do you say that?"

"He must really believe in you if he allowed you to lead a meeting with Walter—or with any client for that matter. Even though you're a Dalton, you're still only an intern, Hannah."

At the time, I'd assumed it was because of my personal connection with Walter. But Dominick had a point. Since that trip, Declan had allowed me to weigh in during several other client meetings. Knowing that he controlled every situation he was in, the only reason he would have allowed this was if he trusted me—trusted that I'd done my research, trusted that I was going to present the correct information.

"With that being said, Declan's mentorship isn't what I want to talk to you about," I admitted.

"All right."

This was the hard part.

And the tightening in my throat, the slickness on my palms only made it more difficult.

"I know Declan was pretty adamant about assigning me to a different litigator at the start of my internship, and I don't want that, in any way, to reflect poorly on him. You see … we have a bit of a past." I looked at the coffee cup, testing my stomach to see if I was ready for a sip. I kept my hands in my lap and continued, "Before the two of us came to work here, he mentored one of my law classes, and that's where we originally met." I paused, thinking of the right way to word this. "And that's where things progressed outside the class-room. You know, we took things to the next level —physically."

"I see."

"But here's where things went all wrong, Dom." I'd worn my hair down, and I gathered all the strands into my hand, my fingers acting like an elastic. "There was a misunderstanding. I thought we were going to continue our night and see much more of each other. That didn't happen because, in my eyes, he stood me up. And then we never saw each other again."

"And then you became his intern, which, I assume, came as quite a surprise."

I nodded. "But it gets worse." I lifted my hair as the back of my neck began to sweat. "As I looked into the eyes of my new boss, I didn't feel comfortable telling him my feelings about the mishap or even my side of what had happened." I took a deep breath. "So, I lied to him, Dominick. I told him I was too drunk to remember anything from that night. And, as you can imag-ine, the guilt started piling up inside him."

As he leaned forward, his cuff links hit the top of his desk, and his stare hardened. "Does Declan know the truth now?"

"Yes. It came to a head last night." I dropped my hair and clutched my stomach. "I'm telling you this because there was a reason why he didn't want me as his intern, and that's my fault. He spent the last semester thinking ..." My voice trailed off. I swallowed. I pushed the emotion away. "He thought he had hooked up with a woman who didn't remember any of it, and that led to some really heavy and really shitty thoughts."

"Jesus, Hannah."

I whispered, "I know." I raised my hand. "But I had my reasoning—a reasoning that I made very clear to him last night. He's not innocent either, Dominick. We're both in the wrong."

He remained silent, staring at me, his gaze telling me he was processing.

"I know you warned him, which I love you for, but that warning came a little late." I uncrossed my legs and moved to the end of the chair. "He tried, Dominick. I can't say I did because after that night we were together, many months ago, my feelings for him have only deepened. But he put in a solid effort to keep things professional between us."

"And now?"

The knot from last night returned. With each breath, it moved higher in my throat. "I love him."

The sound of his exhale was loud enough for me to hear. "Do you know why I warned him?"

"No."

"Declan might be the best litigator in California, and no one in this state dares to fuck with him, but I have an unfair advantage. I'm one of his best friends, and I can see right through him, and what I saw was that he already had feelings for you. The more he tried to hide those feelings, the more obvious they were."

He moved a pile of paperwork, like he needed more space for whatever he was about to say. "My warning wasn't to keep him away from you. My warning was to make sure he knew that I was keeping an eye on him. And what that means in guy language is, if he hurt even a hair on your head, I would destroy him. Limb by fucking limb."

I couldn't help but smile. "And I love you for that too." I got quiet as Dominick took a drink of his coffee. "I honestly don't know what's going to happen between us. What things will look like once everything calms down. But before this internship ends, I wanted you to hear this from me. I don't want you blaming Declan for anything he said about me or his desire to transfer me. I take full responsibility for all of that."

Of course, Declan had played a big part in this, and I hadn't been afraid to tell him that last night. I'd take fault where the fault was due, but Declan wasn't a saint in this situation.

"I'm curious what side of the story I'm going to hear when Declan comes in"—he looked at his watch—"in about three minutes."

Shit.

"In that case, I'd better go." I grabbed my untouched coffee and stood from the chair. "I'll see you this weekend at the graduation party?"

"Kendall and I wouldn't miss it."

I gave him a smile and walked to his door.

"Hannah?"

I turned around. "Yeah?"

"Things get a little tricky when you work for family, and having conversations like the one we just had isn't easy. Nor is it a simple feat to admit when you're wrong. Thank you for being honest with me."

I nodded and opened his door, closing it behind me, immediately seeing Declan walking down the narrow hallway.

Directly at me.

God, timing hated me.

He looked so handsome this morning in his dark gray suit and black striped tie, his scruff a bit thicker than yesterday, his hair perfectly gelled—unlike the way it had looked when he left my apartment last night.

What he couldn't hide were the bags under his eyes, showing he'd gotten the same amount of sleep as me.

As he got closer, I expected hardness in his expression.

Anger in his stare.

A fight in his posture.

Remnants of all three were present.

But there was something else too. Something I couldn't pinpoint.

He came to a stop a few feet from me, the movement sending me a delicious wave of his cologne. That spicy aroma —*oh God*, I'd missed smelling it while I was getting ready for work this morning.

"Hi," I whispered.

He towered over me in this tight space, making me feel tiny and wanted.

"Hannah ..." His gaze moved across my face, taking me in. "What were you doing in Dominick's office?"

My lungs felt so tight as I took a breath, this nervous energy fluttering through my whole body.

I just wanted to wrap my arms around him.

I just wanted to press my lips against his.

"Telling him the truth."

His head cocked to the side. "About?"

"Us." I licked across my mouth. "About the night we met and how my lie caused things to be a bit rocky between us, especially at the beginning. You shouldn't have to tackle the repercussions of my lie, so I made sure Dominick heard the truth—from my lips." I held the coffee against my chest, the only shield I had in my possession. "Why are you going in to speak to him?"

He glanced toward Dominick's door and then back at me. It took that movement for me to see what I couldn't read before. The softness that rimmed his eyelids, the affection that poured out from his emerald irises.

"The same reason," he said. "But I wasn't going to mention the lie."

"You were just going to tell him about ... us?"

"Yes."

Was there even an us at this point?

Before Declan had left last night, he'd asked for time to sort through his thoughts. Pushing him wasn't going to make him move any faster.

He knew how I felt, and he knew where I stood.

I fingered the end of his tie as I said, "You look so tired."

His hands were at his sides, and as he lifted one, it briefly grazed my waist. The touch was light. If I hadn't been paying attention, I probably would have missed it. His hand continued up to his face, his palm landing on his forehead, lowering to his nose, mouth, and off his chin.

"I am."

That was all it took, and I could barely breathe.

"If you need anything, I'll be at my desk."

He didn't respond.

He just stared into my eyes.

But there was emotion that passed between us, lasting for several seconds before he broke our eye contact and walked to Dominick's door.

I didn't turn around to look at him.

I just headed in the opposite direction, and when I went by

Ford's office and saw that he was inside, I stepped in and closed the door, pressing my back against it.

He glanced up from his desk. "Are you all right?"

"No." I shook my head. "Yes." I finally brought the coffee up to my mouth and took a long drink. "No."

He pointed at a chair. "Sit."

I fell into the seat and set the coffee on his desk, freeing my hands so I could wrap my arms around me. "Convo with Dominick—check. Running into Declan immediately after leaving Dominick's office"—I tried to fill my lungs, but I was breathless—"also check."

Since Oaklyn had been at a work event last night and couldn't answer my call, I'd phoned Ford right after I set up the meeting with Dominick.

He knew everything now.

Every. Single. Gritty. Detail.

"This distance between us ... it hurts." My arms squeezed. "I just want to kiss him."

He was smiling. I couldn't imagine why.

"What's with the grin?" I found myself glaring at him. "I'm practically dying over here, and you're all smiley, like Everly when she talks about the color pink."

He rested his chin on his knuckles. "You're in love with him."

I'd admitted that to Dominick just a few minutes ago, and that was the first time I'd said the words out loud.

It had hit me then, but it was hitting me even harder now.

"Yes." I felt pressure against my chest and realized my hand had moved there. "Yes, I love him."

The feeling behind my fingers wasn't an electrical shock; it was more of a slow, burning simmer.

"Does he know that?"

"Not unless he's a mind reader. The thing is, he kind of is."

I sank deeper into the chair. "Ford ..." I reached for the coffee. "God, I wish this were wine," I said before I took a sip. "What if he decides this is all too much? What if I walk out the door on Friday and we don't talk again until much later this year, when I come back here to work as a clerk? What if we're done?"

"Hannah ..." I went to stand up, deciding pacing would feel much better than sitting when I heard, "The man is in love with you," and it rocked me so hard that I couldn't move.

"How do you know that?"

His smile grew. "Because I talked to him last night."

I felt my eyes bug out of my head. "You ... did?"

"He called me after you and I spoke."

"And you didn't tell me? You're the worst bestie cousin in the entire universe, you know that?"

He laughed. "Listen, after Declan and I hung up, Eve needed to be put to bed, and then I found myself in the middle of something."

"*Ahhh*, Sydney. Enough said." When he didn't respond, I added, "No need to say more about the Sydney part. You need to tell me everything about your conversation with Declan."

"Do I, huh?" He winked.

"Ford—"

"All right, all right." He grabbed his coffee and came around to my side of his desk, sitting in the chair next to mine. "He explained that he intended to wait until your internship was over before the two of you got a bit more serious, but things just didn't play out that way. I think he was feeling guilty that he'd had a conversation with Jenner in Wyoming and he hadn't said anything yet to me, knowing how close the two of us are."

"He was being respectful. I like that." My heart was thumping out of my chest. "What did you say to him?"

"I told him if he hurt you, I would single-handedly destroy him." He smiled. "But otherwise, I was fine with the situation and that I'd never seen you so happy." He reached for my shoulder, squeezing it. "Which is the truth."

"Dying. Keep going."

He laughed. "That was it. The convo was short, sweet, and to the point. He said nothing about the weird place the two of you were in or that you'd gotten into a fight or anything about the lie."

My brows rose. "Really?"

"Why does that surprise you?"

As Ford drank his coffee, I thought about his question.

Maybe Declan didn't want to involve my cousins.

Maybe he thought it was none of their business.

Or maybe, in the long run, we were going to move past the tornado that had uprooted our relationship last night, so why even mention it?

"I don't know," I sighed. "I'm not sure I know anything anymore."

He wiped his lips. "Not true. You know how much you love Declan."

I gripped the armrest as those words slapped me over and over again. And once I got past the initial shock, I studied Ford's grin. "You're enjoying this, aren't you? Now that the family is done giving you shit about Sydney, it's like you're passing the baton to me."

"Nothing makes me happier."

I rolled my eyes. "So, what do I do? Help me. I'm lost."

He wrapped his arm around the back of my chair. "You have to be patient and continue showing him why he fell for you. Don't hide your feelings, Hannah. Let him see them. But don't shove them down his throat either."

"I need a manual."

He shook his head. "You just need to be yourself." When he tightened the grip on the cushion behind me, the chair moved. "Listen, Declan talked to Jenner. He talked to me. Now, he's in Dominick's office, talking to him. He wouldn't be doing any of this if he didn't see a future with you."

"Wait ..." I thought back to everything I'd said since I'd walked through Ford's door. "How do you know he's in Dominick's office, talking to him? I didn't tell you that."

He smiled back at me.

"Jesus," I groaned. "Don't tell me; I already know. Dominick told you all in your group text. You're a bunch of clucking hens, I swear. You're just as gossipy and drama-filled as women—maybe even more so."

"Should I take offense to that? I can't tell ..."

I stood from my chair. "No comment."

"Hey," he said as I reached his door. "Don't forget something—something that's extremely important."

"And that is?"

"He loves you."

I clutched his doorknob as his response melted into my body. "Those are words I need to hear from him, Ford."

He nodded, and I strolled down the hallway, passing Declan's door on my way to the kitchen. His office was empty, and that meant he was still with Dominick. I didn't know how I felt about that, but I would do anything to be a fly on that wall.

In the kitchen, I made two coffees and grabbed some napkins and went into Declan's office. I placed his coffee near his keyboard, a folded napkin next to it, and a Danish on top of it. I'd made a special batch of apple ones in the middle of the night when I couldn't sleep. I'd even attempted a sugary glaze, similar to Chef Alex's, that had hints of cinnamon and vanilla that I swirled over the top. Happy with the placement of his breakfast, I took a seat at my desk and checked my phone to see if I had any messages.

Camden: T-minus 2 days until I'm home. I might crash at your place until my stuff gets delivered to my new apartment. Movers said it should take about a week. Oaklyn won't care, will she?
Me: I can't wait. I feel like I haven't seen you in years. And, no, of course she won't care.
Camden: Dude, can you believe our graduation party is THIS weekend? That we're going to be in full-force bar prep by next week? Shit, I can't even believe I'm leaving NY and moving back to LA.
Me: You know what I can't believe? That our schools have the audacity to have graduation on the same day, so our parents have to divide and conquer, and you get Dad, and I get Mom. I want to be in NY for you. I want you here for me.
Camden: You know I feel the same way.
Me: I have so much anxiety about bar prep that I can barely even think about it.

I heard Declan coming down the hallway, and I held my breath. The last thing I wanted was to make eye contact, so I didn't turn around when I sensed him walking into his office or taking a seat on his leather chair. I didn't even look to see his reaction to the Danish or watch if he took a bite.

But, damn, I wanted to.

Camden: If Dom, Jenner, and Ford passed, I'm not worried about us. We can run circles around those fools. :)
Me: Don't be so sure of yourself, Mr. Cocky. It won't be cute if you say that and then you don't pass.

A new message appeared on my screen.
But this one wasn't from my brother.

Declan: Get to work.

The temptation was far too strong, and I was on the verge of turning around when my phone chimed again, stopping me.

Declan: Best Danish I've ever had in my life. Thank you. I'm going to miss these breakfasts.
Declan: I'm going to miss you.

TWENTY-FIVE

DECLAN

I'd spoken to each of the Dalton brothers, and all three had given me their blessing.

Of course, Dominick had doled out plenty of shit before his came. Words I'd expected. Words a best friend would slap you with and break your balls over because you'd not only kept him in the dark, but the person of interest was also his cousin.

What helped with Dominick's opinion, I assumed, was that he'd heard Hannah's side first.

I hadn't anticipated her doing that.

But when I had sat on the opposite side of Dominick's desk and told him what had gone down between us, he had gotten it. He understood. And he hadn't blamed me for what I'd done.

Even though he knew I was an asshole with quite the reputation when it came to women, he also knew Hannah was different to me.

She was mine.

And now that all that was behind me and I'd confessed the truth to her about the night at the bar, I felt zero guilt.

As for the emotions, those were growing by the goddamn day.

What didn't help was that Hannah was giving me exactly what I'd asked for. But she was fucking everywhere I looked. When I peeked out my office door, she would be camped just outside at her desk. When I returned to my office after meetings, she would have breakfast waiting for me or lunch or more coffee. When I went home at night, I would find her things, like her sweater hanging over the back of my barstool, where she'd forgotten it the last time she came over. When I scrolled through social media before passing out at night, I would see her posts.

She wasn't hounding me to talk about us.

She wasn't blowing up my phone.

She wasn't showing up at my house.

She was just making her presence known.

And I fucking felt it.

Everywhere.

The minutes now dwindling down to the end of her internship.

Once we reached that final hour, I watched her get up from her desk and come into my doorway. One arm raised high as she held on to the frame, the other at her side, clutching a notebook and pen. She'd removed her suit jacket, and her tank was tucked into her skirt, revealing the slimness of her waist and the definition in her arms.

"What can I do for you, Miss Dalton?"

The greeting made her smile.

Fuck, that sight was so gorgeous.

"I just wanted you to know that I gave all my passwords to your assistant in case she needs to access my email or the files I saved, and she knows she can always call me if she can't find something."

"You're really leaving us ..."

At the beginning, I'd fucking dreamed of this day. But as the weeks had passed, having Hannah here had turned out to be something better than I'd imagined. Since there was an us, even if things were slightly rocky at the moment, having her on my team probably wasn't the best scenario, but having her in this building was.

She'd be back once she took the bar, working as a clerk until she passed. Now that our secret was out, I highly doubted she'd be a clerk on my team. Something told me she'd be assigned to Christopher.

Still, that was months away.

Months of not seeing her every day.

Months of her locked in her apartment, doing nothing but studying, bar prepping monopolizing every second of her life.

I knew the process.

It was hell.

And, *goddamn it*, I was going to miss her.

More than I already did, and she was standing right in front of me.

She took a seat in front of my desk, adjusting those beautiful legs so she didn't flash me her pussy. "Declan, I have to."

"I know."

She didn't reply.

She didn't have to.

I saw every thought running through her head.

She wanted to know where we stood.

What the future would look like.

When she would wake up with my arms around her.

"Is there anything I can do before I leave?"

Her voice was eager.

Soft.

Sensual even.

I chuckled, pushing my chair back a few feet so I could cross a foot over my thigh. "Don't ask me that, Hannah. You know what that will lead to."

A wave of heat passed over her cheeks.

"You know, something I inherited from my childhood is this inability to forgive. I hold grudges. I'm not proud of that fact, but I'm learning—especially as I get older—that it's something I struggle with. When someone pisses me off in a way that affects me emotionally, I'm done. I close that door, and I don't look back. That's why I don't let anyone get too close to me."

The flush was leaving her cheeks as her breathing sped up, her skin tone almost turning pale. She was thinking the worst, fearing that I was putting an end to us.

She was in for a big surprise.

"Another thing about me, Hannah, is that I don't allow people to fight back. I don't even give them a chance to speak. Their opinion is meaningless to me. When my mind is made up —like it is now—I don't give a fuck about what they have to say."

"But you let me speak the other night."

I nodded. "I did, and I listened to everything you said." My foot dropped to the floor, and I pulled myself to the edge of the desk. "And I even understood why you hadn't told me the truth. It doesn't mean I like it, but given the evidence that you had, I can see how you drew that conclusion."

She crossed her arms. "Why do I feel like there's a but?"

"You're right. There is a but. Because there's a whole other side to this." My head dropped, so she couldn't see my smile. "This brilliant, stunning fucking firecracker came into my life and bulldozed right through every one of my walls." When I glanced up, her eyes were getting teary. "I don't know what you did to me, Hannah, but you made me listen to you. You made me search for forgiveness. And that grudge that I always held, you made it fall."

"Declan ..." She wiped the corners of her eyes.

"You fought for me. That's what you've been doing since our argument. Fighting. Nonstop. For me." I took a breath. "I've felt it every day." I reached across the desk and held out my hand. "I don't want there to be distance between us. In fact, where you're sitting now is even too far away."

A tear dripped down her cheek as she clasped our fingers together and said, "When you love someone, you fight."

Damn it. I felt that one.

It hit.

And then it hit again.

"With the way men are attracted to you, it looks like I'll be fighting for the woman I love for the rest of my life." I clenched my jaw and growled, "Now, go lock my door."

She laughed.

It was the best sound I'd ever heard.

"You have a meeting in ten minutes, followed by another meeting forty-five minutes later. I'll be gone before the first one is even over."

"Cancel both."

"Ford will gut me if I do that." She wiped her cheeks, the tears long gone from her eyes. "The first one is with Stephanie Baxter, one of his wealthiest clients. She's been waiting almost a month to get in with you."

I thought for a second. "All right, then come to my house tonight."

"Tonight?" Her eyes widened. "You do know this is the biggest weekend of my life, right? And everyone and their great-aunt is coming into town to celebrate my joint graduation with Camden."

I squeezed her fingers. "I can't wait until your graduation party to kiss you."

Until now, I hadn't told her I was going.

As the recognition registered, a softness drifted across her face. "You just made it impossible for me to say no."

"Dinner, my place—you know, the house where I've never brought any other woman before."

She moved in closer, pressing her tits against my desk. "And you're going to give me those lips—you know, the ones you've never given to any woman besides me."

I winked. "You're always the exception, Hannah."

She released my hand and sauntered toward the door, glancing at me over her shoulder as she said, "I'll bring dessert."

"There's only one thing I want for dessert, and that's you."

TWENTY-SIX

HANNAH

Butterflies. That was the only way I could describe the feeling in my stomach as I walked up to Declan's front door. This wasn't the first time I'd been here. We'd spent plenty of time together since our return from Wyoming. But this occasion felt different than those previous dates.

It felt more significant.

It finally felt like all the obstacles were moved out of our way now that we'd had conversations with my family, and as of this evening, I was no longer interning at The Dalton Group.

And it felt like our relationship had changed.

Intern Hannah wasn't knocking on his door.

Girlfriend Hannah was.

I'd stripped off my suit when I got home, and after a shower, I'd put on leggings and a tank top, adding very little makeup with my hair in a high ponytail. This was the version of me that I wanted Declan to wrap his arms around.

He opened the door, wearing a pair of dark jeans, a white T-shirt that fit snugly over his incredibly defined chest, and bare feet. His thick lips were outlined in delicious, dark scruff.

I shifted my weight, balancing my overnight bag and two Tupperware containers. "Hi."

As his hand moved up the frame of the door, his eyes taking in the entire length of me, my lungs tightened, a feeling consuming me that went far deeper than just a physical reaction.

"Hannah ..." His voice was deep, growly. "Some women try so hard to look beautiful. You"—his eyes dipped before slowly rising—"do it so effortlessly. Fuck, you're gorgeous."

His compliment made me breathe harder.

"Casual is my favorite." I ran just my fingertips over his abs, feeling the ripples and line of dark hair through the thin material. "On both of us."

He moved to the side, adding more space to the doorway. "Come in."

I didn't get farther than the entrance before he gripped the back of my head, steering my face closer to his.

"I need those lips."

He slammed our mouths together.

Tasting.

Feeding.

And when he pulled away, he roared, "Exactly what I needed."

Standing this close—my lips still wet and tasting of him, the feel of his skin against mine, the wind of his cologne, the heat from his presence—it was sensory overload.

With his hand on my face, he kissed me again. "Fuck, I missed this."

My eyes drifted open.

"This smile"—he tightened his hold on my cheek—"I don't want it to fade tonight."

"I can't see how it could."

Not with the way I was feeling.

How I was still hardly breathing.

"Come on," he said, his hand now on my back, leading me into the kitchen.

As I set the containers on his island, he took the bag from my shoulder and took it into his bedroom.

Every time I came here, I fell more in love with his home. An environment that was pristine, a style that was masculine. Dark art covered steel-gray walls, the floors rich and ebony. Molding and lighting weren't just accents; they were used as decor. I'd once commented on how even his entryway was decorated to perfection, and he'd said every litigator needed a strong opening statement.

Except Declan's entire house was a statement.

One I would love to spend much more time in.

I closed my eyes and took in the aroma, and as I heard Declan rejoin me in the kitchen, I said, "Whatever Peter prepared smells delicious."

"Tonight wasn't Peter. It was all me."

His admission caused my eyelids to open.

Declan's private chef had made us dinner every time I came over. His food was amazing, and his presentation was five-star worthy. I'd had no idea Declan even knew how to cook.

"So, you're telling me that this gorgeous kitchen wasn't just designed for Peter?" I scanned the high-end appliances, the extra-tall cabinets, the island that was the length of my whole bedroom.

He tucked a piece of my hair behind my ear. "In college, I quickly learned that if I wanted decent food, I was going to have to make it myself. So, I did. I just don't have time to do much cooking anymore. Hence why Peter works for me full-time." He moved to the other side of the kitchen, where he decanted a bottle of red before he poured some into two glasses.

"What's the special occasion?"

He returned to my side and handed me a glass. "You."

God, this man.

"Well, whatever you made, it smells amazing." I tilted my face up to him.

He held his glass to mine. "To graduating law school with top honors and the highest accumulated hours of pro bono work during the year." He kissed me. "That's impressive."

"How did you know about my pro bono work?"

He smiled. "You know I have plenty of connections at that school."

"What else did Professor Ward tell you?"

"She didn't know that I'd switched firms and wanted to see if there were any openings at Smith & Klein in case you decided you didn't want to work at The Dalton Group."

I couldn't believe what I was hearing. "She did that for me?"

"She believes in you, Hannah. You're her top student, and she wanted to make sure you had options."

Still holding my glass to his, I said, "Did you tell her I was your intern?"

"I might have skipped that detail, but I did mention that we're dating, and I promised to take good care of you—not when it comes to law. You have that all figured out on your own."

I gave him a quick kiss. "I'll cheers to that."

"What did you make?" A grin spread across his face while he waited for me to reply. "Or is it a surprise?"

I set my glass down and reached for the containers—one blue, one red—and I loosened the top of the red one. "I had some brownies in the freezer that I was going to bring over. Oreo-flavored ones. But since I had some extra time after I left the office, I whipped up something else." I lifted off the lid.

"Everly says my cupcakes are the best, so that's what I went with."

He pulled my body against his, holding the top of my ass. "I thought I made it clear that you were going to be my dessert tonight."

"You can have both."

He looked toward the treats. "Vanilla?"

"There's nothing vanilla about you, Declan."

I swiped some frosting off the side of one, and he sucked the glob off my fingertip.

"Apple," he moaned.

"And there's apple pie filling in the center of the cake part along with tiny, tiny apple chunks mixed into the frosting."

He set my wine down and lifted me into his arms. "Because it's my favorite." He kissed me, a burst of sweetness coming off his tongue. "You're too good to me."

"I also made my favorite; that's in the blue container."

He set me on the counter and opened the other lid, taking out a cupcake. "Nutella, I'm guessing."

"How did you know?"

"I pay attention." He took a bite, and I watched his expression change as he took in the fullness of the flavor. "Fuck, this is good."

He held it in front of my lips, and I nibbled the side before he finished the rest of it and went in for a second one, this time apple.

"You're going to ruin your dinner."

"With an appetite as big as mine?" He dived into my neck, kissing up to my ear, growling, "Impossible." When he finally reached the middle of the apple, his eyes closed, and he groaned, "Hannah, what the fuck is this?"

"You like?"

He gave me a quick glance, eyeing me up and down. "I far more than like."

"Love then?"

Even though there was a small bit of frosting on his lip that he hadn't licked off yet and his hand was full of the dessert, he stood between my legs, wrapped an arm around my back, and kissed me. There was no hurry in the way his tongue slid into my mouth, an explosion of passion following.

And when he pulled away, "Yes ... love," was what I heard.

I knew we were no longer talking about the cupcakes, but I brought us back to the topic and said, "I made a dozen of each flavor. You'll have plenty to savor over the next couple of days."

"I'm afraid they'll be gone by tonight." He finished the rest of the second cupcake and licked his fingers. "Don't move." But he did, leaving me to go to the oven, lowering the door to check inside.

I tried to steal a peek. "Is that homemade bread?"

"Focaccia."

I then attempted to look at the stovetop, where he was stirring a large pot of something. "I smell ... salmon?"

"I sautéed some mussels, shrimp, calamari, lobster tails, and clams in a white wine and butter sauce that I'm going to add to pappardelle. Lots of chefs combine seafood with tomato sauce, but I like the lightness of white wine when you use a hearty pasta like pappardelle." He slid a little to the side and pointed at the cast iron skillet that was right next to the pasta. "This is a piece of salmon and a whole branzino that I've cooked in olive oil and a bunch of fresh herbs." He turned his back to the food. "Fish for the first course, pasta for the second. Apple cupcakes for the third." His eyes narrowed. "And then I'm having you after dessert."

I stared at him, dumbfounded. "Who are you?"

"What do you mean?"

I searched his eyes. "Come here." I waited until he was close to cup his cheeks, his scruff prickling my palms. "You haven't barked at me all day. You didn't hold a grudge after our argument, like I'd feared you would. You even invited me over and cooked this incredible meal for me." I rubbed my thumb over his lips. "And now, you're going to eat me as a fourth course." I glanced back and forth between his eyes. "I'm just wondering who this new guy is and where he's been hiding this past semester."

His arms circled around me. "The barking isn't gone—I can promise you that." He nipped the back of my thumb. "I just wanted to do something special for your graduation, but don't get used to it. Peter isn't going anywhere anytime soon."

He brushed his nose against mine. "And the only thing I've thought about all day is how many orgasms my tongue is going to give you tonight." He started tugging down my yoga pants. "I don't think I can wait until after dinner." He stopped when the waist of the pants was at my knees and looked at me. "Unless you're hungrier for that?" He nodded toward the stove. "In which case, I'll pull these back up."

There was no choice in my mind.

There was only him.

And us.

I ran my fingers through his hair and pushed the top of his head to lower him down my body. "This," I moaned after the first swipe of his tongue, "is what I want."

TWENTY-SEVEN

DECLAN

I parked outside Hannah's parents' house and grabbed the large bag I'd placed on the passenger seat before making my way up to the front door. Based on the number of cars here, there was one hell of a party happening inside, and in attendance were all the people responsible for my paycheck—the three brothers along with their parents, David and Sue Dalton. Although I'd had individual conversations with their sons, I hadn't mentioned anything about Hannah to David or Sue, nor did I plan to. If the topic was mentioned at this party, I'd address it, but not before.

I pressed the doorbell, and a familiar face greeted me on the other side of the door.

Just not the face I had been hoping for.

"Declan Shaw," Camden said, chuckling. "Can't say I'm surprised to see your ass on my doorstep, but after all that shit-talking, maybe I should be." He crossed his arms over his chest. "Funny, my sister says you're one of the good guys. Is that true?" He looked over his shoulder before we connected eyes again. "When I asked my cousins that question"—he laughed—"they had a whole lot to say about you."

"I'm sure they did, especially Dominick. He's got more dirt on me than a goddamn coffin."

"Listen, we all have our pasts. I'm certainly no exception." He reached forward to pound my fist. "I just want to make sure it doesn't interfere with my sister. That one deserves to be treated right."

After our knuckles tapped, I pulled my hand back and said, "She will be; you have no reason to worry." I continued to read his eyes, weighing what he was looking for. "I owe you an apology for that night at the bar. I never should have said those things about Hannah. I especially never should have said them to you. That was fucked up of me."

"It's all good, man." He paused. "Now that I'm living in LA again, we should grab a drink sometime."

"For sure," I answered. "I'd like that."

He shifted, allowing me to pass, his hand patting my shoulder once I stepped into the doorway. "Have you met any of the family?"

"Just the side who works at the firm."

"*Ahhh,*" he groaned, leading me toward the living room. "The brothers are all in here, so consider this your safe zone. The second you head that way"—he pointed to the dining room—"you'll be unprotected, so expect to be bombarded for a solid hour, maybe two. Every aunt, great-niece, family friend is going to invade territories you're unprepared for. If you need to be saved, just give me a look, and I'll come get you."

I laughed. "You're a good man, Camden."

"Food stations are everywhere, and the bar is over there." He pointed one last time to the patio. "Help yourself."

"I appreciate it."

"Hey, Shaw," Camden said as he took a few steps forward

but then turned to face me. "You might have one hell of a reputation in the courtroom, but personally"—he grinned—"you're like an open book, and I saw right through your bullshit that night." His smile grew. "See you around."

Jesus Christ.

Dominick had said the same thing.

I didn't know if they were telling the truth or if they were just trying to get under my skin. Whatever the case was, I didn't let it bother me as I walked toward my group of friends in the living room.

"What's up, my man?" I said to Dominick, reaching around his shoulder to give him a man hug.

"I was wondering when you were going to show up," he replied, slapping my back. "Good to see you, buddy."

"Good to be here," I responded, and I moved on to Oaklyn, giving her a hug. "I know I'm late. I had to stop at the store to find a bag that would fit her gift."

When choosing what to get Hannah, I hadn't consulted with her best friend, but I'd let her in on the surprise. Since Oaklyn was usually home whenever I went to their place, we'd had plenty of time to discuss the present.

"She's going to die when she opens it," Oaklyn said. "And she's going to be so thrilled when she sees that you're here."

"Where is she?"

Oaklyn shrugged. "Around—you know, hostess with the mostest."

I gave her a smile, and then I moved around the rest of the circle, shaking hands with Kendall, then Jo and Jenner, and Sydney and Ford. Lastly, I stopped in front of Hannah's princess.

I knelt and stuck out my fingers, saying, "Hello, Everly."

She held her dad's waist and squeezed my hand with an impressive grip.

"I've seen you at the office before, but I don't think we've officially met," I said. "I'm Declan. I work with your dad, and I'm a friend of Hannah's."

"Hannah had better not be your best friend 'cause she's my best friend."

I laughed. "I would never take her away from you; don't worry. You know, she talks about you a lot."

Her eyes lit up. "She does?"

"She tells me how much you love her cupcakes."

"We make pink ones together. You need to try a pink one, Mr. Declan. Those are the *bessst*."

I could see why Hannah was completely enamored with Everly.

"I'll have to tell Hannah to bring me a pink one," I said. "Sounds like I'm missing out on something amazing."

When she nodded, her little curls bounced. "You are!"

Just as I started to rise, I caught eyes with Hannah. She was outside, chatting with a small group of people, her face glowing as she stared at me. I knew it wasn't from the hot California sun.

It was from this.

Last night.

Us.

She said something to the group she was speaking to, and then she made her way inside, not stopping until her arms were around my waist.

With my only free hand, I gripped the back of her head, holding her against my chest, whispering, "Hello, gorgeous," into her hair.

A quick peek around showed me we had an audience. Family members in this room and the adjoining one were glancing in our direction, and so were the brothers and their girls along with Oaklyn and Camden.

Everyone was taking us in.

Oaklyn even sang, "*Awww*," at some point.

Hannah gazed up at me. "I'm so happy you're here and ..." Her cheeks flushed as she realized we had a spotlight. "Everyone and their mother is staring at us right now, aren't they?"

I tried to ignore all the attention and handed her the bag. "For you."

Emotion began to fill Hannah's eyes.

"Congratulations, baby. I'm so proud of you."

She took the bag from my hand, and I could tell she was surprised by the heaviness of it. "You did not have to get me anything. Last night was more than enough."

"What happened last night?" Dominick asked.

I laughed.

Hannah rolled her eyes and looked at them. "Shouldn't you all be in your own conversation and not snooping into mine?"

"But you guys are just too cute," Oaklyn teased.

"And they're so entertaining," Ford added as he lifted Everly.

"Yeah, I second that," Jenner said.

Hannah's attention returned to me. "Did you meet Everly?"

"*Yesss!*" Everly answered for me. "You owe Mr. Declan a pink cupcake!"

"Is that so?" Hannah said as she looked at Everly. "Maybe I need to bring Mr. Declan with me the next time we bake together, and you can give him one of your cupcakes. How does that sound?"

"Yay! I like sparkles everywhere. Do you like sparkles?" Everly asked me.

"I think Mr. Declan likes extra sparkles," Dominick responded. "And his favorite color also happens to be pink."

"It *isss?*" Everly asked, her mouth hanging open.

I gave Dominick a look and then glanced at Everly. I couldn't disappoint the kid, and I feared the truth would crush her. "Pink's cool," I told her. "I can definitely hang with some pink."

"Hannah, I can bake with Mr. Declan. He's fun."

I smiled at Everly.

And then Hannah grinned at me. "Everly's approval is a huge deal, just so you know. She doesn't let anyone bake with us."

"Not even me," Ford admitted.

"That's 'cause Daddy doesn't bake good, and he likes to leave out ingredients"—she put her hands over her mouth, like she was attempting a whisper—"like the chocolate chips."

"Ford," I said, teasing him, "how could you?"

Jenner pointed at Ford and said, "A strong contestant for the Worst Dad Award."

"Hey, hey," Sydney shot back, rubbing her hand over Ford's chest. "I dare you to find a better dad than this one."

While Jenner and Dominick challenged that statement, Hannah rose on her tiptoes and said softly in my ear, "Is it time I rescue you and take you somewhere private for a second or—"

"Yes."

She giggled. "Thought so." Her arms lowered, and she linked our fingers. "Bestie, I'm going to return Mr. Declan in a few minutes, okay? Make sure to keep this group in line while we're gone. Don't let them do anything we wouldn't do."

"I'm on it," Everly replied.

Hannah led me through the house and up a staircase and down a hallway, where she opened the last door on the right, closing it once we stepped inside.

After a quick peek around, I said, "Was this your bedroom?"

"Yep, and Mom hasn't changed a thing." She sat on the bed, setting the gift beside her. "She keeps saying she's going to redecorate and make it into an official guest room, but she never will. I think she's secretly hoping Cam and I will move back in." Her hand went up in the air. "That'll never happen, in case you're worried."

"If you move anywhere, it'll be into my place, not back here."

Her brows rose. "Do you think you could handle waking up next to me every morning?"

"I'd look forward to it."

I broke eye contact to walk around the space, checking out her swim team trophies and the framed photos of her and her friends. There was a chair in the corner that had bags hanging over the side and several shelves of paperbacks. The door to her closet was cracked open, and there were still clothes inside.

"How many secrets does this room hold?"

"Oh God," she sighed. "Millions."

"Any worth sharing?"

She shrugged. "I plead the Fifth."

"Fair enough." I stood in the center of the room. "If you're still her baby, how is Mom going to react when she finds out you're dating an older man?"

"Mom already knows. I don't keep much from her." She crossed her legs and tapped the spot next to her, inviting me to join her on the bed. "She's dying to meet you, which is going to happen the second we go back downstairs. Dad, too, but I'll admit, he's not the nice one. That's Mom."

"I hear dads never are—not that I have much experience in that department."

She wrapped her arms around my neck. "Uncle David and Aunt Sue have already filled them in on your accomplishments, I'm sure. They're going to love you."

I nipped her bottom lip. "Will they love me as much as you do?"

"Impossible."

"Give me those lips," I demanded.

She slammed our mouths together.

As her taste instantly hit my tongue, her vanilla scent filled my nose, and I breathed her in, listening to each of her exhales releasing with tiny moans.

Fuck, I can't get enough of this girl.

She slowly pulled away, resting her forehead against mine. "I know I already said this, but I'm so happy you're here." She leaned back, taking me in. "Part of me still can't even believe it. Or that"—she ran her thumb across my mouth—"I can kiss this whenever I want."

"It's yours, Hannah."

She was quiet for a few moments. "I hope that's still true when I'm in studying hell and days go by without us seeing each other." The emotion I'd seen earlier returned to her face. "The next few months are going to be hard, Declan."

I gripped her back, pulling her closer. "I know what you're about to go through, and I assure you, nothing is going to change between us."

She searched my eyes. "What if I can only see you once or twice a week?" She took a breath. "Or less?"

"Well, I can't promise I won't turn into a growling asshole" —I gripped her harder—"but I can promise we'll get through it and we'll be fine. There's no reason for you to worry." I kissed her. "I mean it."

She nodded. "Okay."

"Now, open your gift."

She reached inside the bag, taking out the long, rectangular box. The lid then came off, and she moved the tissue paper aside, that glow returning to her face the moment she realized it was a briefcase.

Her hand went over her mouth. "Oh my God, it's beautiful."

"There's a story behind this present." I waited for her eyes to lock with mine before I continued, "When I was a kid, my parents took me on vacation to Maine. We were walking through Old Port, a quaint section in Portland, and we came across this small store that specialized in handmade leather goods. I'll never forget when I passed that window, seeing this huge—at least what had seemed huge at the time—briefcase inside. I made my parents stop and go in and look at it with me, and I said to them, 'When I graduate law school, I want a brief-case just like that one.' " My fingers slid into her hair, holding the back of her head. "Right before I graduated, my father looked up the store. They were still in business, and he asked them to make me a briefcase."

"It's the one you use now, isn't it? The one that has your initials next to the lock?"

I nodded. "I reached out to the owner a few weeks ago, and I had him make this for you."

Her eyes got so big. "I can't believe you had this made just for me."

I rubbed my fingers over the *HD* that I'd had engraved next to the lock. I then opened the top, so she could see the way I'd customized the interior. "I wanted you to have something that was made just for you. Something with superior craftsmanship. That'll last as long as you want it to."

"Declan ..." She ran her hand over each section, the flaps of organization I'd had added to hold her pens and notebooks and files and tablet. She finally landed on the bottom, where the date of her graduation was engraved along with the USC logo.

"This is ... I don't even know what to say." She glanced up. "It's the nicest, most thoughtful gift anyone has ever given me."

My hand moved to her cheek, holding her steady. "Every time you walk into a courtroom is going to feel different. Some days, you're going to feel confident as hell. Some days, you're going to wish you'd had another week to prepare. Some cases are going to be automatic wins. Some, you're going to have to fight like hell. But one thing will remain consistent, and that's your presentation—the suit covering your body, the expression locked on your face, and the briefcase in your hand." I leaned my face close to hers. "If you ever need it—and I'm not saying you will, but if you do—that handle can feel like my fingers, and you can squeeze it as hard as you need to, baby, and I'll always be there for you."

She circled her arms around me, aligning our bodies, burying her face in my neck.

When she held on, she clutched me so fucking tightly.

"I love you, Hannah."

"I love you more," she whispered back.

TWENTY-EIGHT

HANNAH

"I imagined this moment," I whispered to Declan, squeezing his hand as he stood next to me, "when I was in the depths of studying and my eyes just wanted to close and I wanted to throw my books and give up." I turned to him. "Whenever I got to that point, I would think of us, here, and all this beauty. That's what drove me to keep going."

"And now that you're here?"

A breeze whipped past my face, bringing with it a scent that I absolutely loved—an indescribable freshness that I smelled every time I stepped into the mountains. "It's even better the second time."

He released my hand and wrapped his arm around me, pulling me against the side of his body. His lips pressed into the top of my head while we both took in this view.

A view we'd been discussing since the last time we had been here.

A view we wanted to have more time to appreciate.

On my first day of studying, Declan had sent me an email.

The itinerary it'd outlined was a surprise, as was the whole trip, his message saying I just needed to hang in there, that the reward would be worth the twelve weeks of hell I was about to go through. He had us leaving two days after I sat for the bar. We would start in Big Sky, Montana, and then we'd spend several days in Yellowstone before ending the adventure in Jackson Hole, Wyoming.

His goal was for me to unplug once we got here.

My goal was a week of nonstop, uninterrupted time together—something I'd desperately needed.

We'd just arrived in Jackson Hole last night, and now, we were standing in front of the Grand Teton on a road somewhere inside the valley. We'd spent the morning rafting down Snake River, and on our way back to town, we had passed a sight that was so intensely beautiful that I asked Declan to pull over. Here, the mountains were a rich purple, the tips already white with snow, the sky so calm that not even a single cloud interrupted it. In front of us, at least a football field away, was a barn. It was old, weathered, with wonderful trees framing both sides.

There was something about this rickety structure, the fencing that surrounded the property, how it looked in front of the mountains that completely captured me. I couldn't stop taking photos. I couldn't stop fantasizing about what it would be like to live in a home that had a view like this.

"Don't worry; we're coming back again."

I glanced up at Declan as a reassuring look passed over his face. "Why would you say that?"

"I can tell how much you love it here, so we'll make another trip once Walter opens his hotel. And maybe another after I take you skiing in Europe."

I rubbed my teeth over my bottom lip. "Sounds like you're about to keep me very busy."

"You're going to need the time off when you're working eighty hours a week. Trust me."

Eighty hours seemed like nothing compared to the time I'd put into studying.

But in a few days, once we returned to LA, I would take a couple of weeks to get my life in order since the last twelve had been spent off the grid, and then I'd go to work as a clerk at The Dalton Group until the results of my exam came in.

I stood on my tiptoes to reach his lips. "Once a month or so, we're just going to run away to travel the world? Because you think I'm going to need that time off?"

"When we're both working that much, I'm going to need that time with you." He reached under my fleece to grab my ass. "Do you find anything wrong with that?"

I laughed. "Nope."

"Didn't think so."

He kissed me before he moved in behind me, holding my back to his chest, his arm crossing my neck. Warmth came off his body, and I soaked it in, my lungs burning as I inhaled the frigid air.

"Maybe next time, we'll do Glacier National Park instead of Big Sky," he said. "We can even go up to Banff and check out Lake Louise."

I glanced up at him. "My God, Declan, that sounds absolutely fabulous. Those are locations I've dreamed about seeing."

"I know." He rubbed his thumb over my mouth. "They've been on my list too." As I looked toward the mountains, he nuzzled into my neck. "We have no plans for the rest of the day, and dinner reservations aren't until eight thirty tonight, so there are a few things we can do."

Since we'd gotten off the private jet in Montana, every day had been an adventure. Some were spent hiking, some on wildlife tours, and today, we'd experienced the water. What we hadn't done was spend any time in the big, beautiful suites that Declan had booked.

"What if we just went back to the hotel room and relaxed for a bit?" I suggested. "Maybe open that bottle of champagne that the hotel left for us? Put on some robes and hang by the fireplace?"

"*Mmm*," he moaned, giving me a look that I recognized. "I was hoping you were going to say that."

"Oh yeah? Why's that?"

"I already texted the concierge and ordered us room service." He tightened his grip on me. "It should be getting delivered right about now."

"Declan, Declan ..." After I turned toward him, my hands went to his face, and I was consumed by his handsomeness. "We should get going, then."

"Not before I do this."

My eyes closed as he pressed his lips to mine, my body relaxing against him, his hands taking all my weight.

There was something different about kissing in the mountains. About the air. About the way the scenery almost caged us in, hugging us like an extra set of arms. A beauty that matched my love for this man.

"Are you ready?" he whispered, his lips now hovering over mine.

I didn't know exactly what he was asking—if I was ready to leave, if I was ready to eat the food he was having delivered, or if it was something else.

But it didn't matter.

I'd follow Declan anywhere.

I clasped our hands together, and he helped me step into the Jeep.

Since our hotel was right in the middle of town, the drive

there was short, and we pulled up to the front entrance, where the valet met us. Once we were inside the lobby, we took the elevator to our floor.

But when he opened our door, room service wasn't the only thing that greeted us.

"Declan ..." I said so softly as I took it all in.

Rose petals covered the floor, and candles flickered across every surface. There was a buffet of food, including desserts, on a table in the corner. And what created the most romantic ambiance were the flames that licked behind the glass of the fireplace and the balcony doors that had been left open, filling the room with my favorite scented air. There was so much to look at; it even took me a moment to notice the massage table that had more petals spread across the top of it.

I turned toward him. "I can't believe this. That you put it all together. That you did this for me." I swallowed, trying to find the words. "It's absolutely stunning."

His fingers locked with mine, and he said, "Come with me," before taking me out onto the balcony.

The view from up here was as gorgeous as the valley we'd just driven from, but being higher in elevation only added another breathtaking layer.

"Would you like some champagne?"

He broke away from my hand to pour us each a glass, the bottle sitting next to the table that had been set up outside. On top of the table were two place settings with more petals and a scattering of tea lights.

I took the glass from his hand. "I'm blown away right now."

"We haven't even eaten yet." He cupped my face, gazing into my eyes. "Wait until you try the desserts. I worked with the hotel's pastry chef to pick out some I thought you'd love."

"And there's going to be massages?"

He clinked his glass against mine. "There's going to be one massage. That's the one I'm going to give you."

"You're doing it?"

He nodded. "I think you'll be surprised at how good I am." His hand was still on my face, and it lowered to my shoulder, rubbing into the muscle.

I moaned, "My God, you are ..."

He took the champagne out of my hand, placing it on the table before he lifted me into his arms. "What I am is ... in love with you."

I wrapped my legs and arms around him even though, no matter what, I knew he wouldn't let me fall.

And because I couldn't wait a second longer, I kissed him.

It wasn't slow or gentle.

It was rough.

Needy.

In control.

The same demanding way that Declan kissed me.

And when I pulled back, breathlessly, I said, "As much as I want to eat the lunch and desserts that you had delivered, there's something else I want first."

He growled and gripped my ass as he carried me back into the suite. "Is that so?"

I unzipped the top of his fleece, so I could have more access to his neck. It was there, the spot just below his ear, where I started to kiss. "I want you."

"Show me."

He backed us up to the bed and sat on the edge. With my legs straddling him, I wasted no time in unzipping his jacket the rest of the way and removing the shirt he had on underneath. He did the same to me, peeling off each piece of clothing, adjusting our positions so we could take off our pants and shoes.

Once I was naked, I climbed down onto the floor, balancing on my knees as I gazed up at him.

My God, his cock was perfect.

Everything about him was.

Even the sounds that came out of him as I surrounded his tip and lowered down his shaft. I gripped the bottom half, the part I couldn't fit in my mouth, and swiveled my hand around it.

"Fuck yes," he roared, holding the back of my head, guiding me lower.

I took in as much as I could, rising to his crown, where I sucked the hardest.

Where I sucked like I wanted his cum on my tongue.

It was one thing to look at him when his face was between my legs. It was a whole different level of sexy to see the way he stared at me now, how the pleasure spread across his eyes, how the hunger tugged at his lips.

"Just like that," he ordered. "Yes."

With each dip of my mouth, I tried taking him in deeper, my hand working the bottom, my other fingers brushing over his balls. He didn't release the back of my head, nor did he close his eyes.

He watched every bob.

And his crown didn't leave my lips until I heard, "I need to taste your cunt."

The thought of his tongue on me was almost more than I could handle.

But I wanted it.

I always wanted it.

"Come sit on my face."

He reclined on the bed, and I followed him, moving up his body until I was spread across his mouth. Just as I glanced down at him, he licked me.

Hard.

With the whole width of his tongue, like my pussy was the underside of an envelope.

"Oh God." I quivered.

His tongue focused solely on my clit as his finger slipped inside me.

My back arched, and my hips rocked while I screamed, "Yes! Fuck!"

He wasn't just flicking.

He was sucking.

Nibbling the very edge of me.

And I was almost positive there was now a second finger plunging into me, twisting toward my G-spot, grazing across it.

"You taste so fucking good."

There were so many sensations bursting through me as my legs strained to hold me.

My hands clasped together.

My mouth opened, my thoughts so lost as I cried, "Declan ..."

"Do you want to come on my face?"

Oh God.

Yes.

"*Yesss.*"

He picked up speed, not just with his tongue, but his hand, too, the satisfaction growing, building, and spreading through me.

The peak came out of nowhere.

And with it came this fierce eruption, causing me to jerk across his mouth.

"Declan!" A shudder pounded through my stomach, and I yelled, "Fuck, I'm coming!"

His mouth pressed even harder, licking, swallowing, adding that friction I needed. And while he dove his fingers in and out of me, my orgasm churned, exploding, taking absolutely no surrender as it barreled through my body.

I knelt up the moment I became so sensitive that I couldn't even take his breath on me.

"Do you want that again?"

I couldn't breathe.

I couldn't think.

But I looked down at him while I panted, "Yes."

He never got tired of eating me. I loved him for that.

"But I want you."

All it took was those four words to pass through my lips before he flipped me onto my back and moved my ass to the end of the bed. He stood, facing the mattress, and held my legs around him while he slid into me.

"Ah!" I sucked in air. "Declan!"

The tingles were still so raw that when he entered, it felt like tiny bolts of electricity were zapping between my legs.

"Goddamn it," he hissed. "You're so fucking wet."

His voice was as erotic as his tongue, the vibration of his tone whipping across me.

"Fuck, Hannah." He brushed his finger back and forth across my clit. "You feel fucking amazing."

I wanted to moan.

I wanted to scream.

I wanted my reaction to tell him exactly how I was feeling.

But I was locked in this place where his movements had taken over my voice, my emotion, every part of my body, and I could do nothing but squeeze the blanket beneath me and hang on.

"You're tightening," he exhaled. "Fucking pulsing." He leaned over me, our bodies aligned, his hips thrusting back and hammering forward. Over and over. "You want to come on my cock?"

I swallowed, searching.

Digging.

"Yes!" I gasped.

Before I could find that release, he pulled out, turned me onto my stomach, lifted me to my hands and knees, and stroked right back in.

This angle—*my God*—it came with an overwhelming amount of fullness. If there was an end to me, I swore he hit it every time he dived in. But within that deepness was also a special place, and he aimed right for it, his tip caressing that G-spot, teasing my orgasm.

"Declan, I'm going to—"

"I know. I can feel it."

His hands roamed down my back and over my ass and around my hip, and when he flicked my clit, I lost it.

"Fuck!" I shouted. *"Fuuuck!"* It came on even faster this round, grabbing ahold of me, the waves shaking through me. "Declan!"

This time, the tingles started in my thighs, swelling toward my chest.

My nails bit into the blanket; my toes bent into the bed.

"So fucking wet." He slowed, but he continued to give me that combination of pressure and penetration.

It was just what I needed.

What I craved.

What was making me completely wild.

"Feeling you come"—he kissed the center of my back—"is the hottest thing I've ever experienced." His lips were like fire, each kiss another scorching flame. "Do you know what I want?" His voice was sharp, exhilarating.

I wasn't sure I could even form words at this point, so I moaned instead.

"I want to feel you lose yourself on my dick again." He

reared his ass back and gradually slipped into me. "And then I'm going to fill you with my fucking cum."

He gave me no chance to respond.

Not even a second to grunt out how steamy that sounded before he was turning me around and lifting me from the bed, bringing me to the balcony.

We had the entire top floor of the boutique hotel, and there were no balconies beside us, no buildings in front of us.

Just the mountains.

He sat on one of the lounge chairs and placed me on top of him. "I want to watch you come." He took my nipple into his mouth, staring into my eyes while he bit down, simultaneously tilting his hips up, filling me with every inch of his dick.

The outside air made my senses more aware.

The crispness gnawed at my skin.

The freshness made my back arch.

"Jesus, you're fucking gorgeous."

I'd just taken my first dip, rocking forward and back before rising to his tip again.

His eyes didn't leave me even though his mouth was moving to new spots, his hands just as busy.

When I reached his crown, I circled, giving myself that added friction. It was during my second rotation that I felt his finger touch that forbidden place. He'd taken some of the wetness from my pussy, and he sank right in.

"Oh God." I gripped his shoulders, squeezing them. "That feels so good."

"You love me being in your ass. You love me being inside that tight little hole as much as I do."

He was only giving me a finger, but I took it.

I used it.

And my body began to build around it.

"*Ahhh!*" I inhaled. "Yes!"

Even though he'd given me the control, I felt taken.

Consumed.

Raptured.

He was kissing me, and with each swipe of his tongue, he was bringing me that much closer to the edge.

The edge where I was going to lose it all.

"You're almost there. I can feel it." His finger went deeper; it moved faster, and so did his thumb that was rubbing my clit. "You can't fight how good this feels, Hannah." He was moving with me, thrusting up at the same time as I lowered. "I'm filling your fucking ass; your cunt is tightening around my dick, and your clit is hardening." He sucked on my lip, releasing it to say, "Let it go, baby. Give me your fucking orgasm."

How could words be so sexy?

How could they make me feel better than I already was?

But they did.

They brought me there.

And I was gone.

"Declan," I howled, frozen in the air while he pummeled into me. I couldn't tell where the sensations were coming from. I couldn't tell which part of my body was feeling the most pleasure. All I could do was take it. And then all I could do was fall. "Oh fuck! Yes!"

"You want more of this cock? I'm going to give it to you."

I heard myself beg.

I heard myself moan.

I heard myself demand, "Come with me."

Shudders were exhausting my body, but I still felt the change in him.

The roughness in his drives.

The deepness.

"Hannah," he roared.

But he didn't stop.

He didn't slow.

He upheld this relentless pattern, pounding into me while he smashed our lips together.

"You're milking me," he growled the moment he pulled away. "Milking every drop out of me."

The waves were still colliding, but as I heard this, as I now knew what was happening inside him, I felt like I was reaching that summit all over again.

There was a messy combination of jitters and tingles, and, "Declan," came shouting out of me.

"Take my cum, Hannah." His movements were fierce, untamed. "I want your cunt to swallow it."

I screamed when the final shudder passed through me, and then I felt nothing but stillness as we clung to each other, finding our breath again.

When I felt like I could finally form words, I pressed my hands on both sides of his face and gently kissed him. "The mountains just got quite the show."

He dragged his thumb over my bottom lip. "That's just the first round. Wait until I rub the Nutella mousse cake all over you and then pound"—he grabbed my ass with both hands—"this."

EPILOGUE
DECLAN

Three Months Later

"Richie Star is insisting that he meet with you next Friday, the second he gets back from his tour," my assistant said. She was standing in front of my desk, her expression fearful as she delivered the news about one of the largest rock singers in the world whose record company wasn't letting him out of his contract so he could start his own label.

I tapped my pen on the nearest folder. "Do I have an opening?"

She shook her head. "Not for the next six weeks."

"Then, tell him that."

"I did, and he threatened to show up here, Declan." Her lips spread wide. "He actually said he'd camp outside your office and wait until you let him in." She moved her notebook against her chest and held it there like a shield.

My pen stilled as the rage erupted inside me. "That motherfucker."

"I told him it was impossible—"

"I'll slap a restraining order on him so fast that he'll be facing another crime if he steps foot into this fucking building."

"I hinted at that," she admitted.

Jesus.

And I'd thought Walter was fucking needy.

Dominick's clients were proving to be so much worse. Rich, entitled, demanding little pricks, like Richie Star, who expected the world to just kneel at his feet.

I had zero patience for people like him.

"Friday ... Friday," I repeated as I pulled up my schedule and scanned the entire day.

I didn't know why the fuck I was bothering. If I didn't have an opening, there was nothing I could do.

Especially because the following day, on Saturday morning, Hannah and I were flying to Switzerland, where we'd be spending almost two weeks before I returned to LA for Jenner's bachelor party.

If I was going to cave, then I'd have to meet with Richie before I left.

Goddamn it.

I knew the media was going to have a field day with this case.

It would be worse than the Kennedy trial.

"I don't know why—I must be in the giving mood—but you can tell that asshole I'll meet him here at seven in the morning on Friday. If he's late"—I ground my teeth together—"and I mean, even by a second—I'm locking my door, and he won't get another chance with me."

"I'll let him know." She pulled the pad away from her chest, glancing at something she had written, and said, "Declan?"

"Yes?"

"I need to discuss the Montgomery case with you—"

"Hell no." I put my hand in the air. "Only one shitshow at a time. We'll discuss the Montgomery case later. I need to finish the terms of the Spade settlement that I've been trying to work on for the last hour, but I keep getting interrupted."

She nodded and left the room.

Now that I had silence, I returned to the document and began to type, getting through only two sentences before there was a knock at my door.

Fuck me.

"What?" I shouted.

The door slowly cracked open, and Hannah's face appeared in the doorway.

"Hi." She smiled. "Have a second?"

"For you, I have more than a second." As she walked inside my office, my hands left the keyboard, and I leaned back in my chair. "What can I do for you, Miss Dalton?"

As she took a seat, she glanced toward the door she had closed. "What did you say to Alice? She ran out of your office like you'd lit her on fire."

"I might have."

"Ah. The bark is back."

I smiled. "The bark never left, baby." My arms stretched out wide, and then I cupped the back of my head with my palms. "Everyone is getting on my fucking nerves today. I've been trying to draft this settlement for Walter, and I have had no time to finish it."

She cocked her head. "Should I leave, then?"

"Don't you dare."

"Not that I wish your bark on anyone, but admittedly, it's nice not to be on the receiving end of it anymore. Christopher doesn't growl; he whines. That sound is much easier on the nerves."

"What are you saying, Hannah?"

She was holding a folder and set it on the chair next

to her, leaning her arms on my desk. "You should buy Alice something nice for all the hell you put her through."

"It's her job."

"Technically, yes, but she deals with a pit bull every day when she'd rather be working for a doodle."

I huffed. "You're not comparing me to a fucking dog, are you?"

"I'm saying, you should give me your credit card, and I'll pick her up a gift card to a spa, or I'll buy her a new Chanel bag or something that will make sure she continues to show up every morning."

Alice was a good assistant.

If Hannah thought a gift would take away the edge, then it was worth it.

I reached into my pocket, removed my wallet, and tossed the credit card across the desk. "Have fun."

As I settled back in my chair, I was reminded of the days when she had been my intern, when I would come into my office every morning and there was breakfast and coffee waiting for me.

"What I wouldn't do to have you back on my team." I shook my head. "Christopher, that lucky bastard."

"You now have me living in your house, and you get to wake up to my face every morning." She grinned. "I'd say that's even better, no?"

As I thought of the way she had looked just a few hours ago, soundlessly asleep on my chest, I growled, "You might have a point."

"I have another point to share with you." She set my credit card on her lap, her expression changing as she took several deep breaths.

My brows rose. "What is this about?"

"I have news." Her hands flattened on my desk. "Things around here—at least for me—are going to be changing."

My fingers tightened into a fist. "What do you mean ... changing?"

At one point, over the last couple of weeks, Hannah had told me that she was concerned about us working in the same building every day, that she was worried that the business environment would affect our relationship.

She wanted nothing to come between us.

I'd reminded her that she worked on a different floor now, on a completely separate team.

There was no overlap.

And, as far as I was concerned, her new office put her too far away from me.

I wanted her close.

I wanted her in the desk right outside my office, like she'd been in before, so I could look at her every goddamn day.

Change meant something new, and I hoped to hell that didn't mean she was leaving the firm.

I wouldn't stand for that. Neither would her family.

She tucked a chunk of hair behind her ear and took a deep breath before she grabbed the folder off the chair beside her. "I was offered a new position."

I had every intention of destroying that offer the second I got my hands on it.

Shredding the contract bit by fucking bit.

I reached out my hand. "Give it to me."

"Declan ..." She glanced down, breaking our eye contact.

Fuck.

I didn't like the look of this.

I didn't like the sound of it either.

"Hannah, let me see it."

She slowly slid it across my desk, and I clasped the folder

between my hands and opened the top flap. The first thing I looked at was the logo at the beginning of the contract, followed by the position that was being offered.

"My fucking girl," I moaned as I read the start date and the salary, flipping to the end to see the signatures that had already been notarized. "Hannah ..." I said as I met her eyes.

She bit her lip. "I know." She stood from her seat and came around to my side of the desk, sitting on my lap, where she wrapped her arms around my neck.

"I'm so fucking proud of you." I held her so tightly. "Baby, you not only passed the bar, but you also just got everything you'd ever dreamed of."

"I got the bar results about an hour ago and rushed into my uncle's office to tell him. Dominick, Jenner, Ford, and my aunt came in and handed me my contract. I signed it right away." Tears began to fill her eyes. "An associate lawyer at The Dalton Group." She shook her head. "Declan, I can't believe it."

I wiped the bottoms of her eyes. "I can." I kissed her. "I never questioned it for a second. You earned this; you deserve this, and now, we're going to celebrate." I held her cheek, rubbing my thumb across her lip. "What do you want to do tonight?"

When she kissed me, I tasted the hunger on her lips.

The need that pulsed through her body.

She pulled away and leaned into my ear, whispering words that made my dick so fucking hard.

That made me grip her face with a strength that was even more intense than before.

"That's how you want to celebrate?" I asked.

She loosened the knot at my throat, pulling my tie until she could slip it over my head. "Yes." Her lips went to my ear, where she moaned, "I want you. Right now."

"Then, you'd better lock the door."

She dropped the tie on my desk and got up from my lap, walking to the door to do as I'd said. When she turned to face me, she slipped off her skirt and tossed her shirt on the floor.

That body.

That perfection.

Every fucking bit of it was mine.

As she returned to my lap, I gave her one final order, "Keep your heels on."

Interested in reading the other books in the Dalton Family Series

...

The Lawyer
The Billionaire
The Single Dad
The Bachelor
Or check out Signed, which stars Brett Young

ACKNOWLEDGMENTS

Nina Grinstead, the past few months have shown me just how hard you fight for me. It's something I've seen and known since day one, but what we've accomplished, the goals we've achieved, the dreams we've made happen in the latter half of this year are nothing short of amazing. So many happy tears (with palm trees behind my head), all because of you, Nina. *Love you* doesn't even come close to cutting it. Team B forever.

Jovana Shirley, I hope you know how grateful I am for you, how much you inspire me, how every book I send your way is better—how I'm better—because of you. You're an artist, and I'm completely in awe of you. As I always say, I'm never doing this without you. Never, ever. Love you so, so hard.

Hang Le, my unicorn, you are just incredible in every way.

Judy Zweifel, as always, thank you for being so wonderful to work with and for taking such good care of my words and for always squeezing me in last minute. <3

Chanpreet Singh, thank you for always holding me together and for helping me in every single way. Adore you, lady. XO.

Kaitie Reister, I love you, girl. Thanks for being you.

Nikki Terrill, my soul sister. Every tear, vent, virtual hug, life chaos, workout—you've been there through it all. I could never do this without you, and I would never want to. Love you hard.

Sarah Symonds, my friend, you're now even deeper into

this journey with me, and it couldn't make me happier. Thank you for being on this ride, for being the best partner in crime. I wouldn't want to do this without you. Ever. LY.

Logan Chisholm, you jumped right in and literally saved me. I can't thank you enough for all your support, all your wisdom, all your patience, and for always responding to my millions of questions, lol. You're fabulous, girl, and I just treasure you.

Ratula Roy, you always find that one hole, and you ALWAYS know just how to fix it. Thank you for the countless voice texts and for celebrating every bit of happiness with me. I always say, you have my back, my heart, and my love—and it couldn't be truer. Love you.

Kimmi Street, my sister from another mister. Thank you from the bottom of my heart. You saved me. You inspired me. You kept me standing in so many different ways. I love you more than love.

Extra-special love goes to Valentine PR, my ARC team, my Bookstagram team, Kelley Beckham, Sarah Norris, Kim Cermak, Kayti McGee, Tracey Waggaman, Elizabeth Kelley, Jennifer Porpora, Pat Mann, and my group of Sarasota girls, whom I love more than anything. I'm so grateful for all of you.

Mom and Dad, thanks for your unwavering belief in me and your constant encouragement. It means more than you'll ever know.

Brian, my words could never dent the love I feel for you. Trust me when I say, I love you more.

My Midnighters, you are such a supportive, loving, motivating group. Thanks for being such an inspiration, for holding my hand when I need it, and for always begging for more words. I love you all.

To all the bloggers who read, review, share, post, tweet, Instagram—Thank you, thank you, thank you will never be enough. You do so much for our writing community, and we're so appreciative.

To my readers—I cherish each and every one of you. I'm so grateful for all the love you show my books, for taking the time to reach out to me, and for your passion and enthusiasm. I love, love, love you.

MARNI'S MIDNIGHTERS

Getting to know my readers is one of my favorite parts about being an author. In Marni's Midnighters, my private Facebook group, I post covers before they're revealed to the public and excerpts of the projects I'm currently working on, and team members qualify for exclusive giveaways.

To join Marni's Midnighters, click HERE.

ABOUT THE AUTHOR

USA Today best-selling author Marni Mann knew she was going to be a writer since middle school. While other girls her age were daydreaming about teenage pop stars, Marni was fantasizing about penning her first novel. She crafts sexy, titillating stories that weave together her love of darkness, mystery, passion, and human emotions. A New Englander at heart, she now lives in Sarasota, Florida, with her husband and their yellow Lab. When she's not nose deep in her laptop, working on her next novel, she's scouring for chocolate, sipping wine, traveling, or devouring fabulous books.

Want to get in touch? Visit Marni at ...
www.marnismann.com
MarniMannBooks@gmail.com

ALSO BY MARNI MANN

STAND-ALONE NOVELS

Even If It Hurts (Contemporary Romance)

Before You (Contemporary Romance)

The Better Version of Me (Psychological Thriller)

THE DALTON FAMILY SERIES—EROTIC ROMANCE

The Lawyer

The Billionaire

The Single Dad

The Intern

The Bachelor

THE AGENCY SERIES—EROTIC ROMANCE

Signed

Endorsed

Contracted

Negotiated

THE BEARDED SAVAGES SERIES—EROTIC ROMANCE

The Unblocked Collection

Wild Aces

MOMENTS IN BOSTON SERIES—CONTEMPORARY ROMANCE

When Ashes Fall

When We Met

When Darkness Ends

THE PRISONED SERIES—DARK EROTIC THRILLER

Prisoned

Animal

Monster

THE SHADOWS DUET—EROTIC ROMANCE

Seductive Shadows

Seductive Secrecy

THE BAR HARBOR DUET—NEW ADULT

Pulled Beneath

Pulled Within

THE MEMOIR SERIES—DARK MAINSTREAM FICTION

Memoirs Aren't Fairytales

Scars from a Memoir

THE BACHELOR

Don't forget to pre-order The Bachelor, a scorching hot, billionaire, forbidden romance, and the final book in The Dalton Family Series, releasing Spring of 2023.